The Perfect Blend

"C. Kelly Robinson has created *A Perfect Blend* of humor, drama and emotion. Nikki was too real."
—Gloria Mallette, bestselling author of *Shades of Jade* and *The Honey Well*

"What a story! Robinson flaunts his literary skills and spins a tale of love and family that is emotionally riveting and highly entertaining. This is one read you will not want to miss."
—Tracy Price-Thompson, bestselling author of *Chocolate Sangria* and *Black Coffee*

"Captured my attention on page one and kept it until the very end."
—Kimberla Lawson Roby, Author of *Too Much of A Good Thing*

"*The Perfect Blend* is terrific and entertaining, with a rhythm that draws you in. . . . A winner!"
—Victoria Christopher Murray, bestselling author of *Temptation*

No More Mr. Nice Guy
A Main Selection of the Black Expressions Book Club

"Robinson handles his subject matter with plenty of attitude. As in his debut, brisk plotting, snappy vernacular and resilient characters keep things entertaining. . . . [T]his spunky title will please fans of E. Lynn Harris and Omar Tyree."
—*Publishers Weekly*

"Funny, nimble, entertaining storytelling. Laugh out loud moments. Robinson's characters are easily recognizable."
—Marcus Major, author of *A Family Affair*

"Robinson writes another insightful and funny story about black men and the dating scene. Women and men will enjoy this love story."
—*Booklist*

"Young, black, single and mad as hell. . . . [A] lighthearted look at the irrationality of dating."
—*Kirkus Reviews*

continued . . .

Between Brothers

"Not since Spike Lee's *School Daze* and the much-loved sitcom *A Different World* has the Black experience on campus been this intriguing. . . . A spirited tale of four classmates on a mission to save their college while dealing with real-world growing pains."

—Essence

"Good, resourceful characters fight back in a vivid narrative. . . . [A] refreshing variety of characters." *—Kirkus Reviews*

"Robinson has skillfully painted three-dimensional characters that reflect our rich, often misunderstood diversity."

—William July, author of Brothers, Lust and Love

"*Between Brothers* gives a candid and refreshing look inside the lives of four 'together brothers' who transcend stereotypes and restore faith and hope in our black men."

—Tracey Price-Thompson, author of Chocolate Sangria and Black Coffee

"C. Kelly Robinson has produced an insightful, well written novel. Highly recommended."

——Timmothy B. McCann, bestselling author of Until

"[*Between Brothers*] is both an exceptionally well-written and consummate novel of character studies. . . . [A]n engaging, compelling story set in the very real and contemporary world of the Black community." *—Midwest Book Review*

The Strong, Silent Type

"A compelling story." *—Booklist*

"An entertaining, true-to-life story. . . . Robinson's fans will not be disappointed." *—Black Issues Book Review*

THE ONE
THAT GOT AWAY

THE ONE THAT GOT AWAY

C. KELLY ROBINSON

 NEW AMERICAN LIBRARY

NEW AMERICAN LIBRARY

Published by New American Library, a division of
Penguin Group (USA) Inc., 375 Hudson Street, New York, New York 10014, USA
Penguin Group (Canada), 90 Eglinton Avenue East, Suite 700, Toronto
Ontario M4P 2Y3, Canada (a division of Pearson Penguin Canada Inc.)
Penguin Books Ltd., 80 Strand, London WC2R 0RL, England
Penguin Ireland, 25 St. Stephen's Green, Dublin 2,
Ireland (a division of Penguin Books Ltd.)
Penguin Group (Australia), 250 Camberwell Road, Camberwell, Victoria 3124,
Australia (a division of Pearson Australia Group Pty. Ltd.)
Penguin Books India Pvt. Ltd., 11 Community Centre, Panchsheel Park,
New Delhi – 110 017, India
Penguin Group (NZ), cnr Airborne and Rosedale Roads, Albany,
Auckland 1310, New Zealand (a division of Pearson New Zealand Ltd.)
Penguin Books (South Africa) (Pty.) Ltd., 24 Sturdee Avenue,
Rosebank, Johannesburg 2196, South Africa

Penguin Books Ltd., Registered Offices: 80 Strand, London WC2R 0RL, England

First published by New American Library, a division of Penguin Group (USA) Inc.

10   9   8   7   6   5   4   3   2

NEW AMERICAN LIBRARY and logo are trademarks of Penguin Group (USA) Inc.

LIBRARY OF CONGRESS CATALOGING-IN-PUBLICATION DATA:

Robinson, C. Kelly (Chester Kelly), 1970–
   The one that got away / by C. Kelly Robinson.
     p. cm.
   ISBN 0-451-21663-6
   1. First loves–Fiction. 2. Radio stations–Fiction. 3. Divorced mothers–Fiction.
4. African Americans–Fiction. 5. Cincinnati (Ohio)–Fiction. 6. Chicago–(Ill.)–Fiction.
I. Title.
   PS3568.O2855O54   2005
   813'.54–dc22   2005015370

Set in Berthold Garamond
Designed by Elke Sigal

ACKNOWLEDGMENTS

With thanks to my Lord and Savior, Jesus Christ, to my agent, Elaine Koster, my editor, Kara Cesare, and the New American Library staff. As always, I am thankful for Kyra, for my loving family (immediate and extended), the friends who continue to support me personally and professionally, and the Omega Baptist Church family. Finally, my sincere appreciation goes out to all the book clubs, bookstores, and fellow authors.

An hour before events ripped the scales from his eyes, Tony Gooden faced a moment of truth. The screen on his ringing cell phone announced the caller, and it was the last person he expected today: Serena Height-Kincaid, the college sweetheart he'd just seen for the first time in ten years. Though he was no stranger to stress—in three years as the Chicago mayor's chief of staff he'd battled both gangsters and gangbangers—Tony was useless in the face of a simple phone call. Sure, he wanted her back, but then, so did her husband.

An hour before the phone call, Tony had been hip-deep in denial. Making his way through the wedding's receiving line, he took Serena's silky-smooth hand and summoned an emotional force field. He'd spent the night before in a deep pool of his own sweat, choreographing this very moment, but now he radiated nothing but calm. To the groomsmen and bridesmaids surrounding them, he was just another guest, not the man who'd crashed that other wedding years before—Serena's.

Their bumpy, passionate history wafting between them, the two exchanged a civil, curt handshake. He was still trying to ignore the flattering fit of her strapless pink dress when she spoke. "Tony Gooden," Serena said, glancing to his left and right, a forced smile on her face. "No supermodel at your side tonight?"

"Frankly, you're a few years late for that." His romantic history was strewn with the affections of girls with modeling experience, but he'd outgrown that phase by his late twenties. Surprised they'd managed this much conversation, Tony let his eyes rest on Serena's a little longer this time. "I'm just your average bachelor these days."

"Oh, I doubt that." Serena's smile remained, but the grin was artificial. Her gray-green eyes, full of wary suspicion, spoke the truth. "You're not single by accident, Tony. Even your father was married by the time he was our age."

Damn, that's cold. Score two points for the lady; Serena had always enjoyed putting him in his place. *That's what you get for coming stag.* If not for that roller coaster of a heated discussion on Wednesday morning, his most recent lady friend, Colette, would be at his side, dazzling the wedding party with her beauty and shaming Serena into silence.

Colette wasn't there because Tony had finally asked her about the positive pregnancy test he'd found in her trash two months earlier. As each subsequent week passed and she hadn't said a word, he'd prayed that no stork was coming, hoping feverishly that he'd misread the test or that it belonged to one of her friends. Though Colette never ballooned on him or started puking every five seconds, something had finally made him ask the question, and he still hadn't fully absorbed her answer.

Catching Serena's confused glare, Tony realized he'd stayed silent for too long. Standing there outside the Hyatt Regency ballroom, he stood tall—as tall as you could stand at five foot ten, anyway—and leaned in toward his ex, one hand gently holding hers. The passage of ten years hadn't laid a finger on her smooth butterscotch complexion, her alluring little figure, or her cinnamon-apple scent, but he told himself he didn't notice. "Serena," he said, determined to get through his script, "I just want to say—"

"Nice mustache, by the way." Interrupting him, she released

his hand. Her gaze hardened, and filled with contempt. Even her fluttery, bubbly voice had developed a new edge. "Almost makes you look twenty."

Don't take the bait. Tony reminded himself he wasn't there to defend his facial hair, a recent addition meant to offset the smooth, round contours of his baby face. Even now he looked younger than his thirty-two years, but at least people weren't mistaking him for a college kid.

He leaned forward, getting back to his game plan. "I hear the pain in your voice, Dee," he said, whispering Serena's nickname into her delicate, pointy left ear. "For the record, I was out of line with that stunt I pulled. I hope you and Jamie live happily ever after."

Caught off guard, Serena froze in place at his words. As strains of Teena Marie and Rick James's "Fire and Desire" seeped from the ballroom into the hallway, her jaw clenched so quickly, Tony almost missed it. Looking over his shoulder with a cool stare, she said, "Ancient history," while shrugging. Standing straighter, she matched his stare again. "Good to see you."

That was it. She'd left him out there, forced to choose his next approach: a quick nod of the head to end things and shake the next hand in line, or an abject plea for her sincere forgiveness. There were men who might take the challenge, who might shed their pride in hopes of burying the hatchet with the woman they'd lost the most sleep over. On that day, at that moment, Tony Gooden was too much The Man to be that man. Catching Serena's eyes one last time, he shook his head slowly and said, "I'm glad you're at peace, then." Pivoting smoothly toward the next bridesmaid, he extended a hand without waiting for Serena's reaction. He wasn't chasing after anyone anymore. Not even Serena Height-Kincaid.

When he had made his way through the receiving line, he stood alone, searching the crowd for Trey, his old friend and last-minute "date" for the wedding. His brow wrinkling with annoyance, he swept his eyes over the packed hallway. *Bet that fool's collecting numbers.* Here he'd asked Trey to come along for moral support in his hour of need, and the boy was lining up booty calls.

He still hadn't locked onto Trey when the groom, Devon, stepped out of the receiving line and rushed to his side. "See, that wasn't so painful, T," Devon said, his gravelly voice barely audible over the gathering crowd. "You're still standing."

"Yeah, whatever," Tony said, loosening his silk tie and playing with the navy blue buttons on his tapered, professionally tailored suit coat. He shook his college roommate's hand, admiring Devon's sharp ebony tux and tails. "Again, man, I can't tell you how proud I am." He meant every word.

Tony still vividly recalled the night Devon first met Kym, during their sophomore year at Northwestern. Devon, a tall, lanky English major who always slept peacefully while Tony pounded his mattress with the latest conquest, agonized for weeks about the short, shapely honey who'd caught his eye at the library. Bookish despite an occasional crazy streak, Devon had struck up a conversation with Kym but failed to pursue those seven magical digits. With Tony's coaching, his roommate finally tracked the conservative accounting major down and wormed his way into her heart. Their path to the altar hadn't been linear nor without drama, but today represented the culmination of his roomie's dream.

"Hey, we appreciate you celebrating with us," Devon said, giving Tony another firm handshake. "Really wish you could have been in the ceremony, though."

Tony glared at his friend, a deadpan look in his eyes. "Now, you knew that wasn't happening." Kym, who happened to be one of Serena's closest friends, vetoed Devon's initial plan to include Tony among the groomsmen. Devon fought for him, but Tony quickly bowed out. In reality, the thought of standing before God and a crowd of hundreds with Serena just across the aisle wasn't his idea of fun. It was Devon and Kym's day; why infect it with memories of his own ass-baring at Serena's aborted wedding? Tony's last-minute antics kept her from walking the aisle that special day, but the following week she'd tossed his gallant efforts aside, eloping to Las Vegas with Jamie Kincaid. She was right. They were ancient history, and the book wouldn't be rewritten this time.

"Come on," Devon said, throwing an arm over Tony's shoulder and peering down at him. "Let's get inside the ballroom. They're about to have toasts in a few, and I know you got a good one for me."

"Ease up with the hugs, Dev," Tony said, frowning playfully as he shrugged out of his friend's embrace. "You married Kym today, not me. I gotta roll. You don't want me and Serena in the same room for too long, okay?"

"Jamie's not even here, if that's what you're worried about," Devon replied. The placid joy on his face slackened as his eyes grew serious. "Guess he stayed home with the kids. So since your hot date dumped you, it's just you and Serena in the mix here. If you don't start none, she won't. Kym and I already talked to her." It still killed Tony that he'd introduced Serena to Kym all those years ago in school. Without his involvement, Serena would never even have been a part of today's nuptials. *No good deed goes unpunished.*

"I have to jet," Tony said, trying to pretend he wasn't curious about Serena's husband's absence. *He let his wife come here alone, knowing I'd be lying in wait?* He popped fists with Devon again. "I'm out, man, call me when you get back from Aruba. Now let me find Trey before I get charged for another hour of parking." He didn't know why Kym's parents insisted on having the reception at a downtown Loop hotel, of all places: guests not only had to come off with an expensive gift, they had to pay thirty bucks to park their cars, too?

Devon shook his bald head, his bony shoulders quivering with laughter. "What the hell's gotten into you, dog? You used to roll like P. Diddy; nowadays you're pinching pennies like MC Hammer."

"Long story," Tony replied, still scanning the crowd for Trey.

"But, hey," Devon said, "I thought you were getting paid behind Zora's success. I mean, you can't get away from her book." Zora, Tony's half sister, had recently published her first novel, a hip-hop story of a girl gangsta, and the book was popping up on bestsellers lists across the country.

"The books are moving, man," Tony said, "but we ain't been paid for half of 'em yet." He turned away from his old roomie as he finally located Trey, who stood in the dissolving receiving line flirting with Jade, another of Kym and Serena's friends. *That's just what we need*, Tony thought. Since their years as college-age partners-in-crime, Kym, Serena, and Jade had formed an unbreakable trio. He hated to see Trey, the player of all players, get drawn into the web along with him and Devon. As Kym caught Devon's eye, waving him toward the ballroom entrance, Tony popped the groom's shoulder. "Tell my boy to get his ass over here, please."

A minute later, when Trey finally broke away from Jade, a fresh business card in his palm, he smirked at Tony's impatience. "You tryin' to beat the next hour's parking fee, ain't you?"

"Damn right," Tony replied. From a young age, he had been trained to appreciate the finer things in life: five-star restaurants, tailored clothing, front-row concert seats, Rolex watches, not to mention the Boston Whaler boat he co-owned with his father, Wayne. Unfortunately, like his dad's, Tony's income lagged a step behind his tastes.

Trey, who had grown oddly quiet, raised his voice at Tony as they stood waiting for an elevator. "Yo, you hear me? I said, have you gone cheapskate 'cause the station's still not paying you right?"

Worried about eavesdropping guests, Tony waited until he and Trey had stepped aboard an empty elevator to answer his friend's question. Quickly and curtly, he fed Trey the lowdown. A couple of years earlier, he'd retired from politics at thirty and taken a job as manager and minority shareholder at WHOT-FM radio, an attempt to seek his fortune. He earned a salary of a hundred grand, but in a major city that stretched only so far. What really chapped his ass was the phony accounting the station's holding company used to show a net loss; as a result, he had yet to earn a bonus.

Tony's wounded pride got the best of him as he stepped off the elevator, and he realized he was whining. "The station's ratings and ad revenues have increased each of the past two years," he said. "They're pulling the wool over my eyes, man."

Trey, who was just a few years removed from his "wigger" stage and who remained more interested in *Playboy* than *Business Week*, grimaced sympathetically. "That why you cashed out your ride?"

"Damn, I miss that M3." Hands in his pockets, head momentarily bowed, Tony mourned his silver BMW, which he'd sold to avoid eviction from his luxury condo in Lincoln Park. This after having his life threatened by a pesky collections agent inquiring about his college loans, which he'd finally chipped away at by selling half his stock portfolio. As they strode through the garage, Tony allowed himself a rare moment of transparency. "Something's gotta give, Trey. This is killing me."

Stroking his well-groomed beard, Trey glanced toward his boy. "What about that job O.J. hooked you up with?"

"What, working for that school? There was no money," Tony said with a flick of the wrist. What else could he say? His friend O.J., WHOT's star radio personality, had hooked him up with a college buddy, Larry Whitaker, whose family owned a medium-sized conglomerate in Cincinnati. Whitaker Holdings owned a chain of supermarkets and an electronics retailer, but had recently branched out by founding a for-profit school for troubled teens.

"I thought Larry and his dad was high rollers," Trey said as they arrived at his black Dodge Dakota truck, a Quad model roomy enough to hold half his kids.

"Yeah, well, they weren't trying to let me in on the high rolling," Tony replied. "Can you believe they wanted me to work for their *school*? Doing something with media and government relations. The salary wasn't even six figures."

Firing up his engine, Trey grunted. He knew Tony's demands quite well. "Guess you gonna have to go back into the gigolo business, my brother. Hook up with a girl whose daddy can hire you or somethin'."

"Nah, that's you," Tony said, shaking his head as Trey's truck rolled toward an exit ramp. Taking cues from his dad, Tony had often dated girls who worked at fine department stores and clothing chains—thank God for those employee discounts—but he had earned every job he ever had and wasn't about to take a hustler's way out now.

"Don't hate on me for knowing how to pay my bills when needed," Trey replied as he wound his truck toward ground level. Full of blond-haired, blue-eyed soul, Trey was a man with baggage, including six multiracial children by five different mothers. Even with all those mouths to feed and a half-completed college degree, though, his finances were less stressed than Tony's. "There's nothing wrong with getting more than the panties for your ways with the ladies."

"Trey, please, just leave it alone." Tony's breath grew short and he felt the same tingling in his chest that drove him to the doctor last month. Doc Montgomery had the nerve to place him on high blood pressure medication, and Tony had no interest in returning to him anytime soon. He needed to calm down, get Serena's dismissive words and that cold stare out of his head.

Once he'd slipped his friend cash for the parking attendant and they had merged into traffic on Wacker Drive, Trey replied to Tony's stern brush-off. "Ya know, brother, I didn't have to skip Zach's game to keep you company," he said, reminding Tony of his second-oldest boy's baseball game.

"You're right," Tony replied, rolling down his window. With summer still weeks away, the weather was damp and cool but with enough sun to justify a touch of a breeze. Stress had straight-up blinded him to his friend's sacrifice; Trey's absence from his son's game had certainly incurred the ever-present wrath of Janine, Zach's mama. The tension crimping his forehead forced him to drop his head. "I really appreciate you coming along, man. You could have left me to face this whole thing on my own."

"Yeah," Trey said, grunting again. "Why couldn't you talk Colette into coming with you, though? I know you all had some fight, but that's a regular week for you two. No make-up sex yet?"

"She lost a baby. Ours, I guess." Tony was shocked by his own sudden candor. As his friend turned toward him with a jolt, he gazed into his own lap and pulled a toothpick from the breast pocket of his coat. "It was the ultimate wake-up call," he said, voice low as he chewed nervously. "She lost the kid around six weeks, I guess, just when she was about to tell me. Thing I can't figure, Trey, is she seemed more relieved by the miscarriage than I was."

Trey's right eye twitched. "She's lying about that, T. No woman's relieved about losing a baby."

Tony finally raised his eyes, trying to be as sensitive as he could. "I feel you, but I got her point. We'd have raised the child together if the pregnancy had been viable, man, but we knew we weren't in love. Talking about the miscarriage just made us admit it."

Trey, intimately familiar with the bullet his friend had dodged, nodded solemnly as they pulled onto Lake Shore Drive. "Damn, Mr. Too Good almost joined the daddy club. I ain't mad at you, though. If that made you realize you didn't love the girl, best thing you can do is keep your pole out of her pool."

"Thank you, Dr. Phil. I have advice for you, too. That girl you were rapping to just now?"

"Jade?"

"Walk away from that one, player. Trust me."

"I think she's cute," Trey replied, turning to glare at Tony. "Straightforward and real, too. I predict I'll be making some trips to see her in Cincy."

Cincinnati: Serena's city. A part of Tony had rejected the Whitaker Holdings job because it was located there. The last thing he needed was to have Trey drag him along on a trip to see Jade. "Trey, I'm warning you—"

"You've been holding out on me," Trey said, his words coming forcefully as he made a sudden lane change, incurring the wrath of a tall, round traffic officer. The sounds of the agitated officer's whistle rang out, and Trey came to a sudden stop after frowning in the sister's direction. "Jade didn't go into detail," he continued, hands now at ten and two on the steering wheel, "but she kept making smart remarks about you and that Serena babe."

Folding his arms, Tony looked past Trey, wishing he could strip off his suit and take a dip in the blue beckoning waters beyond. Why had he let the boy walk around unsupervised? The plan was to keep Trey with him at all times, to avoid exactly this conversation. Only his friends from the Northwestern years knew he'd crashed a woman's wedding. None of his boys these days, most of whom were childhood friends like Trey or recent acquaintances like O.J., had the first clue Serena even existed. The Tony Gooden they knew wouldn't cross the street to win back a woman's heart; he was renowned for his ability to move on to the next pretty brown round.

"This isn't open for discussion," Tony said, eager to shut the thread down. He'd no sooner tell most folk about Serena than he'd tell them about his birth mother, the woman who tried to give him up for adoption before his father stepped in and raised little Tony himself. A few months earlier he had finally told Trey and their boy Mitchell—who had always assumed that his first stepmom, Stephanie, was his flesh and blood—about his "second" mother, but he could only share so much at once.

The ringing of Tony's cell phone interrupted his pleas for privacy. He grabbed it from his belt, flipped it open, and nearly messed his pants when Serena's name popped up on caller ID.

The phone purring in his hand, Tony was cold with shock. Too stunned to speak, he quickly calculated the odds that this call would lead to happiness and that he'd finally get what he really wanted with Serena Height-Kincaid. Despite all she meant to him, there was no getting around two inconvenient parts of the equation. Her two precious daughters, Dawn and Sydney, who would never understand how close he came to being their father; and Jamie Kincaid himself, the man who stole her years ago with one well-aimed stream of sperm.

"Who is it?" Trey asked, clearly intrigued by his friend's indecision.

Tony settled back into his seat, flipping the phone shut. "Wrong number."

2

As soon as Devon and Kym's limo whisked them from the reception to O'Hare Airport, where they planned to catch the first leg of their flight to Aruba, Serena sprang into action. Coolly worming her way through the muggy ballroom, which was still three-quarters full with partying guests, she locked in on her anonymous tormentor, a shapely, mahogany sister with legs you could ride from New York to L.A.

Rolling her shoulders calmly, Serena reminded herself she was a professional; a less-educated or self-assured woman might go off in this situation. As she rolled up beside her significantly taller antagonist, she caught a whiff of the woman's fumes, confirming her guess the girl was a touch tipsy. A glass of sparkling white wine pitching and lurching in her right hand, the woman stood toe-to-toe with a handsome bearded brother in a charcoal double-breasted suit. Seeing no need to wait until their flirtation was complete, Serena tapped the sister's shoulder. "Excuse me, may I speak to you for a moment?"

The woman turned, looking over her shoulder and down at Serena. Her narrow eyes were full of confusion, even disgust, that this chesty little woman had interrupted her attempt to get macked. "I'm busy."

"It won't take but a minute." Serena placed a hand on the brother's back, smiling pleasantly. "Nice cologne. Don't leave her, okay? I'll bring her right back."

"It's all good," he said, hoisting his champagne flute. "I'm gonna go refill; then I'll see you in a second, Candace."

Candace. Serena smiled, the brother having saved her some effort. As he made his turn toward the bar, Serena ran a hand down Candace's long, toned left arm. "Candace," she said, knowing her smile was nearly as plastic as the one she'd flashed Tony, "I just thought you should know you were very rude earlier."

Candace did a literal double take, a hand instinctively clamping against a hip. "What are you talking about, uh—"

"Serena," she said, sticking out a flawlessly manicured hand. "Serena Height-Kincaid, Jamie's wife." Serena forced the smile again. "That was my husband you were talking about earlier. You know, when you were yelling so loud everyone within a hundred feet could hear you."

A sheepish smirk rippled Candace's lips and the hand dropped from her hip. "Aw, no . . ." The way their eyes locked, Serena could read Candace's recall of her greatest hits from an hour ago, when she began regaling her table of cackling, crooked-weave-wearing hens with tales of her romantic encounters with Jamie. *That man is an Energizer bunny—he can go!* The table aflame with laughter, Candace had plowed on. After musing out loud about why any woman would marry such a "whoremonger," she'd spun her crowd-pleaser. *Forget the ring, Jamie—just keep hittin' me with that big ole thang!*

"Oh, God," Candace said, flicking a hand over her mouth. Jamie had probably enjoyed the sister's wide, sensuous mouth, which Serena could have easily filled with her fist. "I am so sorry. Someone told me Jamie's wife was here, and I just got to reliving the past . . ." She shrugged, a goofy smile on her face. "I'm sorry? I mean, what do you want me to say?"

Her arms still crossed, Serena smiled up at Candace. "Oh, there's nothing more for you to say," she said. "Just a suggestion, though. Next time you know you're in the company of someone you want to gossip about, keep your voice down. I mean, what if my kids had been here and heard all that?"

"Okay, don't go getting all preachy on me now," Candace said, her posture stiffening again. "You gonna tell me you've never talked that way about Jamie with your girlfriends? Everybody know he knocks good boots."

Serena felt her lips flatten as she sucked her teeth. "The point is, watch what you say in public. In case you hadn't noticed, Candace, this wasn't some pajama party."

"Whatever," Candace replied, waving a hand dismissively. "I'm gonna go find that man. Your problem ain't with me, it's with your husband." She looked down at Serena, judgment seeping from her eyes. "How you gonna marry a ho and act surprised when he don't change?"

Candace had her chance, and in Serena's estimation, she'd pissed all over it. Her natural athletic talents augmented by the adrenaline of humiliation, Serena lunged forward, leapt, and struck. Her slap knocked Candace's head back at a thirty-degree angle.

Turned out Candace wasn't a fighter. As Serena stood there trying to believe what she'd just done, the tall woman bent over, felt the growing welt on her cheek, and began to sob. By the time she gathered the strength to stare back at Serena through tearstained eyes, an equal number of defenders had surrounded them. The hens from Candace's table formed a ring around their fallen heroine, while Kym's bridesmaids gathered around Serena. Standing there in the middle as the two groups traded glares and pointed fingers, Serena pulled her palms to her face. *It's official, I'm losing my mind.*

As Serena stepped from the Jacuzzi, she realized the hours since her face-off had whizzed by in a complete blur. She recalled only images. The bewildered looks and questions from her friends, as well as from Candace's gang when they saw the attack. Her own cold, monotone attempt to explain what she'd done. Jade, her

best friend in the world, dragging her into the nearest ladies'
room. Jade dragging her back up to their suite at the Hyatt. Her
head clearing, Serena realized Jade must have drawn her bath in
the Jacuzzi. She'd probably helped her undress, too, because she
didn't remember doing that, either.

As Serena finished toweling off and wrapped herself in one of
the hotel's white terrycloth robes, Jade knocked on the bathroom
door and immediately cracked it, peeking in. "All better?"

In the bathroom's low, soft lighting, Serena smiled weakly.
"Come on in, and leave the door open, please. This steam is driving me crazy." Then after a pause, "So am I gonna get sued, or
what?"

"Well, with as many fools as there are today, you about asked
for a lawsuit, didn't you?" Shaking her head, Jade crossed the floor
and took a seat on the sink's marble countertop as Serena teased
her own hair. After going with a short, professionally tapered natural for the past year, she had let her wavy locks grow long enough
to be styled in a short, layered cut. It wasn't shampoo night, so a
few more laps with the comb and she'd be done.

After Jade comforted her with the news that Candace's friends
had dragged her away, blaming her behavior on too much alcohol
and agreeing to call things even, Serena set her comb down and
looked into her girl's brown eyes, hoping she didn't look too desperate. At work, she had an impeccable game face—she never let
people see her sweat. Even though she occasionally dropped her
veil with close friends, she still had a thimble of pride to protect.
"I can't do it alone, Jade," she finally said, embarrassed at the
water pooling in her eyes.

Sighing and wiping a tear from her own eye, Jade scooted
down the sink counter, close enough to cover one of Serena's dewy
hands with her own crisp, cool ones. From the moment they'd left
Cincinnati on Friday morning, Jade had been asking prying questions, her suspicion of Serena's family troubles written on her face.
Jade gazed at her patiently, as if she knew her friend was finally
ready to get real. "Well, well. Serena Kincaid admits to a weakness,
fancy that. Stop bottling everything up, girl. Just speak."

"You might have guessed this isn't about Jamie's inability to keep his dick to himself," Serena said, her eyes on the counter.

She didn't need to elaborate on that point. Kym and Jade had introduced Serena to Jamie back in their college days, when he was the biggest basketball star Northwestern had seen in decades. The night he first approached Serena at a house party, respectfully asking for a dance just hours after Tony began sawing into her heart by breaking their third date in a row, she figured he was right on time. A tall, handsome, and courteous star athlete seemed just what the doctor ordered.

Unfortunately, Jamie had always been the order of numerous other females, too, a fact she'd tolerated as his lover, baby's mama, and spouse. He had a demanding appetite for women, one that required feeding during his short stint in the bowels of the NBA, where he'd spent half his time on the road, and even once he returned home after being released by the Cleveland Cavaliers. Although Jamie was discreet about his business, Serena had been both disappointed and relieved when he decided to go play ball in Italy for an international league. Disappointed to have her husband and kids' father gone for six months of every year, but relieved that an ocean now separated her from his various mistresses.

"I know it's not about Jamie's wandering ways—we've had those conversations," Jade said, bringing her back. "So what is it?"

"I need to find my husband a real job," Serena replied, meeting Jade's concerned stare. "It's the only way to get him back home year-round." Getting Jamie away from European ball wouldn't be easy, though. The two years he'd spent working conventional jobs had been a tragicomedy. A job selling cars revealed that, while bright and charming, Jamie was too proud to do the ass-kissing necessary to close most sales. A stint using his chemistry degree at a pharmaceutical firm ended when his affair with the company's only black vice president got both him and her fired. There had been other short-lived attempts: a substitute teaching gig he quit when a female student became infatuated and started calling the house every night; a coaching job he quit after discovering today's kids had no motivation; and a maddening month trying to become a financial advisor. In the end nothing made him happy, and in all cases his income was lower than Serena's, a humiliation his pride could only abide from overseas.

Jade interrupted Serena's litany of Jamie's professional failures, abruptly getting her on track. "*Why* do you need him home full-time again? You've managed pretty well all these years."

"Well, when your home turns into a war zone, you need a general to help restore order."

"A war zone? Come on, Dawn can't possibly be that bad."

Jade's immediate assumption that Dawn, Serena's fourteen-year-old, was the problem hurt only because Jade was exactly right. After Dawn's freshman year at a magnet school, Serena had pulled the child out, if only out of respect for the other kids on the school's waiting list. Dawn, for her part, had been too busy skipping class or falling asleep in it to appreciate her teachers' efforts. "She's getting worse," Serena said, tracing an absentminded pattern into the marble counter. "She treats Sydney like they aren't even sisters."

"What did she do now?"

Tears welling up in her eyes, Serena recounted the mean-spirited prank Dawn pulled recently on ten-year-old Sydney. Not only had she sneaked into her little sister's bedroom when the child was changing clothes, she'd snapped embarrassing photos of her sister's naked behind and passed them around to kids in the neighborhood, several of whom attended Sydney's school. As a parent and as treasurer of Cincinnati Public Schools, Serena had been horrified by her own child's actions.

"She tried to say it was payback for Sydney telling on her for talking on the phone to certain boys whose calls I'd forbidden," Serena told Jade, shaking her head. "But there's more to it. I swear, it's like Dawn wants everyone else to be as miserable as she is."

Jade peered at her friend sympathetically. "Does any of this have to do with Brady?" Brady—Serena's high school sweetheart, first lover, and Dawn's father—had been a ruggedly handsome son of army officers who'd enrolled in the corps straight out of high school. In the two years that passed between Dawn's birth and Brady's death by friendly fire in the first Gulf War, he'd been a devoted father and a faithful provider of child support. He was a good man, but at seventeen Serena hadn't been ready to be his wife, or anyone else's, for that matter.

"I know she's struggling with Brady's memory," Serena replied. As she came of age in a time rocked by the current Iraq War, Dawn was constantly reminded of the "prequel" war that took her father's life. "I can't imagine what it's like for her, but that's still no excuse for her to neglect school or treat her sister like an enemy."

Jade leaned forward, her hands gripping the countertop. "I'm not trying to excuse Dawn, Serena, but you know society's also to blame for her behavior. She's trying to cut Sydney down to size."

"What are you talking about?"

"Serena, let's not play blind." Jade was standing now, his intense gaze softened around the edges, a compensation for the frankness in her tone. "Both your girls are beautiful, Serena, but if Dawn looks like a young Angela Bassett, Sydney's a miniature Halle Berry."

Jade's polarizing imagery sent a bristling wave up Serena's back. "And?" She absolutely hated when people tried to divide black folk by focusing on complexion or hair texture. For years, Serena had experimented with ways to camouflage her own Halle-type looks to avoid being painted into the "red bone" or "too light to be right" box. At various points she'd sheared her head bald, visited tanning booths, or wore lipsticks that enhanced the fullness of her "soup-coolers." Anything to hide the relatively recent European strains (French on her father's side, Irish on her mother's) running through her.

The affirming conversation turned testy for a few minutes, as the friends debated what role, if any, complexion played in Dawn's troubling behavior. Jade, whose own ethnicity was a melting pot of Jamaican, Colombian, and Korean strains, insisted on making her point. "Like it or not, girl, we all know this society still ranks people, especially women, by how close we come to the white ideal. And little Sydney is closer to it than our precious Dawn."

"I just don't agree with you," Serena said, shaking her head but wondering whether it wouldn't be easier if her girlfriend was right. The more she thought about it, Jade's theory on Dawn's behavior beat the alternative. There was only one other good explanation for her daughter's acting out: the same demons that stalked Serena's own youth, the ones that left her temporarily unfit to raise baby Dawn. Not only had they made life hell then, they lay in wait for her today, daring her to skip a few days' pills. Were the same demons creeping up on her daughter now? Serena wasn't mentally prepared to go there.

3

As she held on to Jade's embrace, Serena whispered a prayer for mercy and strength. She'd get Dawn and Sydney through this rough period, but she had to have Jamie's help at parenting. At times he acted like Dawn was her responsibility alone, but Serena never hesitated to remind him that while Sydney was his only biological child, Dawn was his, too; the adoption had been a condition of her agreement to marry him in the first place.

"You don't have to solve all this tonight," Jade said, rubbing Serena's back with warm, deep strokes. "Let's get you into bed." A wry smile crept onto her face. "Once you drop off, maybe I'll get a call from that fine man I met at the reception."

Just that quickly, Serena felt the appreciation welling up in her seep away. "Are you talking about that white boy who was with Tony Gooden?" He had been cute, but if he was friends with Tony he was probably trouble.

"Oh." Jade frowned and looked away like a kid caught with her hand in the cookie jar. "Well, yeah. I swear, though, I didn't know he was with Tony until *after* he got my number."

"I don't know the guy," Serena said dismissively, "so do your thing. It's none of my business."

Jade let her comment go, then asked, "You really didn't feel *anything*, positive or negative, after seeing Tony tonight?"

"Jade, did you hear me earlier or not? I've got bigger things on my mind than some man who crashed my wedding a decade ago." Lies, all lies, but she was working overtime to convince herself they were true. After years spent suppressing her most embarrassing emotions, Serena was convinced that had been a complete stranger shaking Tony's hand in the receiving line. Yes, a weak-willed stranger, full of secret hopes that her ex would pursue her all over again, as if the ten years since her aborted wedding had never passed. What a fool the woman was; rejecting several dance invitations from handsome groomsmen, she'd rushed to the nearest ladies' room and dialed Tony's cell number, her mind intent on accepting his apology with a little more class. If she could lie to herself, how could she tell Jade the truth?

"Well, I still think he should have stayed away today out of respect for you," Jade replied. "But I know sometimes the heart overwhelms the head, especially when you haven't seen someone in a long time."

"He didn't even register on my scale, okay?"

"Okay, now," Jade said, throwing a thin, peach-scented arm over Serena's shoulder as they walked toward the bathroom door. "Tell me some lies I can believe at least. Yes or no answers. Do you think he's still cute?"

"Yes, though I'd say handsome now." Arriving at her bed, Serena took a seat and smiled up at Jade.

"I don't know if the mustache helps," her friend replied. "Other than that, though, he was just like I would have pictured. Lean and fit, sharp fade, tailored suit, gold cuff links, you name it. Once he gets over his search for another version of you, Tony just might make someone a good husband."

Serena let Jade's kind words go unchallenged. Her friend was probably right. Tony might still be fleeing the weights of marriage and family, but she knew him well enough to know he wasn't the typical bachelor racking up a bedroom body count. She wondered if he still doubted his ability to be a successful husband; he'd always feared he would wind up like Wayne, his twice-divorced playboy father.

"Uh-oh," Jade said as she settled onto her own bed. "You've got that dreamy look in your eyes. I hope you're not fantasizing about a certain somebody." She smiled, but her eyes burned with a hint of caution. "You're better than Jamie, Serena. Don't go there."

"Girl, I'm fine," Serena said, waving her friend off and clicking on the television. To her right, a large window with an amazing view reminded her of the bustling city below, but she had no energy for adventure. Finding the Lifetime network, she settled back against the bed's fluffy pillows and shut her eyes. *A trip down memory lane never hurt anyone, Jade.*

There were any number of reasons Mr. Tony Gooden got close enough to do his damage, damage he'd unsuccessfully tried to undo at her and Jamie's wedding. Despite the many memories they shared from a romance that lasted barely two hundred days, the sight today of his button nose and the sound of his high-pitched voice—half a notch between Chris Tucker and Chris Rock—brought one particular day rushing back.

It was a rainy spring afternoon, late in her freshman year, when he arrived at her aunt Velma's house in Oak Park. Serena was living with Velma, the only relative willing to take her off her parents' hands after years of crack, DUIs, and Dawn's unplanned arrival. As soon as she stepped onto Velma's porch, Tony spun around and pulled her close. After risking a lengthy French kiss, something he knew Velma forbade on her property, he began pulling her toward his used faded Mercedes sedan. "Let's move," he said. "I promised Devon we'd meet him and the girls at five."

Serena waited until they were safely encased inside the Mercedes before leaning over for another kiss. When a flashback of the previous night's sexual marathon hit her, she snaked a hand into his lap. She had just started a soft stroking motion when Tony started the car, shifting just enough that she lost her grip.

"*What* are you doing?" She wasn't accustomed to her man turning down sex play, regardless of time or place. She and Tony

enjoyed pushing each other mentally—whether the subject was education reform, the authenticity of the Bible, or Clinton versus
Bush 41, they were always bickering—but that energy always
spilled into the bedroom, and anywhere else they could steal a private moment.

"Hey," he said, a chuckle softening his insistent tone, "we
need to get over there, is all. I want to make sure you meet
Devon's date and her friend."

"Oh, God, is this that Kym girl and her friend Jade? Why
would two Northwestern AKAs bother with a girl from UIC who
lives with her spinster aunt?" Serena knew Chicago's University of
Illinois campus had a good rep, but Northwestern was the Har-
vard of the Midwest.

"Serena," Tony replied as he weaved and bobbed toward the
Dan Ryan Expressway, "you gotta work with me here. Kym and
Jade are *thorough*. You start studying with them, you'll be the top
accounting student at your school before you know it."

"That's assuming I can even keep up with them," she sighed,
just loud enough for him to hear.

"Just give it a try, please?" One hand on the wheel, Tony
placed the other on her knee. "You're a natural, trust me."

She still couldn't explain it, but something about the confidence Tony transmitted with his touch seeped into her veins; it
always had. He was the one who got her to admit she'd always had
a knack for numbers, even though she viewed math and accounting as nerd fields. Tony called her out, though, pointing out her
facility with things numerical and mathematical, from her ability
to instantly calculate each person's share of a big restaurant tab to
her uncanny knack for predicting their grocery bill to a near-
penny. His gentle, nearly subliminal prodding convinced her to
switch her major to accounting from general studies. Now that she
was making her way through the coursework but questioning her
ability, he had taken it on himself to introduce her to Kym and
Jade, who were accounting stars at Northwestern and might make
great study buddies.

Tony hadn't always shown the soft touch, though. She recalled one of their first dates after she moved to Chicago, when she lit vanilla-scented candles on his glass coffee table and sang her two favorite standards for him—Patti LaBelle's "If Only You Knew" and Anita Baker's "Sweet Love." Even though they hadn't slept together yet and she'd shared her desire to quit college and pursue a singing career in New York, he said exactly what was on his mind. "Don't take this the wrong way, sexy, but you suck." Singing being her deepest passion at the time, Serena reacted with a stream of profanity, followed by her best attempt to nail him with a carefully aimed potted geranium.

That day as they drove to meet Kym and Jade, who would become not only great study buddies but her best friends, Serena looked at her scrappy, cocky boyfriend and felt nothing but blessed by his contradictions. Foul mouthed, full of himself, and materialistic, he was a man with an earnest, sensitive core.

He would come to cause her great pain, but in a sense Serena owed Tony. Without his influence, she might be waitressing in New York today, awaiting her elusive big break and still burdening her parents with raising Dawn. By now, she'd surpassed her own mentors: although Jade was a successful accounting manager for a manufacturing company and Kym was a vice president at her parents' mortgage bank, they both agreed Serena's job—managing the $500 million budget of an urban school system, along with a staff of dozens—outclassed theirs.

He didn't stand by you. As her eyes popped open, reason warned Serena to release her revisionist history. Propping herself up on her elbows, she turned toward Jade's bed, only to find her girl knocked out, as worn from the day's pace as she felt. Feeling too wiped out to check in with her parents, Serena toyed with her cell phone and considered trying Tony again. She'd sneaked a peek at his cell number during a visit the other night to Kym and Devon's condo, when they'd let her use their home PC to check her work email.

She dialed the first three digits of his number but stopped suddenly. He hadn't answered last time, and she knew Tony Gooden was not the type who hadn't had the phone on when she

called. Cell phones hadn't been that common in their days together, but she had no doubt that a motormouth like Tony abused
his cell, probably taking calls in hushed churches, public libraries,
likely even in the middle of making love, for all she could guess.
If he hadn't picked up, it meant he was as through with her as she
liked to think she was with him.

Accepting reality for what it was, Serena punched her phone
back to life and grimly did her duty, dialing another number. "Hi,
Jamie," she sighed when he answered.

4

A long line of excited young buppies and gangbangers—many of them scantily clad young women—clogged the sidewalk outside Excursions, a West Side nightclub. As Tony bobbed and wove through the crowd, mouthing respectful "excuse me's" to the most belligerent-looking roughnecks, he smiled with pride at the evidence of his success. He had coordinated several "off the chain" book parties the past year, but tonight's would set a new standard. Folk from across Chicago were out in full force, eager to hear his little sister Zora's first public reading from *One of the Boyz*, her recently released novel. The excitement charging the air was unmistakable: after reading *Boyz*, the hottest urban novel since *The Coldest Winter Ever*, Chicago readers hungered for a glimpse of its creator.

Tony's financial ambitions—and debts—had fueled Zora's growing career. Just a year earlier, he started generating extra cash by investing in up-and-coming artists. For his first project, he financed the reprinting of his old friend Mitchell Stone's self-published novel *Out of His Shadow*. The book sold out three additional printings, earning Tony a 15 percent return on his money, a nice improvement over his stock portfolio.

He was hooked after that, carefully selecting writers, painters, and poets with untapped potential and helping them spread their wings. By the time his twenty-year-old half sister brought her first manuscript to him for feedback, he'd already started doing public relations for his artists, scheduling them on local radio like WHOT and V103-FM and coordinating high-profile readings at popular clubs like Excursions.

As the club's head bouncer frisked him and ushered him from the nippy night air into the club's brick-walled, fluorescent-lit lobby, Tony had only one regret. Though Trey had promised to swing through, his other two best friends, O.J. and Mitchell, wouldn't be by tonight. O.J. was away hosting a benefit for the United Negro College Fund, and Mitchell was in Atlanta visiting his older son, Clay. Tony was on his own tonight; he didn't know why, but the realization was unsettling.

Squirreling away his unrest, he coolly surveyed the growing crowd. Brimming with a few excess ounces of Coors Light, he savored the warm sensation flowing through his veins. He was in a much better mood than earlier, at Devon's wedding. The suds distracted him from everything but one fact: Serena hadn't left a message. It had taken a few hours to admit he wished she had.

He should have just skipped the wedding. He loved his boy Devon, but his loyal attendance had done nothing but stir up pointless memories, starting with the chilly autumn day she strutted into Chicago's DuSable Museum, where he was a high school senior giving tours to out-of-town visitors. Looking over the group of students from Cincinnati's Princeton High, he'd considered stepping to several of the girls, but even at sixteen Serena was singular. *Petite, curvaceous figure . . . close-cropped, boyish haircut . . . the face of a young Lena Horne.* Tony applied his charms with the stealth of a panther, sidling alongside her as a movie summarized trader Jean Baptiste Pointe DuSable's early adventures. By the time the auditorium lights came up, he had her hotel name and room number.

Imagine his surprise that night, when an innocent postcurfew stroll along Michigan's shore revealed something beyond Serena's intriguing package. Her cutting, liberating wit tantalized while whittling him down to size. "You're gonna have to work for this," she said before delivering a confident, knowing kiss laced with cherry Blow Pop. "I don't get through Chicago much, so get ready to do some driving."

Another eighteen months would pass before they saw each other again, but Tony's sense that night that a thrilling, occasionally humiliating roller coaster lay ahead was dead-on. Their on-again, off-again tortured romance blossomed when she moved to Chicago to enroll at UIC, then stuttered its way through his remaining years at Northwestern, until the night she met Jamie. No other woman's allure had survived the bearing of another man's child, no other girlfriend kept him faithful while they were exclusive, and there was certainly no other ex whose wedding he'd tried to stop.

His attempts to erase those memories were interrupted when Owen, the nightclub's paunchy, well-dressed manager, rolled up beside him. Throwing a wrist shimmering with gold bracelets over Tony's shoulder, Owen ticked his head to the side. "What's up, young man?"

"You are, sir," Tony replied, knocking fists with the old head. He and Owen had been cool since Tony's days working for the mayor, when Owen ran the city's license bureau. He'd been axed under the new administration, landing at Excursions when a friend bought and renovated the place.

Glancing hesitantly over each shoulder, Owen asked, "Is your girl ready to turn this place out? She's had people talking about this event for weeks. The young girls especially seem pumped up about tonight." Just as Zora had planned, *One of the Boyz*'s feminist message of self-empowerment had connected with the wives, girlfriends, and baby mamas of the streets' toughest toughs.

Tony smiled like a proud papa. "I have faith in her like you don't know, man. She's been itching to do a public reading, meet her fans, the whole nine." He was fronting in a major way, but Owen didn't need to know that.

A sudden darkening in Owen's expression took Tony by surprise. "We've had a situation," he growled in a confidential tone, using a heavily starched handkerchief to dab sweat drops from his full salt-and-pepper beard. "Let's rap."

Tony let the manager lead him to a less cramped section of the bar before asking, "What's the problem?" Owen better not be having second thoughts about letting them hold Zora's party for free; Tony had done his part by ensuring a packed house, and every fan here knew they'd be buying a meal and a minimum of two drinks.

"You all are scaring this old man," Owen said, dropping his arms to his side before dabbing at his forehead. As he stepped closer, he flooded Tony with the stale cigar smoke on his breath and the spicy fumes of his cologne. "I've been hosting readings for your authors for months now, Tony, but something about this crowd don't feel right."

"Owen, let's talk facts, not feelings." Tony stepped back, sweeping an arm behind him. "You're gonna make a mint tonight. What you got to be scared about?"

"It ain't about the money," Owen replied, motioning toward him with a wiggling index finger. As Tony crooked his neck closer he said, "You heard of some fool named J.T. Dog?"

"Oh, yeah. Sure." He religiously held to his poker face, but the hairs on Tony's neck stood at attention. This time last year, he'd been no more familiar with J.T. Dog, a former rapper turned novelist, than Owen was now. That changed the minute *One of the Boyz* hit bookshelves.

Owen wasn't sold by Tony's calm response. "Is this fool as crazy he sounds? I need to know, Tony. Right now."

Frankly, Tony wished he had an answer for the older man. In truth, he was still learning how to play this game of hip-hop chicken with J.T. and other rapper types who resented the message of self-empowerment Zora had baked into her writing. On top of that, while she was too shy to conduct seminars based on *One of the Boyz,* she had conducted several major print interviews—think *Essence, Ebony, Vibe, The Source*—in which she urged young women to use their "power" to enforce change in their men. "If every woman in the community shut her legs for one day and made the same demand on their men before reopening them, we could change the game for real," she said in just about every feature.

There was even talk of a black feminist group organizing a march based on Zora's suggestion, sort of a weeklong Million Women's March designed to give women the courage to leave abusive and unfaithful men. Tony had been proud of her radical stance and confident it would help sell books, but he hadn't been prepared for the insecure reactions of J.T. and his ilk.

Still facing Owen, Tony huffed air through his nostrils and straightened his leather blazer, trying to look unflappable. "Was J.T. actually *here*?"

"My bouncers just shoved him back into his limo," Owen said, his hands on hips now. "You're worried; don't try to tell me you ain't."

Tony crossed his arms. "What did he say? Why'd they have to put their hands on the fool?"

"He was talking crazy! Rolled up in line with a ridiculous entourage of thugs, and when the bouncers got tired of their foul mouths and the mess they were spouting about Zora, they really went crazy." Owen sidled closer to him, sticking a hand alongside his mouth and lowering his voice. "My boys had to flash the hardware at 'em, if you know what I mean."

"Great." Tony reached into his coat pocket and retrieved a plastic toothpick. Once he'd popped it between his lips and calmed himself with the chewing rhythm, he clapped Owen on the shoulder. "It'll be all right," he said, raising his voice over the Kanye West track booming through the club. "Your boys did the right thing. I'm confident there'll be no more trouble." He hit Owen's shoulder again. "Let's get this show on the road, come on."

Owen didn't look convinced, but he sighed and bore his way back into the crowd. Checking his watch and seeing it was nearly time for Zora to take the stage, Tony slipped past the bar and seating area, where he knocked on the faded wooden door of the dressing room.

After ninety silent, uncomfortable seconds, a half-dressed Zora finally swung the door open. She still wore a rumpled white T-shirt, but at least she had changed into the lower half of the outfit he'd purchased for tonight, a pair of black silk slacks. Tony was relieved to see his sister wearing anything besides her usual faded khakis and scuffed penny loafers, which she usually complimented with a mismatched wrinkled blouse.

"Hey," she muttered before sighing and trudging back to the low, dented oak desk and chair across the room.

"Hey yourself, beautiful," he said, striding behind her and placing his hands on her high, tight shoulders as she took a seat. "We only have a few minutes left. You need some more privacy while you finish dressing?"

"It won't take me a minute to throw on that shirt," Zora replied. Staring into the smudged oval mirror before her, she scratched nervously at her close-cropped wrap of a hairstyle, advertising dandruff for the whole world to see. "Is there really a sellout crowd out there?"

Shutting his eyes at a stray flake, Tony took a deep breath. Mitchell's wife, Nikki, had scheduled Zora for a morning appointment with a beautician, one she'd obviously skipped. Given that she shared half his genes, Zora definitely had the raw material to be an attractive girl; for some reason she showed no interest in using it. Eyeing her ragged do, he kept calm by reminding himself of the matching low brim hat he'd bought for her; the girl would be wearing it all night.

Determined to keep his cool, Tony addressed her question. "Zora, a capacity crowd's out there, waiting just for you. Now you know why they call me Mr. Too Good." He was overselling his role, of course; these three hundred folks had piled into Excursions because they knew Zora's novel was all that.

One of the Boyz, which Tony was promoting as "the literary love child of Donald Goines, George Pelecanos, and Zane," told the story of a young girl on Chicago's South Side who plots, sleeps, and bludgeons her way to the head of a major gang. After racking up a body count that would make Shaft blush, the heroine's life is changed forever when she ends up pregnant by a rival gang leader, one she murders before learning of the bun in the oven. A harrowing, sensual, and bold story of "girl power," the book had already made major moves. Tony knew the stats by heart: fifty thousand copies sold in a month, soon to be number one on the *Essence* list and twenty on the *New York Times*. The *New York* fucking *Times*!

Tony's happiness at his sister's success was matched only by a lust for his share of the upcoming profits. If Zora wowed the crowd with a strong reading at tonight's party, the buzz around the book would take on legendary proportions. As his sister stewed in silence, however, Tony remembered his work for the night wasn't finished. One obstacle lay before both him and Zora: the paralyzing stage fright that nearly ended her career before it began.

Shortly before they decided to self-publish *One of the Boyz*, Tony arranged Zora's appearance at a poetry slam in Hyde Park. The organizers had invited novelists to read excerpts as well, and Zora agreed it was a good chance to tackle her fears. Tony still believed she would have killed that night, if she hadn't been struck mute the minute she stepped onstage. After a minute of silent fumbling, she fled the stage in tears. She would have burned the *Boyz* manuscript and diskettes if he hadn't followed her home and stopped her.

"Are you ready for this?" Still leaning over her, noticing she also hadn't bothered to use the Chanel perfume he'd bought her, Tony waited patiently for her answer. Zora was content to play deaf, reading intently from her leather-bound journal.

When she finally turned to look at him over her shoulder, she moved with the hesitation of a beaver peeking into sunlight. Sliding her gold wire-rimmed glasses up and down her narrow nose, Zora frowned as she said, "I'll know when I step onto the stage, won't I?"

Kneading her tense shoulders, he checked his tone. *Catch more flies with honey, Tony.* "If you're nervous, just say so, girl. Remember, we can go over the exercises you learned—"

"Exercises, exercises," Zora mumbled, eyes on the pages of her journal. "Either I'll be able to read confidently out there tonight, or I won't. *Que sera, sera.*"

Realizing an argument would only reinforce her fatalistic attitude, Tony walked to the closet near the door and pulled her shirt off its hanger. "Put this on and meet me in the hallway," he whispered, kissing her on the forehead. "You're gonna knock 'em dead."

"You really think I can do this?" As she stared back into his eyes, Tony was struck by Zora's resemblance to the one photo he had of their mother. Snapped a year before his birth, it captured her in her early twenties. Tony had never met Zora's father—the poor loser who'd stayed with his wife after Wayne Gooden knocked her up with a baby boy—but she'd apparently pulled very little from his side of the family tree.

"I *know* you can do this," he replied, scratching suddenly at his neck. Still climbing the learning curve, he wasn't yet expert at this big brother role. Given that their mother had never properly introduced them, he'd known his half sister for only ten months.

Gripping his hands suddenly, Zora glanced at the worn carpet below. "I just wish that *she* would be supportive," she said, her own voice lowered now. "I still can't believe she wouldn't come tonight."

"Well, just remember—her problem's with me, not you," Tony said, embracing his sister in a gentle hug. For a day at the most he'd hoped their mother would break down and drive in from Schaumburg to support Zora. Of course, that would have also meant meeting him face-to-face for the first time in thirty-two years, so he wasn't surprised when she took a pass. This was the same woman who handed him to Wayne Gooden, three weeks after his birth, and returned to her own husband. Zora's father.

A surge of adrenaline shot through Tony as he held his sister. Before the day Zora called to introduce herself last year, blithely mentioning she'd enrolled at Loyola in order to be near him, Tony had never felt a protective instinct toward another human being. All of the significant females in his childhood had been older, self-possessed women—his grandmother, his stepmother, Stephanie, and his three aunts. By baptizing him into the role of Big Brother,

Zora had brought a deeper, more complex texture to Tony's daily life.

She shrugged her way out of his hug. "All right. Let me get dressed now."

He stepped back, snapped his fingers, and pointed toward her confidently. "I'll be back in five minutes."

As Tony paced the perimeter of the seating area, now teeming with laughter, shouting, and tables sagging with food, a doughy brother with dreadlocks tugged at his elbow. Stopping to make conversation, Tony extended his hand. "What's up, bruh?" As Zora's publicist and informal manager, he was all about keeping the crowd happy. "You ready to have a good time tonight?"

The last word had barely left Tony's mouth before the man yanked him to within an inch of his own lips. "I'll have a better time," he said, his beer-spiced halitosis stinging Tony's nostrils, "if Miss Zora apologizes proper for the way she dissed J.T. Dog." He looked up at Tony, his upper lip rigid with anger. "You might tell her that. It could save you both a cap in the ass."

5

Tony decided not to play along with the would-be hoodlum, turning away as the brother's threat hung in the air. *Not this J.T. Dog shit again.* From the moment of Owen's earlier warning, he'd known he had reason to worry. He'd quickly learned that while the "ghetto life" novel was a booming art form, the market carried a little more risk than writing Harlequin romances.

Despite the fact Zora had never met him, J.T. Dog's handlers had convinced him that D. Money, a pivotal character in *One of the Boyz*, was based on him. Seeing how D. Money was a drug lord who used his profits to buy a rap label, J.T.'s fans assumed this was a reference to similar rumors about him. In hip-hop lit, this was apparently the equivalent of calling out a rival on one of your rap songs. Coming from Zora, Tony figured it felt like a double insult to J.T. Dog; here she was telling women to exercise power over the no-good men in their lives, all while exercising public power over J.T.'s own image.

Tony also suspected J.T. Dog's anger at Zora was fueled by their respective book sales. *Boyz* had knocked J.T.'s recent novel, *Gots to Get Mine,* out of the number one bestseller spot at black bookstores across the country. With each passing week, as *Boyz* took a larger slice of the urban novel pie, J.T.'s threats had grown increasingly intense.

He'd unveiled his hardest shot just last week, on one of the countless BET video shows. "We know this trick Zora is tryin' to be real down-low, acting like she can speak for all the sisters," he'd sneered as the host looked on quizzically. "I got peeps everywhere, though. I hear she ain't even from the hood," he'd said, ticking points off on his fingers. "Ain't never lived in no project, ain't never held a gun, ain't even had no baby. How she gonna keep it real?" J.T.'s attacks, of course, had the opposite effect: Zora's sales jumped 30 percent the next week as young girls hungry for affirmation and self-esteem lapped her story up.

As J.T.'s campaign against his sister ramped up, Tony had carefully shielded her from the hoopla. It really wasn't that difficult; the girl listened religiously to hip-hop CDs but watched no TV and was only into satellite radio. With each passing day, he accomplished two important things—building Zora's self-confidence, and lining both of their pockets. At times he'd question whether things were moving too fast, but such concerns were erased by the next day's sales report. If *Boyz* kept up its current pace, Tony's share would pay off his credit card debt and get him approved for another car loan. *Good-bye, Taurus; hello, Jaguar.*

All good, as long as he could shield Zora from J.T. Dog and comparable fools like the idiot who'd issued his cryptic warning. Coolly striding away from J.T.'s messenger and trusting the brother just had too much to drink, Tony returned to the dressing room.

Five minutes later, Owen completed his introduction and welcomed Zora to the stage. As Tony took a seat at a crowded table down front, he scanned the crowd again for potential troublemakers. When he saw nothing to worry about, he swiveled back toward the stage.

"Thank you," Zora said as she positioned herself before the microphone stand. Her hat leaning languidly to the left, her arresting cocoa brown eyes blazing, she seemed transformed by the spotlight. Clearing her throat, she folded her hands as if praying and then spoke with the tenderness of Janet Jackson. "A lot of people have been talking about this book," she said, voice fluttering softly. "Tonight you'll get to hear the *author* talk about it."

From the back row, a hearty female voice seconded Zora's motion. "That's right!"

"Thank you," Zora said again, chuckling and staring at her feet for a second. "Anyway, I'll read two chapters from *One of the Boyz* tonight, but first I'd like to clear up some questions about it—"

"Phony punk bee-yatch!" The words burst from the center of the crowd before anyone could tell where they'd come from. With Zora verbally stopped in her tracks, peering into the crowd anxiously, heads turned in search of the heckler. With the room buzzing in amused anticipation, Tony caught Zora's eye, mouthing, "Go on, play it off." Pausing would just encourage the heckler, probably another J.T. Dog fan that slipped under the radar.

Clearing her throat nervously, Zora took a tentative step closer to her mic. "As I was saying—"

"You just another sister tryin' to bring a brother down!" This time the heckler stood, proudly claiming credit. A tall, solid brother with a bald head, he exchanged high fives with the other men at his table. "J.T. Dog's *got* your number, girl."

"Brother, you need to sit down." Before Tony could beat him to it, Owen had hopped onto the stage alongside Zora. Taking her mic, he stepped to the edge of the stage. "These folks paid good money to hear this young lady," he said, he pointing a finger toward the heckler. "Now are you gonna sit down like you have some sense, or do I gotta escort you out of here?"

"Escort this, partner!" As the heckler stood again, a shiny black pistol in each hand, the crowd scattered like grains of sand. Streams of frantic folk knocking him to and fro, Tony stood but rejected the urge to follow the fleeing crowds. He couldn't leave Zora to fend for herself.

Struggling to his feet, taking knocks to his forehead and shins from the fleeing crowds, he looked anxiously between

Zora and the impulsive Johnny Two-Guns. The heckler stood fifty yards from Zora, guns still raised, when the crowd behind him convulsed suddenly. As some people fell to the floor and others flew through the air, the club's two largest bouncers burst into sight. In seconds they wrestled the gunman to the floor, but when the loud report of a pistol shook the club, the crowd's anxiety only increased. Calm pleas for people to keep moving became frantic shouts, insistent nudges became desperate shoves, and a survival of the fittest vibe filled the cramped space.

His ears ringing at a second burst from the pistol, which had either been fired into the wood floor or into the heckler's chest, Tony steadied himself against the nearest table. Craning his neck, he caught sight of Zora, who stood alone on the stage with arms crossed and feet tapping anxiously. Breathing a sigh of relief, Tony turned back toward the flailing heckler, who was overpowered by the bouncers and Owen, who'd joined in. Satisfied they were beyond serious danger, Tony stayed put. He'd be hard-pressed to get through the panicked crowd, which had nearly morphed into a stampede. Besides, with the gunman apprehended, why risk getting his pretty head bashed in? He'd wait for Zora where he was. Turning back toward the stage, he prepared to wave in her direction. . . .

Where'd she go? His heartbeat rocketing, Tony stared at the empty stage. Had she slipped back to the dressing room, maybe? Climbing onto his table, he scanned the crowd for signs of Zora and finally located her. Pressed nearly flat between a crowd near the bar, his sister fought to keep her balance, shifting uneasily against the mishmash of frantic women and angry, agitated brothers. Elbows flew, legs kicked, and Tony finally realized that some people were literally *walking over others*. This was a genuine stampede: people were going down.

His brain spinning emptily, trying to believe his eyes, Tony stood there atop the table, foreboding creeping up his spine. That's when a football-player-sized brother *thwacked* the back of Zora's head with an out-of-control elbow. Her hands in the air, clawing for a lifeline, Zora was sucked beneath the churning crowd.

Without calculation or thought, Tony dove off the table, landing halfway between it and where he'd last seen Zora. Shoving aside the two brothers who broke his fall, he blazed a path to his sister, who lay on her stomach, arms splayed wide. The back of Zora's blouse was smeared with blood, sweat, and dirt stains, stamped together by several sets of footprints. His breath coming in shorter clips, his eyes full of stinging sweat, Tony screamed for space and knelt over her. Turning Zora over, he slid his arms underneath her torso and lifted her as he stood. Before he could move forward, a booted foot landed hard on his leather loafer, sending a fiery spike of pain up his leg. He didn't even hear his own shouted profanity, but he immediately felt his grip on Zora slacken. *He couldn't drop her, not in the condition she was in. . . .*

His grip restored, Tony's neck pivoted this way and that, seeking the clearest path forward, only to find swarms of fear-crazed folk everywhere. That's when he made the only choice he could. With Zora nestled in his arms, he lowered his head and made like a battering ram, pile-driving his way past two bodies, then one, then three. . . . "We're almost there, Zora," he whispered, knowing she couldn't hear him. "Just hold on—"

The smack of a closed fist against his temple cut him short. His head filling with showers of sparks and fireworks, Tony felt himself sway before he went down. *Zora, hang on, baby.* His last clear memory, after they had plummeted to the floor, was that they were about to become human rugs. Sharp heels and bone-crunching boots colliding with his chest, cheeks, and thighs, Tony felt like a swimmer who'd suddenly been swept over a waterfall; any illusion of control was gone. His body pockmarked with stinging pain, the rush of oozing blood bringing a chill to his brain, Tony lost the will to fight.

His arms falling to his side, his own screams filling his ears, his blurring eyes rested on the vision materializing above him.

Still wearing her strapless pink bridesmaid dress, Serena floated through the panicked crowd and knelt at his side. As his vision of the one that got away steadied his head and whispered calm assurances, Tony tried to form the words floating through his head. *Stay with me. I won't lose you this time.*

6

A momentary load lifted, Serena relished the end of another painful press conference. In order to frustrate the media's focus on the failure of the Cincinnati schools' latest levy attempt, she'd been enlisted to wow the reporters with a summary of the financial restructuring plan she'd recently coordinated. Her job finished for the evening, she felt like sprinting out of the auditorium as her fellow administrators and the local journalists mingled around her. Levi Little, the newly hired director of security, short-circuited that idea.

Appearing at her elbow as she stepped off the low platform stage, the barrel-chested, bowlegged brother leaned in. "Made it through another one, huh?"

"Tell me about it," Serena replied, shaking her head wearily. Before taking the podium, she'd had to watch Kevin Kellogg, her boss and superintendent of schools, take his customary abuse from the geniuses in the media. Dr. Kellogg had a big heart and the knowledge to back it up; in the three years since he had taken over, he'd led with a down-to-earth warmth and unquestioned competence. Test scores system-wide were up 10 percent, absenteeism was down by another 25 percent, and graduation rates had improved in all but two high schools.

In the eyes of the press, though, all that was meaningless in the face of the recent levy's failure. Their view: Kellogg hadn't proven himself to the parents of Cincinnati, and they now had a new vessel for their children's hopes and dreams.

The Rowan Academy, a local for-profit school run by the privately owned Whitaker Holdings corporation, was putting the city schools to shame. Using a radical curriculum designed by a nationwide task force of young educators and academics, the academy had taken some of the most abject losers from the city school system—pregnant teens, dropouts, kids who'd spent more time in juvenile detention than in junior high—and transformed them into teachable students. Its kids' test scores had increased by two hundred percent in some grades, owing to the fact many came on board with scores that were nearly negative. Everyone had his or her own conspiracy theory about Rowan's apparent success, but the press wasn't about to argue with its results.

"Yeah," Levi said now, moving closer to Serena, "these reporters have drank deep from the Rowan Kool-Aid."

"That's the truth," Serena replied, taking a step back before Levi invaded her personal space. She wasn't just tiring of these press conferences; surviving Levi's daily flirtations was an adventure in its own right.

Not that she had a loyal husband sitting at home waiting on her. Jamie had gone out to Colorado three days after her return from Kym's wedding last week. She took his excuse—hooking up with the American teammates from his Italian team for an early start on preseason conditioning and seeing to some issues at the nonprofit foundation they ran together—at face value, but the blind faith that required was a humiliating burden.

Add to that the fact that Levi, a thirty-year-old former pro boxer, was very much a brother in his prime, and he should have had a chance with her. The problem, Serena reminded herself as the security director matched her every step toward the hallway, was his overconfidence. It seemed Levi sensed he was just the sort of brother who'd gotten her into trouble night after night during her free and easy youth. He wasn't even working hard in his attempt to woo her; he clearly believed that simply popping up at her side—smelling of baby oil, sporting a tight fade, flashing that wickedly arresting smile—would do the job, ultimately inducing her to collapse into his arms.

As they neared Serena's office, Levi ran his eyes over her outfit, a black pinstriped pants suit. "Did you, uh, have that tailored?"

She shook her head, chuckling. "Please. Don't you know I'm a public servant, not to mention one with two mouths to feed? I'm strictly off the rack, brother."

Levi put his hands behind his back and swayed in place. "Hard to believe, as well as that hangs on you."

Arriving at her office door, Serena slapped Levi's arm. "Cut it out; you're going to make me blush." She knew Levi was exaggerating; for years now she had worked carefully at dressing like a true professional at the office. Fleeing a youth full of low-cut tops, see-through shirts, and Wonderbras, the Serena Kincaid who showed up for work each day was cloaked in a conservatively bland wardrobe, one designed to smother something as pointless as sex appeal.

"Well, I wouldn't want you blushing on my account," Levi said as Serena retrieved her office key from her pocket. "So tell me, what's it gonna take to wake the people of Cincinnati up, get them to approve the next levy?"

Serena rolled one eye toward Levi, then took it back. "It's after five, baby. Ask me tomorrow at eight a.m., please."

"Ah, come on, I'm just making conversation." Levi shook his head, chuckling. "Working here is proving to be a trip. Never know what the day will bring. I still don't know how I'm gonna keep these ghetto folk from busting a cap in Champion's ass next week."

"Shouldn't he have his own security?" Arthur Champion was one of the most famous black businessmen in the country. A former protégé of Donald Trump, in the eighties, Champion used that rarified air to build a network of major media contacts before forming his own venture capital firm. By the late nineties he had amassed enough wealth to engineer a leveraged buyout of Weller

Industries, a Fortune 100 multinational corporation with fifty thousand employees and plants in eighteen countries.

Although running his company took plenty of time, Champion also made time to follow in his old boss's footsteps, building a side career as a media presence. He'd been very crafty about bringing attention to himself: dating a string of famous (white) actresses and singers, flying a hot air balloon around the world, and appearing in controversial commercials for his company's most popular products. One even featured a lean, half-dressed Champion working one of his company's power drills before a worshipful audience of scantily clad young women. NBC, CNN, and Fox News loved him for his attitude and excess, while *Ebony* and *Essence* worshipped him for his wealth. Champion had everything a black man could want—the respect of his people, the envy of everyone else.

While on tour to promote his recent book, *A Real Champion: Forget Mike, Be Like Me,* the mogul had blithely tossed it all away. Appearing before the Cincinnati NAACP, he was asked his opinion of the struggles facing Cincinnati's and other public school systems. "It's simple," he'd been quoted in the *Enquirer.* "Bad kids with even worse parents. Unless you show me the proof, I'm giving the teachers in these schools the benefit of the doubt. They're not the problem. The problem is a generation of kids being raised by parents whose heads are stuck up their asses." Based on accounts Serena heard from several folk who'd been on hand, Champion hadn't backed down as the night went on. He'd stomped out every last ember of political correctness, sparing no one: teen parents, truants, single mothers, two-income families with no time to raise their children, and a black culture valuing sports, rap music, popularity, and fame over education.

The black community—not just here in Cincy, but nationally—was still aflame with resentment. Who was this uppity Negro to call folk out and air dirty laundry, all with cameras rolling and representatives of The Man on hand? Talk swirled of boycotts against Champion's company's products, along with demands that he be publicly spanked by the Sharptons, Jacksons, and Farrakhans of the world.

Too headstrong to let the firestorm blow over, the self-promoter had come calling again. Word was he'd be speaking next week at Cincinnati's juvenile detention center. Champion's publicist had put out the word that the loudmouth planned on bringing gifts—rumors were he'd be donating up to five million to the school system—but that he'd also be delivering a stern warning to urban schools nationwide.

"Champion should have his own security," Levi said, answering Serena's halfhearted question as she took a seat at her desk, "but Kellogg and the board told me I better make damn sure things go smoothly." As she tapped her PC monitor to life, he walked over behind her, letting his cologne wash over her as he growled into her ear. "If anything happened to him, it would just prove him right about our kids, know what I mean?"

"Levi, thank you so much," Serena said, turning and crossing her arms. Tapping a finger against her desk, she smiled as pleasantly as she could. "See you tomorrow?"

"Okay, sure." An eyebrow raised, Levi took the brush-off in good spirits. Too good. "You have a blessed night now, Serena. Give your hubby my best."

She let her silence respond to his wisecrack and admired the sinewy muscles rippling through the back of his shirt as he strode off. *Don't be mad, Levi.*

Half an hour later she had straightened up her office, changed into a pair of flats, and made the drive over to Angus King stadium, where Dawn and Sydney were competing in an area track meet. After being confined to her air-conditioned office all day, Serena was surprised at how hot it was. Wearily pushing her door open, she climbed from her maroon Ford Explorer and reached back for her cell phone. She'd had it off since going into this afternoon's press conference; no telling whether she'd missed an important message, especially given the drama her girls were putting each other through.

As she put the phone to her ear, Serena felt a sinking realization: there would be no message from Tony Gooden, not five days after she'd made that ill-advised call. In seconds, she was proved right. The only message was from one of Dawn's teachers, Ms. Bright, a wonderful woman whose younger sister graduated high school with Serena. As always, Ms. Bright was crisp, professional, and clearly concerned about some new antic Dawn had pulled. "I'm not writing her up, *yet*," she said on the message. "I know you're doing the best you can, and we'll get her through this time. Just call me, please. My home number is . . ."

Huffing out an exasperated sigh, Serena tried to calculate how best to take Dawn on over this latest screwup. Dawn didn't tend to take counsel very well, usually preferring to shift the spotlight back onto her mother.

"How many of my track meets have you made it to the past year, Mom?" This had been her response last week when Serena got on her about an F on an American Government test. "Maybe if my mother spent less time at the office working for all the kids in the city schools and focused on me once in a while, I'd be a happier child. And maybe, just maybe, I'd be able to concentrate in class better. Ever thought about that?"

Serena had reared back with a prepped open-hand slap, then aborted it and opted instead for a stream of muttered profanities. Her child was driving her crazy, but that was no excuse; she'd just have to keep plugging away at the girl and maybe start praying a little more at the same time.

Standing before her open car door, Serena was startled by the sudden slap of a hand on her shoulder. She nearly dropped the phone as she turned away from the car. "Daddy?"

"Precious." Serena's shoulders slackened as her father, a tall, broad man oozing peace and calm, took her into his arms. Professor Charles Height was the best man she knew, a constant advisor and a perfect complement to Jan, her tough, protective mother.

Deep down, Serena's devotion to her imperfect marriage had as much to do with her parents as with her desire to protect her children. After the hell she'd put them through from age fourteen to twenty-one, holding her marriage together was like a thank-you note to her folks. She couldn't think of a better way to reward them for standing by her all those years.

"You're here just in time," her father said now, his voice an authoritative whisper. "Dawn's event is up first. She'll be on the track in a few minutes." Squinting against the sunlight, he held her back at arm's length, surveying her with his gray-green eyes. "You look worn around the edges, honey."

"It couldn't be helped today, Daddy." Looking at her father before her, dressed in a pair of knee-length plaid shorts and a bright white rugby shirt, she realized her friends were right: her father and Colin Powell could have been separated at birth.

"If I need to call Dr. Kellogg myself," Charles replied, rubbing Serena's arms lovingly, "I will. You can't let him run you ragged, Serena. It's not good for your health."

"Daddy, I'm fine," Serena replied, shooing away his protective tone, though she wondered if he knew how right he was to worry. Stepping back, she shut her car door before taking his hand. As they walked toward the stadium, she punched him playfully in the side. "I love my job, Daddy. That's the easy part of life." As it fell out of her mouth, she knew immediately that she'd said too much.

"The . . . easy part." Charles gripped her hand a little more tightly, stopped where he stood. "As opposed to what?"

She laughed nervously, looked around the parking lot. "Daddy, never mind."

"This is about Jamie, right?" Charles sized her up again through the lenses of his bifocals, then lowered his voice. "Serena, I wasn't going to bring this up, but if he's running around again, you need to let me know."

"Daddy, we are grown adults. It's not your business."

Charles smacked his lips before saying, "It is if you're thinking of cheating on him."

It may have been the heat or it may have been the question, but Serena felt herself sway, her sense of balance slipping away. "Cheating? Me? Why would you think that?"

Charles's neck swiveled discreetly, making sure no one was nearby. "I hear things, Serena." The anger beneath his words let the last embers of his Liberian accent out to play, adding a judgmental bite to his tone.

"Well, you're talking to a bunch of lying assholes, Daddy." As Serena stared at her father in shock, an independent-minded tear squirted from her left eye. It was halfway down her cheek by the time she croaked out the rest of her response. "Mr. Jamison, your friend who works in the administration building, right?"

Nodding slightly, his eyes still locked onto hers, her father's usual shield of calm certainty seemed like an act.

"He thinks I'm carrying on with our head of security, right? Levi Little?"

Still struck mute, Charles confirmed Serena's words with a clearing of his throat.

"Oh, Jesus," she whispered before raising her voice. "Levi flirts with *me*, Daddy. That's it." She stepped so close her forehead bumped up against her father's chin, then folded her arms to help fight back two new tears that had sprouted against her will. "I have never cheated on Jamie and never will. I thought you knew me better than that—"

Her self-defense was interrupted by the purr of her cell phone. "Dammit," she said, still looking her father dead in the face. She felt like throwing the life-interrupting device against the hot pavement, but instinctively raised it to her ear. Her father, for his part, stayed right where he was, his only show of emotion the slow scratching of his nose.

"This is Serena." When silence greeted her, Serena huffed a curse under her breath. "Hello?"

"Serena?" The voice was shaky, barely audible, but she instantly recognized her girl Kym's voice.

"Hey, it's my favorite newlywed," Serena said, stripping the bitterness from her voice. "You two are back safe from the honeymoon?"

"Yes," Kim said, sniffling, "but we came back to some bad news, Dee."

"Oh, God, Kym. What happened?"

"Devon and I argued about it," Kym replied after pausing to blow her nose. "You need to know, though. It's about Tony."

Two Months Later

7

Nursing his father through a mild heart attack hadn't done it. Turning thirty hadn't done it. Same for the sight of Colette's positive pregnancy test, and his own doctor's warnings about his high blood pressure; they'd all failed miserably. For thirty-two years, Tony's confidence in the life he led survived shake-ups that provoked self-examination and even transformation in his closest friends. Untouched and unchanged by the passage of time, impervious to trials and tumult, Tony had proudly proceeded with his life game plan.

Within hours of his trampling on the dance floor of Excursions, though, Tony Gooden met his match. When he came to, he was strapped to a mattress on wheels, a bed hurtling down a crammed hospital hallway.

"Move aside, please!" The impatient shout rang from over Tony's left shoulder, the impassioned instruction of a man draped in a baggy pale blue shirt. The word "orderly" flitted across Tony's mind before a sharp pain in his chest bum-rushed his thoughts. *C-Can't breathe,* he thought, wishing he could form the words for the four people surrounding him, each with a hand pressed to his bed's railing.

As they shoved him into a waiting elevator, Tony began

coughing violently, his pain intensifying. Tears sprouted in the corners of his eyes and he picked up snippets of the staff's conversations about him. *All this from a club stampede?*

None of the others are in this type of shape, damn!

You know how those fools get at the clubs over there. I mean, I love my people, but . . .

Punctured lung . . . fractured ribs . . . left leg must have been trampled by everyone in the club, so mangled . . .

Maybe it had been horror at the extent of his plight, or maybe he was just eager to shut them the hell up, but that's when Tony shot forward and let loose the stream of vomit he'd felt convulsing within. Within seconds he saw the flash of a needle; then all went black again.

He'd had time now to recount this experience to several people, but as he sat across from Nana Quay, the chief of the southern Ghana village where he'd been assigned, Tony could see that it impressed even a man who'd survived war and famine. "For a privileged child of middle-class America," Nana Quay said once Tony had replayed his brush with death, "coming face-to-face with your mortality must have been a life-changing experience."

Leaning back on the couch they shared in the local office of the Searchlight Mission, Tony felt too shy to maintain eye contact with the chief. "Nana, I can't say I've lived up to that description quite yet. I'm still sorting a few things out."

The short, round man stroked his grizzled beard, grinned. "But you are here, young man. That was a big step for a capitalist heathen such as yourself."

"No argument there," Tony replied, chuckling at himself. A week after his final surgery at the University of Chicago, he had submitted his letter of resignation to WHOT. From the moment those doctors and nurses pronounced him near death, he'd been haunted by the thought of an obituary listing increased radio ad revenues as his chief contribution to this world.

With the resignation behind him, his path to a life of meaning was cleared, if only he could figure out what path to seek. Two nights after his resignation, he had seen a local news feature about Searchlight Mission. The Christian evangelicals were in the last week of a fund-raising campaign, recruiting sponsors for volunteers headed to Ghana for an economic development project. Turned out they also needed someone with administrative skills to organize the laborers and serve as liaison to the local villagers; the assigned staff member had gone down with a brutal case of pneumonia. They were thrilled first by Tony's call, then by his resumé; not only were they willing to let him sign up as a late volunteer, he got to earn his way by serving as the on-site project leader. His complete ignorance of scripture meant he couldn't present the gospel to the villagers, of course, but the senior missionaries were confident he'd eventually be converted through osmosis.

The strong, comforting grip of the chief's hand on his shoulder interrupted Tony's reflections. "You are already half of the way through this project, Anthony," he said, insisting still on using everyone's birth name. "Please do not even think of cutting your mission short, regardless of what Ama says."

"She's hurting, Nana," Tony said. "And it's probably my fault somehow. I don't want to jeopardize her support of the Searchlight Mission, all the good she's helped accomplish for you and the village."

"Nonsense," the chief admonished. "Your first instinct in coming here was correct. Already the Lord has used you in ways you do not appreciate. The construction of the new health clinic and the new school are weeks ahead of schedule because of your leadership."

"Simple management skills," Tony replied, sighing and pawing at the side of his short Afro. "But given my missteps with Ama, sir, it looks like my presence here is more disruptive than helpful."

"Well, I was a bit surprised to see such, eh, drama?" The uncharacteristic smile on the chief's face reminded Tony of how ludicrous the past few hours had been. He was here at this moment because Ama, an activist from the nearby metropolis of Kumasi and an invaluable liaison between the Mission and the village, had fallen in love with him. Tall and lithe with angular features and skin the complexion of freshly poured peanut butter fudge, Ama was a world traveler with a master's degree in public policy from Princeton. She'd been immediately fascinated by Tony, and while he'd been a total gentleman, he hadn't done much to discourage her interest, either. That is, until the night before, when she'd cornered him in the master suite of her three-bedroom split-level home.

When he politely declined the invitation to climb into her towering four-poster bed, poor Ama—the type of woman who'd been worshipped sexually by men of French, German, Japanese, and Arab descent—was outdone. As his answer to her intimate offer set in, the educated, cosmopolitan woman morphed into a sister on the corner of your nearest hood.

"You like men, Tony, is that it?" She asked the question with the full force of accusation, her usual efforts to flatten her accent gone. "No sin being gay in my book, honey, but, please, just be honest about eet. Won't hurt my feelings."

Even now, not twenty-four hours later, Tony couldn't recall his response. In truth, he was still processing the mental image that had blocked his path to Ama's bed, to her overheated, half-dressed body. *Serena.* The same vision of her in the pink strapless gown from Devon's wedding, the same one that had followed him from the night of his trampling through those weeks in the hospital. The vision he'd thought would recede once he enacted his plan to do something important with his life. Once he slept with a new woman.

Tony had come to admire Nana Quay in the few weeks they had been acquainted, and the next minutes cemented his opinion. With very few words, the chief not only got him talking about the previous night's controversial events, he lured the complete truth from the very pit of Tony's evolving soul. Words poured forth as he talked about Serena, about his impression that there was unfinished business there, an agenda demanding to be addressed even as they stared each other down in that receiving line. He'd convinced himself into ignoring her cellular call by reminding himself of Jamie's presence, but why was he respecting that pimp's rights, exactly?

Before he knew it, Tony had told the chief about the baby: Colette's, the one that never saw the light of day. Thoughts of that precious, preempted life visited him at odd times, but they didn't end there. For a man who was still childless at thirty-two—as far as he *knew*, that was—Tony found himself occasionally dreaming of what his first child might look like. There was only one problem; the children never resembled him. They were, however, always the spitting image of their mother. Serena.

"There are two answers to your quandary, young man," the chief said in a near-whisper as Tony's confessions wafted through the air. "The first is to immerse yourself in the Christian faith and in your work here. You could take a newfound focus on Christ and a focus on community service back to Chicago with you, and trust that in time God would free you of these thoughts of this woman from your past."

Tony let the chief's silence separate them for a minute before finally meeting the elder's gaze. "And the other answer, sir?"

"Resolve the unanswered questions," Nana Quay replied, his brown eyes growing increasingly somber with warning. "Very dangerous in this case, but there is a respectful way to find out whether her feelings match yours, to learn whether her marriage is bound to end regardless of your involvement. But tread with great care."

"Nana," Tony replied, scooting forward to the edge of the couch, "I'd love to think I could pursue her, but I'd have to be nuts. We don't even live in the same place. I'd have to invent some reason to even visit her city. Have you heard of Cincinnati, Ohio? It's not exactly the center of the universe. I'd look pretty suspect showing up just for the sightseeing."

The chief's eyebrows arched, flexed. "My impression, Anthony, is that you are neither lacking in creativity nor in the ability to withstand a little scrutiny. You mean to tell me there's no other reason you would have for visiting this city?"

Who could explain it, but somehow the chief's words popped loose a fact embedded in Tony's memory. *Larry Whitaker*. O.J.'s friend, the one who'd extended him a job offer days before the accident. *A job in Cincinnati*. At the time, the connection to Serena had been a mere coincidence, a "what do you know?" of no significance while he was still spending his nights romancing Colette and his days fleeing collection agencies. Everything had changed now; Tony found himself speechless at the opportunity lying before him.

"Mmm, not so fast," Nana Quay said, waving a chunky finger in front of his face. "Whichever road you choose, you do owe Ama an apology first. After that, may the good Lord be with you."

8

*H*e wasn't quite sure it qualified as a real city. As his taxicab rolled north on I-75, leaving downtown Cincinnati in the rearview mirror, Tony pulled out his BlackBerry handheld. Three days after his discharge from the hospital, he had vowed to keep a daily journal for the rest of his days, and he had plenty of motivation as he took in what some called the "nasty Nati" for the first time.

He jotted down his immediate impressions, rewinding to the moment the cab hit the expressway: the rolling hills of Kentucky, the wrought-iron and cement bridges and railways connecting Covington and Cincinnati, the Reds' Great American Ball Park, the circular stone face of Union Terminal, all of which bled out into a blander landscape dotted by rows of aged manufacturing plants.

Tony was still taking notes, trying to count how many billboards for Fifth Third Bank he'd passed, when the taxicab bounced to a sudden stop. The cabbie, a forty-something grizzled white guy with flawless grammar, whispered calmly without turning to face him. "This is it, sir. That will be forty-nine dollars."

"This is Blue Ash, huh?" A quick look around confirmed he'd missed the crossroads from urban Cincinnati into its affluent suburbia, but he was clearly on the other side of the line now. Leaning forward to pass three twenties to the driver, he stared at the spotless sidewalk and the gleaming six-story glass office tower before saying, "Keep the change."

"Do you need any help getting out?" The flicker of concern in the man's eyes surprised Tony, though he'd seen it numerous times since his release from the hospital.

"Hell, no—I mean, I'm fine." Tony reached to his left, grabbed his leather satchel and shoulder bag, and slid out of the cab. As he stood, his weight hitting his left leg with full force, he winced at the pain for a second before blocking it out. He was still shifting his weight and getting his balance when he heard the cab door slam. The cabbie had climbed out and shut it for him, before hustling back to the driver's side.

Tony stifled a twinge of humiliation and took careful, barely competent steps toward the lobby's double doors. He was halfway there when they swung open, revealing a tall, voluptuous woman with rich brown skin. Dressed in a bright maroon pants suit flecked with gray, her gold-highlighted hairdo gleaming in the early-morning sun, the sister smiled and held the door open. "Tony Gooden?"

"That's me," he replied, stopping as he stepped to within a foot of her. His left leg felt like acid had been poured through its veins and he was struggling to keep his shoulder bag steady, but he wasn't copping to that. He was a new man and all, but he was still *the* man.

"Let me take that satchel at least," the sister said, extending a hand and sending a shot of relief through Tony's soul. Grabbing it with one hand, she reached out with the other. "I'm Audrey Jacobs, principal of the Rowan Academy. Mr. Whitaker sent me down to get you."

"Beautiful," Tony said, shaking Audrey's hand and reveling in her beaming, confident eye contact. "I mean, that's beautiful of Larry to have you here to greet me, that wasn't necessary. I'm sure you have more important things to do at the school."

"Everything's important at this company," Audrey said as she ushered him across the lobby's black-and-gold marble floor. "Day-to-day business matters, but things since Mr. Champion's announcement have been crazy." From his hospital bed months earlier, Tony had read of Champion's now-legendary visit to Cincinnati, where he'd simultaneously announced large matching donations to the Cincinnati public schools and to the Rowan Academy, which he called the "brightest light of hope" for American education. "Right now," Audrey said, "with Champion pumping us full of cash and insisting we expand Rowan into a nationwide phenomenon, we need someone with your skills more than ever."

"Okay, then," Tony said, stroking his bushy beard as they stepped aboard an elevator with black doors. "No pressure, though, right?"

The elevator whisked them to the top floor, allowing just enough time for Tony to trade thirty more seconds of small talk with Audrey and bask in the smooth jazz piping over the building's speaker system. When the elevator doors opened, they stepped off and nearly ran over their boss and his slightly wealthier friend. Larry Whitaker, the executive vice president of Whitaker Holdings and CEO of the Rowan Academy, stood opposite the increasingly infamous Arthur Champion. Hoisting twenty-ounce cups of Starbucks coffee and carrying on with boisterous, lighthearted conversation, each man looked as if he had stepped off the cover of *Black Enterprise*.

As Tony limped off the elevator, Larry cut his joke short and swiveled toward his new employee. "Tony, welcome aboard, man. Got someone here you need to meet."

"This man needs no introduction." His nostrils tingling at the smoky vanilla scent permeating the office, Tony matched Larry's firm handshake and glanced respectfully at Champion. On the outside he was cool, but inside his heart raced. Ever since Champion had held that press conference announcing his multimillion dollar donation to Rowan Academy, Tony knew this job would grant him the chance to meet his hero in the flesh.

On his first day of work, though? *Damn.* Very impressive, but he wasn't prepared to maximize the moment. Improvising, Tony squared his shoulders and resisted the urge to behave like an ignorant fan. "Mr. Champion," he said calmly as he turned toward the legend and applied his best power handshake, "it is an honor."

Champion squeezed back, then pivoted toward Larry. "Uh, little Whitaker," he said, glancing in Tony's direction, "you didn't tell me you hired a dark-skinned Cornel West as your chief operating officer. You want your organization represented by a man who hasn't shaved in weeks?" Champion threw his hands into the air. "If I didn't know any better, I'd think you didn't hear a word of what I've been talking about this past year."

As Audrey cleared her throat, clearly embarrassed for Tony, Larry rocked back onto his heels, arms crossed. "You heard the man," he said, flashing a smile as he stared toward Tony. "Defend yourself, big guy. Prove you're up to the job."

Tony planted his feet and met Champion's judgmental glare. "Help me understand, sir," he said. "If I may be frank, I'm wearing a suit tailored in Paris, one that's probably worth more than Mr. Whitaker's—no offense, Larry. My hair and beard are combed, my hygiene impeccable. So, your problem with my look is what exactly?"

Champion crossed his arms, bobbling his cup loosely in one hand. "For hired help, you've got quite an ego, son," he said. "In case you missed the idea here, Larry has hired you to implement the vision I've laid out for Rowan Academy." Champion set his coffee cup onto the smooth marble counter of the receptionist's desk and stepped forward until he nearly stood atop Tony's shoes. "Your role, if I let little Whitaker bring you aboard to fill it, will be to get shit done. You should see to it that we're able to establish a branch of the academy in every major city across this country." His voice rising, he jabbed a finger toward Tony's Adam's apple. "While Larry and Audrey focus on the educational aspects, you'll be making sure we can get buildings purchased or constructed, hire good people, get positive media coverage, all that. You will *be* Rowan Academy in the eyes of most politicians, contractors, suppliers, and journalists before they meet any of the rest of us. You've done this before, right?"

"Get shit done?" Tony flinched, but only because another spasm of pain had traveled up his left leg. "Oh, I've done it many times, sir."

"That's absolutely great," Champion replied, "but it doesn't excuse that mess on your face. Are you really telling me you ran a mayor's office and a radio station with a scraggly forest sprouting on your cheeks?"

Though Champion was no taller than he was, the man's forceful energy drove Tony to plant his feet again. Neither his voice nor his stare wavered as he replied, "You're gonna have to excuse me, sir, but shaving wasn't exactly a priority in the Volta Region."

"Volta Region?" Champion paused for a beat, thrown off his game, then recovered. "Ghana, right? I've been there." He crossed his arms, leaned forward again. "Have you?"

"Barely been back a week," Tony said. "I spent the last two months there, doing economic development work for a mission. I actually split my time between three different communities."

Champion raised an eyebrow suspiciously. "You a do-gooder by nature, or trying to assuage a guilty conscience?"

Tony expelled a brief but hearty laugh. "Quite frankly, sir, I can't answer that. I'm not really the same man I was a few months ago." Calmly, with as much nonchalance as he could muster, Tony gave Champion a thumbnail sketch of the night that landed him in the hospital. Larry had already heard it, but Tony wasn't surprised to hear Audrey gasp several times. She even interrupted Champion, who listened with respectful intensity before getting off a question.

"How's your sister?"

"She's fine," Tony said. "Recovered a lot more quickly than I did, at least physically." Tony caught his breath, determined not to get worked up about Zora. "Psychologically, she's had a harder way than me."

"Well," Champion said, arms crossed, "maybe I judged you a little too quickly, Tony. That said, you've been back in the States a week." He rubbed his own cheeks playfully. "Chop, chop, eh?"

Chuckling, Larry slapped Champion on the back and smiled

at Tony. "Already passed your first test. I'm impressed." He turned back toward Champion. "Why don't you and Audrey go on into my office? Audrey, you can pull up the strategic plan. We'll review it as a team after I take Tony on a short tour."

As Audrey and Arthur walked off, Larry led Tony on a tour of the top floor, where the hallway floors were the same color as downstairs, the walls to every office except the executives' were made of glass, and the thick maroon carpet was accented with golden-colored leaves. Their last stop before arriving at Larry's office was his father's corner suite. "The old man's vacationing in Rome with my baby sister and stepmom," Larry said. "Even when he's back, though, he won't bother you much. To the extent he still runs things around here, the academy is his last priority. He says it's the last gasp of my 'bleeding-heart liberalism.' Still, he may put you through your paces just for show, so be ready to sell him on your skills."

"Larry," Tony said, cracking a grin as his boss pointed him toward his own office, "you sound like I still need to close this deal." During his last month in Ghana, he had chased O.J. down via phone, who hooked him back up with Larry. Tony had pitched Larry hard over a patchy phone connection, seemingly winning back the same job offer he'd spurned months earlier.

Sliding his hands into his pockets, Larry looked down at Tony. "I haven't forgotten your wisecracks from last time about the salary being too low, about wanting to work for the corporate office instead of the school."

"And I explained," Tony replied, reaching up to slap the taller man's back, "that I've come to see life in a different light since then. I'm for real about this." Tony stopped in his tracks, forcing Larry to do the same. "I've shed my life back in Chicago," he said, shrugging. "Rented out my condo, passed up several corporate job offers. I'm here because what Rowan Academy does *matters*. And I want the rest of my life—life I wasn't so sure I'd have a few months ago—to matter."

"Well, I guess this was meant to be," Larry said, nodding and shaking Tony's hand firmly. "You may as well know, if I'd found a better candidate by the time you called back, I wouldn't have paid you any mind."

"That would have been fair." Tony rubbed his hands together, anticipation overriding the needle-like sensation spiking through his leg again. "Let's get to work, then."

"Most definitely," Larry replied. "We'll spend the morning with Arthur, updating our strategic plan for the school's expansion. His entourage will be here to get him around noon, then you and I are doing lunch with my wife, Sheila, and our kids." He grinned in spite of himself. "They're the most important part of my life; if you're going to understand me and support me well, you need to know them."

"I'm flattered," Tony replied. "Sure you don't mind me being an extra wheel?"

"It's cool," Larry said, pausing just outside his office door. He glanced inside, where Audrey and Champion stood in front of his computer screen, discussing something of concern. "I tried to look out for you, partner. I invited Audrey to accompany us, but she wasn't comfortable staying away from the school all day."

"Totally understandable." Tony looked into Larry's eyes, players exchanging glances. "She's available, is she?"

"She's a good lady," Larry replied, his voice a near whisper. "I'm not trying to match make, but if you promise to treat her right, well, I sense she wouldn't be offended." Larry chuckled suddenly. "Damn, that's presumptuous of me. You might already have a lady here, for all I know."

Count on it, Tony thought. *Maybe not today, maybe not tomorrow, but eventually.* "I have no lady here, in Chicago, or anywhere else," was what he told Larry. That was the definite truth; after his disastrous attempt to romance Ama in Ghana, he'd decided to swear off any women until things were resolved with Serena. After his counseling session with Nana Quay, Tony had apologized to Ama and won her forgiveness, but it hadn't been easy.

"Okay, so maybe you are actually straight," Ama had conceded. "But you don't want any woman other than this one. You need to go to her."

"She's married."

"Tony, please. If that mattered, we wouldn't be having this conversation. Go to her."

His memory of Ama's cold tone faded as Larry motioned him into his office. "All right, let's see what these folk have been up to."

His brain clearing, Tony couldn't withhold the question he burned to ask. The answer was too important, too central to why he'd made this trip. Even in a town as small as Cincy, he couldn't count on crossing paths with Serena by chance. "Larry," he said, pulling alongside his new boss. "Are you still in the market for a finance director? I know someone you should definitely speak to."

9

Ms. Wilson, a short, glamorous woman with a round, healthy shape, nodded respectfully as she took Jamie's hand. "Mr. Kincaid, it's a pleasure to finally meet you."

As she watched her husband stoop low enough to take Dawn's homeroom teacher's extended hand, Serena resisted the urge to speak her mind. *Yeah, it's about time.* Not only had Jamie conveniently been in Italy during her first two parent-teacher conferences this year, he hadn't made a single conference of Dawn's last year. The past few weeks, though, she'd put him on notice: he'd either help shoulder the load of Dawn's struggles or be harassed about it daily. Apparently Jamie figured it wasn't worth the trouble to keep ignoring her. He'd even called his coach in Italy, informing him he'd have to report to Rome a few days late in order to attend this meeting.

As she took a seat across from them in the empty classroom, Ms. Wilson seemed more anxious than Serena felt. Leaning forward in her seat, planted on the balls of her feet, the teacher politely cleared her throat. "Well, as you know, we were all hoping this meeting wouldn't be necessary. However—"

"You don't need to apologize, Ms. Wilson." Looking up from her desk's cracked manila-colored face, Serena couldn't manage a smile, but she kept the flames in her gut from flaring into her eyes. "We made a deal, or should I say *I* made a deal with you." She ignored Jamie, who swiveled in his seat defensively. "I'm sure you wouldn't have called us in if something wasn't wrong."

"Well," Ms. Wilson replied, her gaze shifting slowly between the couple, "I felt it was best to discuss this in person. You know that in addition to our concerns about Dawn's grades and her lack of attentiveness in class, I was concerned about her tardiness?"

"Ms. Wilson," Jamie said, nodding reassuringly, "my wife has already filled me in. We can cut to the chase. What has she done now?"

"Jamie!" Serena punched Jamie's shoulder before she could stop herself.

Mrs. Wilson drew her back straight. "Well, if we're getting right to it, Mr. and Mrs. Kincaid, we now have a problem bigger than being tardy for class. Dawn has been skipping homeroom altogether for the past three weeks, and I understand from her algebra and English teachers that she's a rarity in their classes, too."

"I don't understand," Serena said, crossing her arms as a calming mechanism. "Where is she when she's not in class? Shouldn't school security or someone be herding her and other kids back into class? Why would you let her hang out in the hallways?"

"To be honest, Mrs. Kincaid, there's only so much we can do along that line." Ms. Wilson dropped her gaze for a second, then recovered it. "Either the children are in the school building somewhere so that a teacher or security guard spots them or they're off campus."

"Out in the street." Serena shook her head slowly. "You don't secure the building, do anything to make it difficult for a student to just walk out during school hours?"

"Though we're a traditional school here at Western Hill, Ms. Kincaid, I've found that my students are generally as well behaved as those at the magnet schools," Ms. Wilson said, sighing. "I've found that with increased parental involvement we can usually decrease behaviors like Dawn's."

His lips pursed, Jamie narrowed his eyes. "All due respect,

ma'am, I don't appreciate where you're going with this. My wife does all she can to keep Dawn motivated. We tried everything with her before we transferred her over here."

"Don't take me wrong," Ms. Wilson said, her voice rising in volume. "You both seem to be wonderful parents, meeting me like this, not to mention I'm very aware of your professional accomplishments. I also hear that your younger daughter is a complete joy for her teachers over at Clifton Elementary, so I realize some of this is out of your hands. I'm just telling you that we have a shared challenge when it comes to Dawn, in getting her to appreciate school."

Serena desperately pinched the bridge of her nose, momentarily cutting off the smell of the room's stale air. She just didn't understand. "She's made so much progress in other areas," she whispered, the best she could manage without risking a crack in her voice. The weight of parenting—the one job with no training, no pay, and countless forces working against you—pressed her shoulders toward the ground.

Ms. Wilson's eyes softened further as she reached forward for Serena's hand. "The family counseling you've been having, it's helped her relationship with her sister?"

"Yes," Serena said, gripping the teacher's hand but glancing at Jamie for validation. "She's stopped picking on Sydney, and she and I have had some really open talks about her biological father."

Jamie, his long legs uncomfortably splayed wide, his head down, nodded. "It's true. Life at home has been much more pleasant since the therapy started."

Ms. Wilson cleared her throat again. "And was it determined whether medication was necessary?"

Serena's nostrils flared as she replied, "The psychiatrist found no signs of clinical depression." Serena had feared a diagnosis similar to her relatively mild manifestations of bipolar disorder; Dawn's doctor's findings were exactly what she wanted to hear, and she wasn't about to have them second-guessed. "Dawn's made this progress without any medical help."

Ms. Wilson folded her hands together, drew her back straight again. "So, before I have to recommend Dawn for suspension, is there anything else you think we should try? Anything you want to do at home first?"

Her brow wrinkling, Serena huffed anxiously. Sister might as well ask her how to climb Mount Everest.

His eyes glued to Ms. Wilson's empathetic stare, Jamie spoke before Serena could form an answer. "If she was your daughter, what would you do?"

The teacher smiled gently. "I don't want to give up on any child, Mr. Kincaid, least of all one as attractive and bright as Dawn. Unfortunately, there seem to be other factors—things beneath the surface—at work here. I don't know that I have the resources to address them, but with your help I'll try."

Jamie bit his lower lip, then lifted his long arms overhead before standing. "We'll get back to you in a day or two, ma'am. Will that be okay?"

Still seated, Serena looked up at her husband, then at the teacher. What did he think he was doing? Like he had the final word or something.

Reading her mind, Jamie extended a hand toward her. "Come on, baby. We have to make a decision, one between us as Dawn's parents."

Ms. Wilson smiled at them, seemingly touched by Jamie's show of leadership. "I can wait another day," she said. "Just please call my extension by five p.m. tomorrow."

Once Jamie had shut her passenger door and walked around to the driver's seat of their Explorer, Serena turned to him and calmly asked, "So what's your plan, Mr. Big?"

"I'm not trying to step on your toes, Dee," Jamie replied, his voice softening. Backing the Explorer out of its parking space, he said, "I could just see you were drained back there, and there's no sense hashing this out in front of Dawn's teacher. Besides, I thought someone reminded me that Dawn is legally my child, too, or did I misunderstand that?"

"Oh, Jamie, whatever," Serena mumbled. "What do you think we should do?"

"I don't want you to slap me, okay?" Jamie smiled wryly as he sped into traffic. "I know I'm not home much, but whenever I get to talking with the brothers at the mosque about the state of the local schools, they only have love for one secular institution in town: Rowan."

"Rowan Academy?" If her husband hadn't been hurtling their car down the interstate at seventy-five miles an hour, Serena would have slapped him. "You want to send our child to the place working overtime to put my employer out of business? Dr. Kellogg would kill me."

Jamie shook his head, a self-satisfied grin twisting his lips. "Dr. Kellogg doesn't have to turn Dawn into a productive citizen, now does he? We have to make the best decision for her, Dee, not for your boss's ego."

Serena shut her eyes, letting her husband's undeniable logic flood her.

"I'm just trying to be real," Jamie said. "Of course the brothers say the Nation's schools are the best way to go, but failing that, they give Rowan real props." He paused, chuckling as he relived one of his recent conversations with the local Nation of Islam leadership. Intrigued by the brothers' record of pursuing justice but unwilling to make the sacrifices inherent in the faith, Jamie enjoyed soaking up their energy from the sidelines. "Now, they're not fans of Arthur Champion, understand. They think he did nothing but air dirty laundry with his verbal bitch-slapping of our community, but they respect what that school has accomplished."

"That place is a fad," Serena said, frowning as if she'd gotten a whiff of chicken livers. "Their success is all hype: bringing in LL Cool J to deliver motivational speeches, having Mekhi Phifer lead workshops in English class, and other showy stuff. It may look good for the evening news, but that can't bring lasting change to kids' hearts."

"You can hate on Rowan if you want, Serena," Jamie said, sighing rebelliously, "but they're getting results. I can't think of a better school to kick some sense into Dawn."

"You don't need to say it like that."

"Let me clean it up, then. I'm confident Rowan will be an edifying environment for my lovely stepdaughter." Shifting lanes suddenly, he pursed his lips again. "Better?"

"She's your *daughter*, Jamie," Serena replied, feeling her neck swivel. "Get rid of that 'step' business, okay? That may be part of the problem, for all we know."

"Damn," Jamie said, sighing and slapping the wheel loudly. "You're absolutely right, Dee. I guess I was just defensive for so long about her, the fact she's not naturally mine. We men are a proud lot, you know?"

"I'm not having that conversation again," Serena said, waving a hand and looking out the passenger-side window. "I understand though, babe. You love me so much, you wish you could have been the first man to get between my legs and make a baby."

"You're cold," Jamie replied, chuckling through clenched teeth. "A brother opens up his heart, and gets nothing but mockery. Maybe I should just tell you now, Dee."

Her curiosity aroused, Serena peered over at her husband. "What are you talking about?"

Without slowing the roll of the Explorer as it sped down the highway, Jamie glanced at Serena with a face-splitting smile. "I was saving it as a special surprise for your birthday, but you need some good news to get you past this drama with Dawn. This is my last season over there, Serena. Six more months and I'll be home for good."

Hearing the words, Serena knew instinctively that she should smile, so she did. Her eyes glued to Jamie's, she touched his knee gently.

"Look at that," he said, his smile beaming even more brightly. "I've struck Ms. Serena Kincaid *mute*. That overcome by joy, are you, girl?" His eyes back on the road, he lowered his voice. "I'm excited about this, Dee, I really am. I know Sydney will be thrilled; what do you think about Dawn? Should we tell her now, see if it helps her shape up a little faster?"

Nodding in support of Jamie's suggestion, Serena stared ahead, eyes on the evergreen trees lining the highway. Her eyes fixed to the passing foliage, she couldn't muster the will to turn back toward her husband. Despite the smile plastered across her face, she feared he'd eventually see the truth in her eyes: the truth of the cold, blank cloud expanding throughout her heart and the face nesting its way into her mind. The same face that had lain in wait the past three months: Tony's.

10

"I thought it was time I return your call."

He paused, apparently listening to the anxious rhythm of Serena's breathing. Her brain told her lungs to slow down and stop exposing the emotions this man's voice stirred, but it was too late.

Gulping, she asked, "I'm sorry?"

"Serena," he said, "this is Tony."

"Oh." She sat up straighter in her chair, subtly frosting her tone. "Kym and Devon told me about your accident. You've been in everyone's thoughts." *Especially mine.* For the first two weeks of Tony's hospitalization, every detail of it relayed by Kym, she'd cried herself to sleep, wishing she had the simple freedom to send him a card or to even call. That was a pipe dream, of course; the painful nature of their breakup as well as the prickly question of why she called the night of his accident stood in the way. "How are you feeling?"

"I'm definitely worse for the wear, but happy to be around, if you know what I mean."

Serena touched a hand to her throat. "Well, that's the right attitude. God, Tony, it sounded like a nightmare." She let the sentence lie there, unsure whether to expound. "What can I do for you? Is everything all right with Devon and Kym?"

"I think they're fine," Tony replied. "Actually, I haven't talked to them since I moved here."

Tapping out an email to a colleague—an attempted distraction from the quivers in the pit of her stomach—Serena cleared her throat. "Oh, where are you living now?"

With no hesitation, no stammer, he said, "I need to see you today, Serena."

"You're . . . here?"

He told her about his new job—chief operating officer for Rowan Academy, the bane of her employer's existence. The place she and Jamie were secretly considering for Dawn. The news didn't register at first; questions poured out of her before she could second-guess them. She had friends who'd interviewed for the Rowan COO job, and she knew that despite the boost the school had received from Arthur Champion, the pay wasn't in the range somebody like Tony would insist on. What the hell was he doing working there, of all places?

Coolly and crisply, he knocked down each of her questions, even insisting he'd always been intrigued by Cincinnati's contradictions—a slower-paced town with a few major-city trappings, enlivened by its infamous struggles with race. "There's problems everywhere, I figure," he said. "But at least here, I'm free from the real headaches of a big city."

Clearly confident about his choice, Tony sounded like a man at ease, seemingly oblivious to the one inconvenient fact about his relocation. Serena couldn't put her finger on it, but the more he talked, the more nervous she became. Too proud to just hang up but too frazzled by an already stressful afternoon to protect herself, she decided to face the music, get it over with. "Tony, I really don't have much time to talk. Is this about the wedding, when I called you?" She braced herself for his answer.

On his end of the phone, standing before his desk at the Whitaker Holdings office tower, Tony sighed. *Don't press her. Not yet.* "It's only about that," he replied, "when you want it to be." Against his every ounce of instinct, he shut his mouth and held the phone.

Serena's defensive reflexes filled the silence instantly. "I am at work, Tony." The grinding of her own teeth made her wince in pain.

"What I'm calling about," Tony responded, stifling any sense of embarrassment, "is a career opportunity you can't afford to pass up."

"Oh, really? Ten years pass and you still know more about my life than I do, is that it?"

"Stay cool," Tony said, grinning to himself. He really hadn't realized how much he missed the challenge of her—the intellect, the strength, the defiance. If he ever won her heart again, that would make it that much more impressive. "It's something you might want to consider. Will you just hear me out?"

Serena shook her head, working her neck to release the tension balling up within. "What is the opportunity?"

"The Rowan Academy needs a finance director. Between our booming bank accounts—thanks to Champion's cash, of course—and the rapid expansion we've planned, Rowan needs a dedicated financial professional—now. The Whitaker Holdings accountants have their hands full on the corporate side."

Serena couldn't deny the flicker of interest Tony had already ignited, though she worked to conceal it. "That sounds like a step down for me, frankly. I already manage an entire school system's finances, you know."

"Yes," Tony replied, "but what do you get for that, besides bragging rights about overseeing a large staff and dozens of crumbling buildings? At Rowan you'll have the chance to truly make a difference. Face it, Serena. As a finance person, you don't have much say over how successful the schools actually are, whether you're here or there. The question is, do you want to steer the finances of a ship that's sailing over a cliff, or one that's on smooth waters?"

"Maybe I like the chance to keep a ship from going over the cliff," she replied, shedding the nerves from the conversation's first few minutes. "It's easy to come off like a success in the first few years, Tony. I'd like to see how Rowan's doing ten years from now. In the meantime, the majority of poor Cincinnati kids are relying on *my* employer, not yours."

"I'm not going to argue with you," Tony replied. "Just send Larry a resumé, please. He's choosing finalists to interview within the next couple of weeks. I think he needs to consider you."

Serena's nose wrinkled as she said, "From what I hear, you all couldn't afford me."

"Don't be so sure. Larry got me cheap, but that was mainly out of spite, since I passed on his first offer a few months back. If he's convinced you're the best candidate, he'll make it worth your while. Let me give you the address to mail the resumé to—"

"Don't bother," Serena said, exhaling forcefully, eager to make her escape. "I'm not interested. Enjoy Cincinnati, okay?"

Taking a seat in his slick leather executive chair, Tony tapped his right foot anxiously. It wasn't like he'd expected a different reaction, but *damn*. "Fine," he said. "If you're a spiritual person, Serena, all I can do is ask you to pray on it. I'd hate to see you pass up an opportunity that could land you in the executive suite of a powerful black-owned company, all to spite me." He paused, considered retracting the last four words. "But, whatever."

On her end of the phone, Serena's temples pulsed with rage, a rage she let fly free and far. "I'm going to tell you this one time," she said. "Don't ever call me at work again—as a matter of fact, you don't need to ever call me *anywhere*. Did I call you the night of Kym's wedding, Tony? Yes. Why? Because in a lot of ways, my life is jacked up. Happy?"

Caught off guard, Tony simply held the phone.

His silence did nothing to cool the embers of her anger. "You couldn't even begin to live up to what the man in my life would have to handle. My daughters are at each other's throats, Dawn may be as screwy in the head as I was when we were together, and regardless of what I think of him, you better believe Jamie wouldn't give me up without a fight."

"Wait a minute," Tony said, on his feet now. "Back off for a second, will you? We all have problems, Serena. You think my life's some cakewalk?" When she didn't answer, he plunged ahead.

"If what we had was real, none of the things you mentioned would stop me from standing by your side. You know that."

"Oh, sure," she replied. She'd promised herself not to go there, but she was off the rails now. "Just like you stood by me back in the day, huh?"

Tony shut his eyes. "We should discuss this in person. Where can we—"

"I'm not meeting you anywhere, don't care to talk to you again once we hang up. Answer my question, Tony."

"I saw the both of you with my own eyes, Serena. Heard you, saw you, damn near *smelled* you."

Just referencing that afternoon made Tony shrink where he stood. Sixteen months into their roller coaster of a relationship, they'd been in a vague period. Together for three weeks, apart for two, together for one, apart for four. In the midst of all that, his stepmother, Stephanie, had been diagnosed with breast cancer.

She had never been perfect, but since the age of four she'd been the only mother Tony ever knew. For nearly a month he lost touch with Serena, spending more time at the hospital with Stephanie than his own father had. Of course, it was no coincidence he saw less of Serena during that time. Stephanie had played a small role in that.

"Don't wind up like your father." Looking weary and worn, his stepmom croaked the words out hours before her most critical surgery. "You're such a fine young man," she said, fingering his chin, "but you're repeating Wayne's mistakes when it comes to women, honey. In case I don't make it through this, do something for me, will you? Leave the bimbos alone. Date one girl at a time; focus on girls with promise. Girls who can offer you more than tits, ass, or a deep throat."

Tony still recalled leaning over her hospital bed, gripping Stephanie's hand and smiling through teary eyes. "I'll try, Steph. I really will."

"Don't just try," she whispered. "Start small. Today. Who's the girl from Cincinnati, the one you bring by the house every now and again?"

"Serena?"

"Mmm," Stephanie had mumbled, shaking her head in recognition. "A tramp. Already has a child she can't raise, scandalous history, gets around more than you do? You can't keep wasting your time with her, baby."

Though Stephanie survived her surgery and still walked the earth today, living nicely on Wayne's alimony checks, it was as close as Tony had ever come to making a deathbed promise. As a result, he stood Serena up on one date after another until Stephanie came through surgery with flying colors and doctors were confident of her recovery. Only then did he allow himself to seek Serena out again, driving to her aunt's house that fateful afternoon, hoping to apologize for dropping off the face of the earth.

That visit bought him a hell of an eyeful. Through the curtains of Serena's first-floor bedroom, Tony watched her and Jamie Kincaid merge into one eight-limbed human being, rattling her poor twin bed with a force Tony had managed on only a handful of nights. Then there was the obvious familiarity between them; this was not their first time.

She had only made love to Jamie once in her aunt's house, so despite the fact they hadn't noticed Tony that day, Serena now knew exactly what he'd seen. The memory sobered her up; it occurred to her anew that she was reliving all this on her work phone.

"Tony," she said, "that was one weak moment, one unfortunate coincidence. I guess because I never saw you with anyone else, that means you were spotless as Jesus, huh?"

"I didn't say that." Even if Serena had other lovers in addition to Jamie, Tony knew that during their nonexclusive period he'd had three for every one of hers.

"I needed you," she said, sucking a rebellious tear back inside her eyelid.

She had arrived at his apartment a few weeks after that afternoon with Jamie, newly diagnosed with her second pregnancy. Devon and Kym had relayed Tony's awareness of her dates with Jamie, but she'd already been through too much to live in shame.

She'd kept it real the second he opened his apartment door. "You may be a daddy."

He let her in, and she broke down the math: she had conceived within two weeks of her last encounter with him and her first time with Jamie. Paternity would be an open question for the next seven months. One thing was certain, though: she was homeless, kicked out by a too-through Aunt Velma. "I'm all for second chances, baby," Aunt Velma had said, head shaking in frustration, "but I'm no saint. My grace has limits."

Serena still didn't know exactly what she expected from Tony that day, but his response was definitely not it. After she'd poured out everything within, painting the picture without asking for anything in particular, he'd clasped his hands and met her eyes with an icy stare. "Call me when you get the test results."

As he shifted anxiously in his office chair, that very sentence rang in Tony's ears, just as it had the morning he burst through the doors of the church where she tried to marry Jamie. "I know you needed more than I gave you that day," he said, his voice ringing hollow in his own ears. "I was a young, self-absorbed ass. If I could have that day back—"

"What does it matter?" Serena pinched the bridge of her nose, stemming a trickle of tears. "Sidney turned out to be Jamie's, so it's really not relevant. Besides, Tony, I know everything about your mom, the way she convinced you that you were too good for me."

Freshly back on his feet, Tony found himself struck mute. *How did she know that?*

"Everything worked out just as it was meant to," Serena said, her tone officially business again. "Thank you for the call, and best wishes finding the right finance director." She inhaled sharply, then slammed her phone down.

On his end of the phone, Tony simmered impatiently, his cell phone still pressed close to his ear. The line had gone dead, which was fine with him. He had no need to flee the pain flooding him; it was nothing but motivation.

From the edge of death, to another continent, to your backyard. Serena, I've come too far to quit.

11

Whinen the time came for a "come to Jesus" sit-down with her older daughter, Serena knew she would need help. Given her own impatience with Dawn's antics and Jamie's aloof parenting style, a conference among the three of them would have ended with nothing but shouting, screaming, and someone inevitably storming off with hurt feelings. To head this off, the intervention occurred on neutral territory—her parents' massive ranch home out in Glendale, the suburban enclave where she'd made all the same stupid moves her daughter was intent on reliving.

With her mother, Jan, away from the house at Sydney's ballet practice, Professor Charles Height was on hand to serve as sole judge and mediator. One thing was certain; as jumpy and rebellious as Dawn was, she'd never "ack" a fool with her poppy.

Seated comfortably in his puffy leather rocking chair, Charles listened calmly as Serena and Jamie summarized Dawn's recent truancy and attitude issues. When they were finished, he tented his fingers and looked across his family room, where Dawn sat on a bright green beanbag chair, her head resting in her hands. "Pumpkin, these are serious matters. Tell your parents why you're doing these things. They're going to set you on the right path, but you can help them out by explaining yourself."

Scooting forward and placing her elbows on the knees of her snug jeans, Dawn looked straight at her grandfather. It was like she didn't even see Serena and Jamie, who sat to her left on a beige sectional sofa. "Poppy, I just get bored in class sometimes. Some of us girls like to kill time in other ways. We don't go out and do drugs or nothing crazy."

"Dawn," Serena said, turning an intent gaze onto her daughter, "life is not always going to be about your amusement. There are rules, child, and until you can support yourself, you're going to have to follow them."

Dawn's nose wrinkled up at first, as if offended by her mother's words, but a glance toward her poppy reminded her to dial it back. "Mom," she said, sighing and picking her words with admirable care, "I've told you about this. Everybody at school feels the same way. They're teaching us out of twenty-year-old textbooks half the time, and the teachers spend so much time making the goof-off kids shut up, they don't have time to challenge us with anything new."

"Well, then, take good notes," Serena replied, a sarcastic grin creeping across her face. "When you get your Ph.D. in education some day, you can use your experiences as evidence of what *not* to do. In the meantime, you need to get as much as you can out of your teachers."

Dawn responded by blowing air through her lips, then standing while keeping her eyes trained on her grandfather. "Typical," she said, shrugging and pointing toward her parents without looking in their direction. "That's all I get from her, Poppy. She acts like she's never been in my shoes!"

"Okay, that's enough." Serena stood, clenching her fists instead of getting in her disrespectful child's face. "Don't talk like you don't see me sitting right here."

Jamie reached up, tugging at the elbow of Serena's suede sport coat. "Be cool, Dee. Focus on the positive in what the girl just said." When his wife instinctively jerked out of his grasp, he bit his lip but continued on. "She's bored at school, you heard her, and Ms. Wilson says she's one of the brightest kids in her class.

She just needs to be somewhere that will challenge her, but also teach to her in a way that feels relevant, up-to-date, you know?"

As Serena boiled in her own stew of creeping rage, her father nodded and began stroking his beard. "You're thinking of Rowan Academy again, right, son?"

"Well, yeah," Jamie said, tugging at Serena's elbow again. "Why not try it, Dee?" Standing, he lumbered over to Dawn and draped an arm over her shoulder. "I'm going to be brutally real right here, in front of all of you, okay?" He turned toward Dawn, pecked a kiss onto her cheek. "I've failed you so far, young lady," he said. "Dawn, I know you think sometimes I favor Sydney over you, just because she's actually my flesh and blood."

Jamie paused long enough to acknowledge Serena's warning stare, then regained his momentum. "I've been guilty of that," he continued. "I get caught up in my own issues and struggles sometimes, and as a result I haven't always fought this male ego thing that makes me put Sydney first. Bottom line, I want you to know that from this day forth flesh and blood don't matter anymore. You are my child, mine. All due respect to your father, may he rest in peace, when he left his earth the creator pulled me off the bench and substituted me in for Brady. I'm going to live up that call from now on."

Serena was impressed with her husband's touching speech, but the disrespect she'd just suffered at Dawn's hands complicated her emotions as she watched her daughter's face flush with a bald, shocked glee. Reaching to wipe a tear away, Dawn spoke in a newly husky voice. "You didn't have to say that, Poppa Jamie."

After kissing Dawn again, Jamie turned toward Serena. "What do you say, Dee? Why don't we let Dawn try out a new environment—"

"She's *not* going to Rowan!" Serena's interjection burst from her so fast, she wondered whether she'd actually said it out loud. The boom in her voice, matched by the acid anger lacing the words, left the room eerily silent for several seconds before Jamie removed his arm from around Dawn's shoulder. "Why don't you just trust me on this one, Serena? Let me lead. You don't have to bear every weight. That's why I made the decision we talked about the other day."

As Serena tried to ignore Jamie's knowing wink, her initial warning to Tony hit her square in the chest. She'd told him he couldn't handle it, *it* being the grown-up challenges of raising a troubled family. Hell, at times like these she wasn't sure she could handle them herself.

Serena heard the tremors in her voice as she looked past Dawn's frown and stared into her husband's pleading eyes. "Let's not talk about your *news* right now, okay?"

"Yeah, you're right," Jamie said, flinging his long arms heavenward. "You weren't impressed by it anyway." The next thing she knew, her husband had an accusing finger leveled at her, just like her daughter had minutes earlier. "You're carrying grudges, Serena, and that's real sorry of you, real sorry."

Searching for a calm and serene response, Serena took a beat but came up empty-handed. "Who the hell are you to pass judgment on anyone? Are you kidding me, Jamie?"

Serena's words ringing in the air, Charles hopped to his feet. "Sounds like you two should have your own conversation," he said, walking over to Dawn and taking her by the hand. "Get out of here. I'm not playing." He reached into his pocket, tossed a set of keys to Jamie. "You know you've been coveting that Navigator since the day I brought it home," he said, referring to his spanking-new SUV. "Knock yourself out with it, just bring it back it back in one piece, please." He turned toward Serena as he tightened his grasp on Dawn's left hand. "When you get back, your daughter will accept your decision about where she'll go to school."

As she slammed the passenger-side door of her father's luxury vehicle, a cloud of new-car smell engulfing her, Serena decided she was too worn around the edges to be evasive. "Look, you may as well know why I'd just as soon keep Dawn out of Rowan."

Backing the Navigator out of her parents' long driveway, Jamie flicked an eye her way. "Dee, I realize it wouldn't look good to your cronies at work, but—"

She laid a finger on the shoulder of his leather bomber. "That's not it." Twisting a finger through a stray curl of hair, Serena gave her husband a thumbnail sketch of Friday's call from her first love. As sweet as Brady, Dawn's father, had been, he was simply her *first*. Love had first come calling in the person of Tony Gooden, and the very sound of his first name was all Jamie needed to hear.

He raised his eyebrows, but Serena could swear she saw the hint of a smile on her husband's face. "You're kidding me. Gooden's actually working for the academy?"

Still trying to read his reaction, Serena stuttered out her answer. "I-Isnt' that what I said? You sound like you already knew he was working here, Jamie."

Jamie let Serena stew for a couple of silent minutes, until they were zooming down Springfield Pike. "Wondered how long it would take you to fess up to that nigger being in town."

Her brain trying to calculate the possibilities, Serena didn't bother to respond.

"If you're wondering, one of the bros at the mosque knows Larry Whitaker," Jamie continued, as if she'd asked. "He mentioned meeting a new hire of Larry's earlier this week. I just knew I heard the brother wrong when he said the guy's name. Even once I confirmed it was 'our' Tony, though, I figured he was working for the corporate side of Whitaker's firm. Tony was always a soldier of fortune, not a do-gooder."

Looking out her window, Serena nodded. "I was surprised, too."

"So, uh, when were you going to tell me about lover boy's call?"

Serena whistled hot air from between her lips. "Please. It was a phone call, Jamie, nothing more. Damn."

"Yeah," Jamie replied, eyes locked onto the road as if she wasn't there. "A call you took two days to mention. But as you like to say, whatever."

"Yeah," Serena said, a fake chuckle rattling her tone. "Whatever."

"Sounds like your boy's a little worse for the wear, though, Dee. Apparently he's got some funny-looking limp, wears a short 'fro, and this scraggly beard." The twinkle in Jamie's eyes betrayed a joy at the thought of his battered rival. "I'll bet he's lost that cocky little swagger he had when he tried to take you from me."

"He tried"—Serena raised her eyebrows, letting her eyes spray plumes of fire—"to take me from you, huh? As if I was some *thing* of yours, is that what you're saying?"

"Don't go getting all feminist on me, Serena." Jamie replied, glancing dismissively in her direction. "You know what I meant. He tried to replace me in your life, in front of our family and loved ones. He's a selfish, smug ass."

"Well, for better or worse," Serena said, sighing, "you won that battle. So, can we talk about how to get Dawn back on track?"

"We'll handle that in a minute," Jamie said, opening up on the gas as he exited the ramp leading onto I-275 west. He rolled his right eyeball in her direction. "How'm I gonna go back to Italy next week, without worrying you're laid up with Gooden?"

"Oh, you have got some nerve." Serena looked away, out her window. "If I based my life around worrying whether you were laid up with folk, I'd never make it out of bed."

"Okay, dammit! Just stop it, now." The forceful volume of Jamie's voice slowed Serena's rebellious spirit. He'd never hit her or made her fear for her safety, but he knew how to show when he meant business. "I'm not perfect, Dee, but I've done right by you for a while now."

Serena shut her eyes. "Jamie . . . please."

"No, I'm not going to leave it alone." Jamie kept his eyes on the road but his voice grew even louder. "I know I was a damn stereotype for years, especially when I was overseas. I never once lied to you about how I rolled, though, did I?"

Serena sucked her teeth and looked out her window.

"Most men cheat; there's nothing unique about my weakness. But that doesn't mean I felt good about it, baby. I mean, I could make excuses—plenty of 'em. But I won't. I owed it to you to stop laying up left and right, and I have."

Serena crossed her arms, keeping her eyes on the road as if she were the one driving. "Well, bravo. Gold star for Jamie, okay?"

"My point," he said, barking his words and slapping the steering wheel for emphasis, "is that you don't get to reset the clock now that your ex is in town. I mean, I know women, and I know if Tony sidles up to you and whispers about how you deserve to be happy and shit—" Jamie waved a hand suddenly, silencing himself. "Forget it."

"Uh-uh," Serena replied, a bitter laugh pouring forth. "Let me finish your thought for you. You're scared Tony will tell me about whatever time he caught you out somewhere with some ho, aren't you?" She couldn't know for certain, but either Tony and Jamie had crossed paths under embarrassing circumstances, or her husband was crazy with paranoia.

"What happened years ago is not the point." A vein popped out on Jamie's right temple, confirming Serena was right on target. "I'm just saying that our slate should be wiped clean. I can tell you haven't let all that go, and Gooden's just the type to play on it."

"Oh, my God." Serena shook her head and blinked as if banishing a bad dream. "Tell me you're not serious. You're preemptively accusing me of planning to have an affair, when I've always been faithful to you? I think you need to get some serious help."

Smoldering with frustration, Jamie couldn't meet her eyes. "There's a lot I've never told you, Serena, but it's not what you'd expect—"

"I don't care, " Serena replied. "I don't care why you stopped cheating. I don't know if I care whether you ever cheat again, okay? I got pretty used to assuming you were with other women, to insisting you use a condom every time we make love." She hunched her shoulders. "So spare me."

"That's it." Jamie spat the words from his mouth, slammed on the brakes, and in seconds they were careening down the shoulder of the expressway. Jolted forward in her seat, Serena grabbed the passenger door's handle for leverage and stared in shock at the intent grimace on her husband's face. Hotels, corporate towers, the occasional grove of trees and fields: they all hurtled past, then the Navigator came to a jarring, skittering screech.

Staring at her husband, her hand raised and ready to strike him, Serena hovered in position. "What the hell are you doing?"

"I won't take these constant insults, not when I've tried to clean up my act," Jamie said, the words escaping in a growl as he pierced her with edgy eyes. "But you know what? I have kept two things from you, Serena. You want to hear 'em now, just get 'em out of the way once and for fuckin' all?"

Serena's hand dropped to her side, but she drew her back up, ready to wrestle her husband if necessary. "What?"

"First of all, from a young age I've been running. Running from what he did to my momma."

"Who?"

Jamie's voice caught for a second as he stared over her shoulder. "Bailey. One of my momma's boyfriends, when I was in junior high."

Serena heard the softening in her own tone. "What did this Bailey do, Jamie?" She knew Jamie's mother, who died while he was at Northwestern, had been a fast and loose lady with a revolving stable of "play uncles" for her young son, but Jamie never talked much about the men in her life. "Did he beat up on her?"

Jamie licked his lips and fixed his gaze on some point over Serena's head. "He did that and worse, until I checked his ass."

"What, you had to fight him?"

Moaning, Jamie shut his eyes. "I had to fight his worthless butt just about every day he lived with us, for close to a year. The man was a domestic terrorist in today's terms. Every night I came home ready to box, and had to sleep with my bedroom door locked so he didn't try to get revenge. It didn't end until I shot his ass one night, when I caught him basically raping Momma. He was too embarrassed to file charges, of course; he just disappeared after that."

"Jamie, Jamie . . ." Her eyes wide, Serena leaned forward to touch a hand to his face. Deep inside, a spirit whispered. *You always knew he'd been abused in some way, didn't you? Not that it's an excuse, but . . .*

He stopped her outstretched hands short, gripping them tightly but respectfully. "I don't deserve any sympathy, because I'm not done yet. The second thing you don't know is why I promised to stop seeing the other women."

The rumble of a passing truck in her ears, Serena was too shocked by Revelation Number One to encourage another.

Jamie's cheeks caved in as he inhaled deeply. "Two years ago a, uh, fan in Italy gave birth to my son. His name is Andrea." Jamie's words picked up in pace, tumbling forward in a seeming attempt to keep Serena mute. "His mom is one of the team's former cheerleaders. No one knows I'm the father except me and her family; we could have both gotten fired."

Serena heard the words but had the sense she was watching their conversation on a movie screen. This wasn't real life. "So," she said with a calm that she knew made no sense, "knocking someone else up was what made you a faithful husband again?"

"Wait, there's more." Eyes shut again, Jamie ran a hand over his bald head, his cheeks twitching. "Andrea's sick, Serena. Really sick. He's had heart problems, lung problems, you name it. From one day to the next I don't know if he'll make it. The weight of all that . . ." He drew a deep breath. "He wouldn't be living such a struggle if I hadn't made him, and he wasn't made out of love, like what you and I produced with Sydney. It woke me up, baby." Jamie opened his moist eyes, his voice beginning to quiver and shake. "It really did."

As Jamie gave in to a wave of guilty tears, Serena sat watching the movie, fully engrossed. Sitting there like a fan in a theater, she watched the wife on-screen, an actress closely resembling her, reach over and pat the husband's shoulder lightly, almost absent-mindedly. "I'm glad you learned a lesson from all that, Jamie," she said, her voice fluttering as she bit her lower lip. "You should be so proud of yourself."

With that, Serena opened the passenger-side door, slammed it behind her, and began strolling down the busy highway's shoulder. When the force of a passing eighteen-wheeler nearly knocked her off her feet, she yelled instinctively at the woman in the movie. *Move, fool! Gonna get yourself killed out there.*

12

"See, that wasn't so painful." Tony whispered into his sister's ear as she stepped away from the podium in Rowan Academy's cavernous auditorium. For the past fifty minutes, Zora had treated Rowan's four hundred upperclassmen to a reading and discussion of *One of the Boyz*, which continued to sell at a brisk pace in book-stores across the country. Tony was especially impressed by the book's success, considering that not only had he retired from the world of literary public relations, but Zora herself had been a com-plete recluse since the night they'd been trampled in Chicago.

But then, maybe her disappearing act had fed folks' appetite for *One of the Boyz*. Because the gunman at the club and several other troublemakers from that night turned out to be employees of J.T. Dog, the nightclub had filed lawsuits against the hip-hopper and his entire empire, drawing nationwide attention. Mil-lions of J.T. Dog fans were now familiar with *One of the Boyz* and the accusations that it had been inspired by the real-life exploits of their favorite rapper. Their curiosity had been fueled even more by Zora's silence, turning her into a Greta Garbo for the MTV crowd.

As usual, though, Tony's sister showed no awareness of this as he led her from the stage. "I don't want to take any more questions," she quipped hastily as he took her hand and waded into the maze of students at the bottom of the steps.

"I know, I know," he replied, hugging her against him and smiling broadly as he hustled her through the crowd. "We'd stay longer, kids, but she has a plane to catch," he shouted apologetically, hustling her past one eager student after another. A general truth, if tweaked: her plane didn't leave for another four hours, but nearly five months after "that night," his sister's fear of crowds was far worse than his.

Escaping out to Rowan's main lobby, they ran into Audrey, Rowan's principal, and Tony's father, Wayne, who had flown into town over the weekend with Zora. As several vocal teachers herded students back toward class and the lobby emptied, Tony read the body language between his father and Audrey. Standing toe-to-toe and gesturing vigorously, likely comparing notes on the differing challenges of running a high school (Audrey) versus a college (Wayne), they made a striking pair.

His devotion to Serena notwithstanding, Tony had already acknowledged a growing physical attraction to Audrey. An inch taller than him and twenty pounds too heavy to ever grace the pages of *Vogue*, Audrey was a beautiful black woman with nothing to apologize for. For Tony, who had loved a wide range of women and body types, she was a definite catch. There'd been a time he would have wormed his way into Audrey's heart and bed so fast she'd have never seen him coming.

For the past six weeks that he had known her, though, such reckless behavior had been out of the question. Many might pass judgment on him for pursuing a married woman, but at the very least Tony drew the line there. He wouldn't further his sin by stringing another woman along at the same time.

So why did it bother him to see his father standing there with Audrey, clearly working his charms with each passing minute? At six foot even, Wayne was both taller and more muscled than his look-alike son, and wielded an even more potent brand of the charisma he'd passed down to Tony. *Let it be,* Tony told himself. *You didn't move here for Audrey, after all.*

"There you are," Audrey said, beaming at Tony and Zora as they neared. Audrey's shoulders shook with laughter, clearly the result of Wayne's latest quip or joke. "Your father is a handful, but I think I've convinced him that Rowan's students are just the type he'd like to have at Chicago Technical," she said, referring to the community college Wayne had run for eight years.

"Audrey, you're not all the way there yet," Wayne said, flashing freshly bleached teeth and stroking his meticulously groomed, gray-flecked beard. "But I respect what you all are doing here." He straightened his Armani suit and winked at Tony. "Never thought you'd follow me into education, did you, son?"

"I'm proud to be here," Tony replied, looking more at Audrey than at his father. Little cracks like that one reminded him: those who knew him best still didn't understand how much the past few months had changed him. He pressed a hand against the small of Zora's back. "You all hear this young lady school these students?"

Audrey took Zora's hands into hers, her mouth set firm but her eyes smiling. "That was beautiful. I've already heard the kids raving about the chance to meet you. And thank you for honoring us with your first reading in months. I'm sure it wasn't easy."

"Well, thank him," Zora replied, smiling gingerly and nodding toward Tony.

"Trust me," Audrey said, her smile taking on a naughty edge as she winked at Tony. "I plan on it."

"Well, uh, we'll let you kids work that out once Zora and I are on the way back home," Wayne replied, chuckling as he fiddled with the gold cuff links on his white silk dress shirt. "So where are we going for lunch? We don't have long before we need to roll to the airport."

Tony smiled innocently at Audrey, wary of encouraging her too much. "Are you joining us?"

"You all are welcome to go out," Audrey said, "but if you're interested, I did have some extra meals catered in from the Lunchtime Gourmet. There's space to eat in my office, if you all want. I have to tend to a couple of fires but can join you before you finish."

Zora and Wayne exchanged glances, shrugging shoulders. "It sounds like a fine offer to me," Wayne said. "That way we keep Tony from spending away his itty-bitty paycheck."

"Come on, Pop." Tony shook his head. The jokes about how he'd "sold out" his dreams of living well were wearing thin. "We'll take you up on your offer, Audrey."

After a hasty tour of the rest of the school, Tony guided Zora and his father into Audrey's spacious office, where a corner table sat piled high with box lunches. They made their selections and got comfortable, reliving the past weekend's house-hunting trip. Wayne and Zora had strong opinions about which house Tony should pursue, and didn't hesitate to share them. He considered their points and humored them, knowing all the while he'd already made up his mind about the one he liked best.

"Well, whichever crib you choose," Wayne said, wiping an errant spray of brown mustard from his cheek, "more important than where you live is what you do. Remember that, will you, son?"

Tony set his fork alongside his Cobb salad. "I don't know that I follow you, Pop."

Wayne glanced at Zora, who had her head down, before saying, "Zora and I had agreed to bring this up with you over the weekend, but we couldn't find the right moment." He took a swig from his bottle of Evian and said, "To hell with it. Here goes, Tony. Trey told us why you really moved to Cincinnati, and we're concerned."

"Oh, really?" Tony smiled as if he found the idea amusing. "Concerned about what?"

Wayne leaned forward, ready to plunge ahead, when Zora gently touched his wrist. "Tony, it's about this woman who lives here . . . Serena?"

There had been a time when Tony's response would have been that of a car salesman—dodge and weave, play stupid, write Trey off as misinformed or misdirected. Instead, he squared his shoulders and shifted his legs, throwing one over the other. His face betraying no emotion, he asked, "What have you heard?"

Somehow, they knew everything: that she lived here, that her marriage was on the rocks, that he had never truly gotten over her. Trey knew most of this on his own, but then, as Tony recalled, his old friend had another source: Serena's girl, Jade.

"Uh, Tony," Wayne said, easing back into his seat, "I think your injuries damaged your common sense." He looked into Tony's eyes as if assessing his son's soul. "I mean, I remember meeting this girl and all—she *was* fine—but you got to know when to say when, son."

"Tony," Zora said, again touching Wayne's wrist as if to wave him off. "I-It's just that we're worried that what you went through—what *we* went through—has made you reach for something that's really not good for you—or for this Serena, for that matter."

Tony felt his forehead bunch as he replied. "Sorry, kids, we're not going there." He paused and, when they were silent, continued. "Nothing personal. If I would talk to anyone about it, it would be you two. But right now, no, this is on me."

"Son, we're just worried that you're chasing after ghosts," Wayne said, his tone as close to begging as he was known to get. "I mean, you know I'm not one to judge you on how you handle women. Hell, you haven't done anything to a woman I didn't do five times over when I was your age. But chasing an old flame who's moved on with her life, when this country's teeming with well-educated single young women? I'm not feeling it, son."

"Big brother," Zora said, eyes on the table again. "There's something you should know before you try anything with this Serena, or with anyone else."

"Zora, what the hell?" Ignoring his father for the moment, Tony stared at his sister, letting the curves in his brow communicate the betrayal he felt. Time and again he'd been Zora's cheerleader and protector; this ambush was her idea of a reward?

She gripped the edge of the table and leaned toward him. "Mom's finally agreed to meet you."

Steeling his insides, Tony forced a smile through his eyes. "A-And?"

Zora's crooked grin felt like a well-meaning pat on the back.

"With all you've done for me, I have to tell you: I think you should humor her. Not for her good, but for yours."

"What?"

"Aren't you angry at her, for the way she deserted you?" When he didn't answer, she continued. "And, don't you get angry at other women as a result?"

Tony tucked a fork back into his salad. "Wrong time, wrong place, sis. It's not like she'd actually show, anyway." Millie had already stood him and Zora up that fateful night at Excursions, a rejection that Tony knew had nothing to do with his sister.

Shutting his emptied sandwich container, Wayne shook his head. "Zora, baby, you should probably let that go for the moment." He swung his gaze toward Tony. "You know my view, son, but I'll let you and Zora work this out on your own."

Clearing his throat, Tony stifled his response when he heard Audrey's doorknob turning. They all shifted toward the doorway so swiftly, she froze in place when she saw the looks on their faces. "Oh, sorry. Am I interrupting a family moment? I can come back in a few minutes."

"No, you're fine," Tony replied briskly, standing and forcing a smile. "We'll just get going. I need to get them out to the airport and get back to the office."

Standing over them and eyeing Tony and Zora's half-eaten meals, Audrey placed her hands on her hips. "Are you rushing your family out of here?" Her pleasant smile confirmed she was picking with him. "You know you're not right."

"It's all right, Audrey," Wayne said, winking playfully. "We know when we've overstayed our welcome, right, Zora?"

His nerves jangled by his family's attack, Tony was still trying to make light of things when Audrey's cell phone rang to life with an instrumental version of Cameo's "Word Up!" She slid it off her belt and punched it to life. "Yes? What? These kids just want to be expelled, don't they?" Her eyes narrowing with growing exasperation, she bit her lower lip. "Lord Jesus. I'll be right there."

Tony tilted his head, smiling at Audrey warily as she slid the phone back onto her belt. "Anything you need help with?"

"Oh, just some antics from a few of my problem babies," Audrey replied with a weary chuckle. "We enrolled a new sophomore this morning from Western Hill, a young female who's already drawn the attention of every male student who's rubbed shoulders with her. Already got these knuckleheads fighting over her, apparently."

"The teens are a volatile age," Wayne replied, chuckling and punching his son's shoulder. "This one was a handful back in the day."

"I know," Audrey said, shaking her head defiantly. "It comes with the territory. We take pride at Rowan for showing more patience with these kids than the average private school, but—Lord."

Tony turned toward his family. "You all mind waiting here while I accompany Audrey?"

"Security's already involved, but I wouldn't mind some extra male company," Audrey said, tugging at the sleeve of Tony's suit coat. "I won't keep him too long."

Tony had his hand on Audrey's office door when Zora called after him. "Hey."

The look in his sister's eyes as Tony faced her was so dependent, so pleading, Tony had to drop his gaze to keep from being overwhelmed. He and Zora had talked nearly every other night since he'd pulled through his surgery the week after the Excursions nightmare. While he'd kept a few things—namely, Serena—from her in order to preserve the respect she held for him, she had opened herself up to her big brother.

These recent months, Tony had coached Zora through too many irrational fears and insecurities to count. Still struggling with exactly how to use the fame that *One of the Boyz* and the trauma she'd survived were providing, she had leaned heavily on her extroverted brother for inspiration. She was here today because Tony had convinced her to stop hiding. "I'll be at your side the whole time," he had said when first talking her into her Rowan speech. "This is your first baby step, sis."

When Tony had gathered his will and returned his eyes to hers, Zora's whispered, nearly silent words carried the precious force of a kid sister's love. "Be careful."

13

As Tony and Audrey raced toward the school cafeteria, she sighed playfully. "I'm curious to see what role your boys are playing in this."

The "boys" were Glenn and Ben Hampton, a pair of twin brothers in Rowan's junior class. During his first week at work, Audrey had introduced Tony to the Hamptons while giving him a tour of the school. It hadn't exactly been a prearranged introduction; the first time Tony laid eyes on Glenn, he'd had a long, muscled forearm wrapped around a bigger kid's neck.

It wasn't as bad as it had first seemed. Once Glenn and the others in the fight were separated, and Ben and other witnesses offered their testimonies, Audrey was convinced that Glenn's role was a peaceful one. Apparently he'd held the kid in place to keep him from getting into the thick of things and really hurting someone.

Regardless, Audrey took advantage of the moment to convince Tony to serve as the twins' informal mentor. Although she considered them two of her "neatest" kids—Glenn was a star wide receiver for Rowan's football team and Ben was both a local sprinting champ and a talented poet—they were short on male role models. Their mother, Evelyn, a former plant employee for

Chrysler, had seen better days. As Glenn liked to say, she raised them "when she felt like it." The boys' motivation seemingly came from an older aunt who was in poor health, but with no strong man around, Audrey summarized their dating habits as "canine" at best.

Smiling despite himself at the thought of his growing friendship with the two young bucks, Tony tried to deny the pain in his left leg, keeping close step with Audrey as they pushed open the cafeteria doors. "Well, let's see whether my boys are even in here."

As they came to a stop at the top of the steps leading down into Rowan's airy, state-of-the-art cafeteria, Tony and Audrey were surprised to find a peaceful situation. A dozen people remained—four security guards, two teachers, and six students. Five of the kids were males, all of whom sat before a scolding guard or teacher. The one female student, a cinnamon brown–skinned girl with long legs running out from her navy Rowan skirt uniform, sat alone nibbling on a fingernail. Audrey took the girl in with stern but sentimental eyes.

"Well, there's the first bad habit of hers that I'll break," she said. "Mr. Gooden, see to the twins, will you? If they were in the midst of whatever scuffle occurred, just leave them with one of the security officers. They'll bring them up to my office and I'll handle them as necessary."

Dressed in their Rowan uniforms of white rugby shirts, navy cotton slacks, and solid white gym shoes, Ben and Glenn sat speaking in hushed tones to Monty, the tall, beer-bellied officer standing over them. As Tony approached the twins, he was struck by the physical blessings that seemed a small compensation for their family challenges. With clear almond complexions, muscled, sinewy builds, and sharp, tight facial features, the twins could have been the estranged fruit of a secret rendezvous between Denzel and Whitney. Identical, their only distinguishing features were their hairstyles; Ben's low, sculpted fade was the antidote to the bushy jungle sitting atop Glenn's head.

"What's going on, Monty?" Tony shook hands vigorously with the security guard, whom he'd met once before in passing.

Slapping the big man's back, he glanced at the twins with playful disdain. "What've they gone and done now?"

"Oh, you know them well enough by now," Monty replied, showing his every tooth as his belly vibrated with laughter. "Ole Glenn here especially got himself a hero complex. Can't just let stuff *be*, know what I mean?"

"Mr. G," Glenn said, his voice full of volume, his head cocked playfully to the side. "All I did was tell Billy over there to leave the new girl alone, give her some space, nah mean?"

Tony leaned against the twins' table, crossing his arms. "In clear, concise English, Glenn."

"Come on, sir." Glenn smiled, clearly both embarrassed and pleased at the attention Tony paid to his grammar. "All I was saying is, Billy's been following that girl through the halls all day, then he sat by her during your sister's presentation today. He was on her, too. Breathing all into her face, putting his funky arm around her."

"Okay," Tony replied, nodding before turning toward Ben, who sat back in his chair with his legs crossed and his lips pursed. "Take it from there, Ben. What did your brother do to diffuse the situation, cool things out?"

Ben fought a grin, but got his response out. "I think his exact words to Billy, before the big ox took a swing at him, were, 'Even if she was feeling you, it ain't like you could handle it anyway.' Things were pretty much downhill from there, sir."

Sighing, Tony looked over his shoulder to an adjacent table where the student who had to be Billy sat with a bag of ice pressed against his cheek. The security officer standing over him gestured wildly, delivering a blistering lecture. Turning back toward Glenn, Tony asked, "Finish the story yourself, now."

"He took a *swing* and a *miss*," Glenn said, as if imitating an announcer at a baseball game. "I ducked once, twice, then three times, Mr. G, before defending myself. You want me to be a punk?"

"I saw it," Monty said, clamping a hand to Glenn's shoulder. "Glenn was actually in the right. He gave Billy several chances to walk away, let things end peacefully. Poor Billy, though, his rage had him open like a bull chasing a matador. Didn't even see that knockout punch coming."

Suddenly aware of his comparative frailty, Tony looked at his mentee with new eyes. "You did that to him with a single punch?"

Before Glenn could answer, Audrey materialized in their midst, the striking new female student now at her side. "Okay, I've heard everything. Sounds like you two are in the clear. One thing." She turned to the girl, whose auburn-highlighted hair was sculpted into a pageboy. "This young lady wanted to tell you both something."

As the girl, who was nearly as tall as Audrey, glanced from one twin to the other, Tony felt his nostrils flare suddenly. *Something . . . familiar.* "You both looked out for me," she said, a welcoming smile on her face. "You all didn't have to do that, it was way cool of you."

"This is important," Audrey said. "Whenever a young brother or sister goes out of their way to help you or affirm your worth, you should give them their just due, right? I'm proud of you two."

"Hey, it's nothing but a thing," Glenn replied, a warm and inviting smile softening his features. He trained his gaze on the young lady. "I hear your name's Dawn," he said, snapping his neck back coolly. "I'm Glenn. Number forty-two on the field, number one everywhere else."

Dawn didn't smile back, just lifted her gold necklace to her mouth and began fiddling with it. "I know who you are," she said.

"Move it along, then," Audrey said, clearly realizing like Tony that things had crossed over from sweet affirmations to naked hormones. "I'll take Dawn to her next class, and let Mr. Gooden see you two to yours."

"Let's move, young cats," Tony said, turning both twins around before they could ogle Dawn—and maybe Audrey too, for all he could tell—any longer.

"Fine with me," Glenn replied, chuckling and tapping Ben's shoulder. "Class is gonna fly by for me now. I'll be counting the minutes till I can step to Dawn properly. That's mine, dog."

Laughing, Tony shoved the twins forward. "Glenn, quit while you're ahead. She's a young lady, not a possession for you to claim. You're sounding like Billy already."

Ben turned back toward Tony, a playful grin on his face. "Oh, so you've never said that exact same phrase about a honey, Mr. G?"

"In our short time together, what have I taught you boys if nothing else?" Tony grabbed a hunk of each one's shirt, shuffling them forward as they neared the steps leading back toward the hallway. "Do as I say, not as I do."

The thought did cross his mind; it already had the second his nostrils first flared. *Serena's daughter was named Dawn.* He shrugged it off, convinced it was simply proof of the work he'd left undone. Serena hadn't called him since that one phone conversation, hadn't contacted Larry Whitaker about the finance director position, hadn't so much as bothered to acknowledge Tony's existence. She was fighting her feelings, but Tony was confident she couldn't stay away forever.

14

Serena hadn't had a full night's sleep in the weeks following Jamie's revelations, but she told herself she was thinking clearly. However tired she might be, this morning she'd admitted it to herself: she was through.

Through being the primary breadwinner for a husband who spent his time playing a child's game for what might as well have been play money. After travel expenses and his newly revealed paternal obligations, Jamie's take-home paycheck was barely half of hers.

No doubt, after years spent swimming upstream, she was through. Through pretending that her youthful sins and indiscretions meant she should never experience true romantic love.

The hard truth: she'd married Jamie only because his sperm won the lottery. Had he not beaten Tony to the punch in creating Sydney, she would have rushed to the man who truly touched her heart, assuming he'd have had her. There was every chance Tony would have fled the scene, proven less willing to tie himself down than Jamie had been. But, hell, Jamie hadn't exactly tied himself down, now had he?

Through. The word echoed inside her head as she sat in her bathroom, Sydney sitting in the chair in front of hers. "Sit still, baby," she said between pursed lips as her little girl squirmed.

"My hair looks fine, Mommy," Sydney said, drawing her shoulders up and twitching again. "All the girls at school *always* like it."

"Oh, Sydney," Serena sighed. "Those white girls only like your hair because it's as long as theirs. How many times have we had this talk?" She poured another dollop of pink oil into her hands, rubbed them together vigorously, and proceeded to massage the oil into Sydney's half-straight, half-curly locks. "They like any black girl's hair that doesn't have to be permed."

"But they like my hair, and they like me," Sydney said. "What's wrong with that?"

"Honey . . . Lord Jesus." Serena shook her head. Her sweet ten-year-old, a talented ballet dancer, was so trusting it scared her. She had to pump some street savvy into the child before she bloomed into a complete dingbat. "Sydney," she said finally, "it's time you learn that your hair does not define you, okay? Look at your daddy. Do you like his hair?"

Sydney's shoulders hopped with laughter. "No, silly. Daddy doesn't have any hair."

Serena massaged another round of oil into her baby's scalp. "But you love Daddy with his bald self, don't you?"

"Of course!"

"Well, that's just one example. Sydney, have any of the girls who like your hair ever said anything nice about your sister's hair?"

Sydney shook her head violently. "Dawn doesn't like my friends."

"Answer my question," Serena said, jerking the child so that she sat straighter in her chair.

"Ouch, Mommy." Sydney turned over her shoulder briefly, a look of betrayal in her eyes. "No," she said, in a belated reply to her mother's questioning. "I've never heard Amber or them say nice stuff about Dawn's hair."

Serena leaned forward until her mouth was level with her daughter's left ear. "Well, next time they start talking about hair, you ask them what they think of Dawn's. Then we'll talk about what they say, okay?"

Sydney's neck drooped forward. "Okay, Mommy." Nearly choking on a sob, the child's next question startled her. "You think Dawn's right to hate me, don't you?"

"Oh, Sydney, no. No." Serena reached forward, hugging her daughter against her breastbone and pecking a kiss onto her cheek. She'd gone too far. The fatigue, combined with her growing disinterest in taking her lithium as religiously as she should, was catching up to her. She had done her best to shield her children from the impact, but other than that Serena didn't care whose feelings she might step on. She was too through to be bothered.

As she finished braiding Sydney's hair, Serena worked at taking a more positive tone. She assured her daughter that the family counseling they'd had, along with Dawn's own private therapy and the family's recent decision to enroll her in Rowan Academy, had paid off.

After just a week there, Dawn was already surprisingly enthusiastic about her new school. Two of her former classmates and another friend from their neighborhood were already enrolled there, and had only good things to say about it. Serena also suspected that some of Dawn's willingness to switch schools had to do with Stevie, a roughneck knucklehead at Western Hill who had dumped her around the end of the summer. Serena was glad to have that kid in the rearview mirror but knew from experience that he wasn't the last; a girl as cute as Dawn would be drawing unwelcome attention for years to come.

The thought of her little girl in some young fool's arms made Serena dizzy with worry. She and Jamie weren't letting Dawn go out on actual dates with boys yet, but one punk after another had rung the family phone off the hook since the child's thirteenth birthday.

"Things are going to be better, baby," Serena said to Sydney as she surveyed her handiwork on the child's hair. "Dawn will be able to get a fresh start at Rowan, and she'll get better at expressing herself when she has a problem with you. All you have to do is keep loving her, and show her that you understand why she gets mad when the other girls praise your hair and ignore hers. Okay?"

By the time Serena's mother, Jan, arrived to pick up her grand-daughter, Sydney was a bouncing ball of joy again. As Sydney wrapped her in a hug, Jan smiled at Serena. "Well. Either she's eager to see me, or Mommy's been an ogre today."

Serena bit her lower lip, then smiled wanly to hide her resentment at her mother's playful accusation. "She hasn't seen much of you and Dad this week," she replied. "Dawn's looking forward to spending the night with you all, too. You have the directions to her friend Tina's house, right?"

"It's all here," Jan said, patting her black leather purse. She looked down at Sydney. "Why you still standing there looking silly? Go get your overnight bag, please."

"Okay." Suddenly choosing to hop like a kangaroo, Sydney bounced toward the front hall's steps.

"Now tell me," Jan said over the faint rumble of Sydney's footsteps, "are you sure this is a good idea? Being alone on a Saturday night, after the past few weeks you've had?" Serena's mother and father knew about Jamie's revelations, only because he chose to share them himself, the morning after his initial confession. Whatever he was, Jamie wasn't stupid; though her parents were disgusted with his actions, they gave him points for being a man and owning up to the whole thing. Like Serena, they'd always known he wasn't much for the monogamy thing.

"I'll be fine, Mom." Serena shut the door behind Jan and accepted the hug her mother offered. "I am so glad Jamie's already back in Italy. I need tonight off just to get over the stress of sharing this house with him."

"You can't avoid him forever, honey," Jan said, smiling and stroking Serena's cheek lovingly. "You two will have to make a decision."

"I know that, Mom," Serena said. "And believe me, I want to do the right thing. I want this marriage to survive." The words sounded good, sounded noble, sounded like what she figured Jan would want to hear, so Serena kept her true thoughts to herself. *A sister is through. Through. Jamie's not the only one who gets to do his own thing anymore.*

"Maybe we should talk some more," Jan said as she pulled out of their hug. Serena suddenly sensed that her mother was picking her words with care. "Why don't I let your father have quality time with the girls on his own this evening, and I'll come back over here? I just want you to make sure you're processing everything clearly, dear."

Serena glanced at her own open-toe shoes, smiling grimly. *You think I'm manic, don't you?* Serena didn't even try to convince herself that her mother was wrong; all that mattered was that her "episodes," as her psychiatrist called them, were always on the mild end of the spectrum. Not exactly the end of the world. "I'm fine, Mom," she said with the most casually reassuring tone she could manage. "Don't worry. Besides, more than anything what I need tonight is a good sleep. Soon as you all walk out that door, I'm going to bed."

"Well, if you're sure," Jan replied, glancing up at Sydney as she bounded down the steps with her bright-colored overnight bag bouncing on her shoulder.

When Serena had locked the door after them, she breathed a sigh of relief and slumped against the door. Six weeks after nearly getting run over by a semi while processing Jamie's roadside confession, she'd embraced the very reaction she first resisted.

She had come too far in life to simply snap upon hearing Jamie's news and immediately go running toward Tony. No, before embracing just how through she was, she had gamely struggled to keep it together. Up until thirty-six hours ago, when she'd confronted Jamie's baby mama, she'd tried to respect her marriage, labored to resist the chemistry that sparkled between her and Tony the day of Kym's wedding.

The other woman's name was Angelita, and not only was she predictably breathtaking—she was nearly as tall as Jamie, her pitch-black curls scraped the small of her back, and her olive complexion was unnaturally spotless—but she failed to stoke Serena's anger or sense of betrayal. When they first met, at a Bob Evans near the hotel Jamie had stashed her and little Andrea in, she was immediately apologetic, insisting that Jamie never admitted to being married until she was pregnant with the boy.

"I don't do these bad things," Angelita had said repeatedly in heavily accented English. "I know you must hate me, and I don't blame you. I just ask you not to hate my boy, Jamie's boy." When she stopped to wipe her tears, Serena noticed Angelita's one blemish: dark circles underneath her eyes, evidence of the maternal stress associated with tending to a sick child.

She'd clearly been a vibrant woman when she first drew Jamie's attention, but Serena looked at the woman across from her and counted her blessings. Motherhood had been a struggle for her in many ways, sure, but she knew from an hour's conversation about Andrea's dozen surgeries and team of specialists that she had it easy by comparison. Truth told, she had it easier than Jamie; given that he was too much of a human being to walk away from his own child, she knew he was as tormented by Andrea's illnesses as Angelita.

As she left the Bob Evans, Serena realized that she shouldn't end her marriage out of spite; she should just release Jamie, free him up to provide Angelita and Andrea with the steady strength and support they so desperately needed. He'd never shown it for her or the girls, but maybe he'd find it for his new family.

Her mind made up, the house finally empty, Serena hustled to the kitchen's cordless phone. Even with the growing fog that had descended the past few days, she knew she had to act fast to beat the gremlins of caution and guilt. She picked up the phone and dialed Tony's cell phone number. She stood there in her family's kitchen, breath growing short, as she relived the last time she dialed this number.

It was not déjà vu, though. This time, he answered.

15

He had offered to simply meet her at a nearby restaurant, but Serena was in a zone that laid her feelings flat against her sleeve. "I don't want to eat a meal with you, Tony," she'd snapped when he first suggested a rendezvous at an Applebee's. "I want to talk. Where do you live?" Minutes later, she drove out to Sharonville and zoomed her Volvo into the parking lot of his Extended Stay hotel, her inhibitions loosening with each passing second.

When Tony answered the door, any doubts about the wisdom of her impulsive move faded. The man before her was not the same one she'd traded wisecracks with at Kym and Devon's wedding. Dressed in an unbuttoned white dress shirt, navy dress slacks, and an expensive-looking pair of dark brown shoes, Tony looked at her as if he'd known this meeting was inevitable. A calm, self-assured peace radiated from his every pore. He smiled slowly, rolling out his pleasure at seeing her in small bits. "Hello."

"What's up?" The words slid from Serena with a tempting ease she hadn't allowed herself to feel in years. Leaning against Tony's doorway in her thigh-high plaid skirt, black heels, and white silk blouse, she recalled a striptease routine she'd done for him in their youth.

Gripping his doorknob and trying to deny a new flash of pain shooting up his left leg, Tony did a double take at Serena's casual tone. It seemed the past eleven years had been erased. This wasn't Jamie Kincaid's wife; it was his "boo" of years ago.

When he stayed silent, stepping aside to let her in, Serena strolled past him, hips in motion. "I appreciate you taking my call," she said, smiling with her eyes as she passed.

"Guess we finally felt like talking at the same time." Admiring her walk, Tony stood at the doorway, hands in his pockets as she took a seat on the small couch in his front room.

Serena leaned back against the couch, spreading her arms wide and crossing her legs with sass. "You might say that."

Once he had shut his door, Tony took a few steps toward her, choosing for the moment to suppress his delight at the trail of perfume she'd left behind. One of the newer Obsession concoctions, he'd smelled it on other women but it was a perfect match with Serena's natural scent. "So, I asked Larry who all he had interviewed for that finance director job—"

Serena shook her head, chuckling. "And he mentioned my change of heart."

Poised a few feet from her, Tony crossed his arms. "It didn't sound like you, Serena. He said you submitted your resumé one minute, then called a couple days later to say you were too busy to interview?"

"Yeah, I know," Serena replied, shrugging. "Flaky as hell, wasn't it?" She reached for her purse. "Would you mind if I smoke?"

Tony felt his eyebrows draw up. "I thought you—"

"Quit? Yeah, well, there's quitting, and there's cutting back. I can only be so good, Tony."

He sucked his teeth, not appreciating the defeat in her tone. "This is a no-smoking room. If you gotta light up, let's get out of here." He paused. "Unless you can't afford to be seen."

Serena rolled her neck anxiously. "What kind of question is that?"

Welcoming her familiar defiance, Tony turned sideways. Downstairs he was growing, extending, pulsing. He hadn't had sex since his hospitalization, partially because thoughts of Serena had rendered him no good for other women, partially because he was afraid his hobbled leg would disrupt the sexual rhythm he'd mastered over two decades of experience. With Serena of all women here before him, his unplanned abstinence made it hard to think straight. As much as he wanted her now, it wasn't yet time, and if Tony had ever wanted to have a woman at the right time and in the right way instead of just any old way, Serena was that woman. "Let's just get out of here, please?"

Insisting on something more adventurous than a lame meal of chicken fingers at the nearest TGI Friday's, Serena used Tony's laptop to pull up the night's happenings on AroundtheNati.com. Her search quickly yielded a concert at Bogart's featuring Glenn Lewis and Avant. The show started in minutes, but Serena called and confirmed they were still selling tickets.

She drove his red Passat to make things simple. As Serena maneuvered them toward the city limits, Tony probed her gingerly. "You didn't sound happy to hear from me a few weeks ago. What's changed?"

"Come on, Tony," Serena replied, huffing and pushing her lower lip out for emphasis. "Do we have to get deep tonight? What if I just came to my senses?"

Tony tipped his neck back against the headrest. "What did Jamie do?"

Staring at Tony like he'd distracted her from a more important task, Serena zoomed through a yellow traffic light. "Jamie's just being Jamie. You knew that; that shit's not news."

"Serena, please." Tony's ears rang at the sound of her foul language. It was beneath her.

"What?" She flicked a nasty glare toward him, then put her gaze back on the road. "Am I not enough of a challenge when I act like the girl you knew? Huh? You want me to be a happily-married mother and professional, don't you? A prim grown-up that you get to *turn out*." Her shoulders jumped as she said, "Yeah, it's all about what feeds Tony's ego."

Tony tried to ignore the dig, but failed. "That's not fair, you know it." He saw no point in arguing this out; he recognized Serena's trash talk from moments in their past, moments when the manic depression she managed so adeptly tightened its grip. There was no setting her straight when she was in this space; best to play along and fight another day. He'd always found these moments fleeting with her, and they'd never dampened his belief that he could help her fight through the haze.

Inside Bogart's, they downed rum, Coke, and vodka before standing toe-to-toe on the club's crammed dance floor, fifty yards from Avant as the singer crooned about reading a girl's mind. It was too loud for most meaningful conversation, but that was just as well. The hypnotic rhythm of swaying couples gave them the motivation, the privacy, to simply rest in each other's arms. From up-tempo numbers where they matched dance moves to slow jams that merged them at the groin, Tony and Serena snapped into place. "Like we've never been apart," he whispered into her ear. This, he thought, was what God intended when he formed woman from man.

In the midst of the moment, Serena felt the first peace she'd experienced in months. Here she was, surrounded by any number of folk who might recognize her with this man who was not her husband, and she couldn't have cared less. Whatever his other issues, Tony Gooden had tried to keep her from marrying the wrong man, and she'd always known that. Maybe tonight was her first step toward correcting a bad decision.

"So," he said into her ear, louder than a whisper but with too much cool to sound like a yell. "Does this mean you're willing to interview with Larry now, maybe work for Rowan?"

"Not so fast, Mr. Gooden," she replied, smiling and pulling him closer with a firm grip on his chin. "The hard part comes later." Shutting her eyes, she let her lips go slack as his arrived to meet hers.

Meeting Serena's kiss and gripping her close, Tony felt his eyes fill with tears. It was as if he'd arrived home after years imprisoned overseas, been fed his first meal after weeks of starvation. *I'm home,* he thought as his mind emptied of everything that had come before this moment, everything that might follow. *Home.*

16

*F*inally indulging the desire that had first gripped her at Kym and Devon's wedding, Serena was so overcome with joy that she nearly sailed out the front door of Bogart's once Tony helped her slip on her light overcoat. One hand clasped to his, she didn't take her eyes off the star-lit sky overhead until they reached Tony's car. When he tried to steer her toward the passenger-side door she resisted, resting her backside against the driver's door and drawing his chin close. "Burnet Woods," she said in reference to a nearby park. "It's too much of a pain to tell you how to get there, so I'm driving again."

The grown-up in Tony fought back a pleased grin. Serena didn't have to connect the dots for him; she was ready, in that willing state that teen boys and most grown men lived for. Tempted as he was to take advantage, he wrapped figurative arms around his pulsing loins; he was in this city because he loved Serena Height-Kincaid, and she was far too precious to just slide up in without any forethought or planning. He pulled his car keys from her reach. "Let me chauffeur you this evening, okay?"

Her back arching defensively, Serena wrapped her arms around Tony's neck. "Is that the sound of you blowing me off?"

"This," he replied after kissing her quickly on the lips and lowering her arms from him, "is me savoring every moment. I'll make you a deal."

Growing suddenly suspicious, Serena tried to read Tony's emotions through his slightly damp, glowing brown skin. She *had* showered before leaving the house, hadn't she? Something felt wrong about his restraint, but she decided to roll with it. "What's the deal?"

"You go for a little ride with me, I'll give you a nice surprise."

Humming with laughter, Serena opened the driver's side door and held it open, an arm extended. "Climb in, kind sir. I'll ride wherever you go."

They were ten miles north of downtown, speeding up I-75 toward Dayton, when Tony completed his part of the deal. "Look underneath your seat there."

"Hmm," Serena chuckled, leaning forward as her head filled with images of a silk teddy, a pair of lace panties. "Let's see whether I'm still as small as you remember."

"Uh-oh." Smirking, Tony stole a glance in her direction. "If you were expecting something sparkling and off the rack, you may be disappointed."

"Oh, shut up," Serena replied, rustling around beneath the seat. "You're so—" She was struck dumb as she slid the "gift" from beneath the seat.

"Your senior favorites book," Tony said, referring to the thick pink-and-white scrapbook holding Serena's most precious high school moments. "You had left it at my place just before you started seeing, uh, Jamie. I never got the chance to return it, for obvious reasons."

"Oh, Lord," Serena said, feeling the light of the smile radiating from her own face as she flipped through photos of herself cheerleading, playing in the band, attending prom with Dawn's father, Brady, and cruising the halls amidst a pack of girls she always cut class with. Taking a deep breath to ward off the sentimental feelings flooding her, she couldn't meet his eyes. "Tony, I thought I had lost this altogether. I never even realized I'd left it at your place."

"Well," Tony replied, "before I apply for sainthood, it wasn't like I didn't know you'd left it there. I was still in a spiteful place when I first found it."

Serena cut him up and down with a *tsk-tsk* of a stare. "Oh, so you let me pull my hair out thinking I'd lost it, huh?"

Tony shrugged. "I wasn't exactly going out of my way to return your things. That said, I did have it out in my car when I crashed the wedding." Slowing the speed of his Passat and hopping over into the right lane, he turned to face Serena nearly full-on. "If you'd made the right choice that day, you'd have gotten this back then."

"Don't go there," Serena said, her voice dropping. "I'm not ready to get deep, Tony. I just want to have fun tonight." She took a look around, frowning when she saw they were nearing Cin-Day Road. "And where do you think you're taking us? You may not realize, but we'll be in Dayton's suburbs in a few minutes."

"Yeah, I know," Tony replied, his tone calm and patient. "Isn't there an area up ahead called Centerville, has a nice mall and a lot of other shopping?"

"Yes, it's your typical midwestern middle-class suburb, packed with Olive Gardens, Applebee's, and Starbucks. Why are you driving there? We've already passed five other exits just like it."

Tony kept his focus on the road, but in the light of a passing Jeep Serena could see his eyes flash with the precision of a planner. "You don't know anyone who lives in Centerville, do you?"

"You'd be right with that guess," she said, catching his calculation instantly. "Once you get past Monroe, you're out of my community. Thank you for preserving my reputation, Mr. Gooden."

"I know, never mind that we just bumped and ground our way through Bogart's, right? At least this way we can talk away from prying eyes. Unlike some of these other redneck communities, I'm assuming Centerville is the next area I can roll through without being pulled over for Driving While Black?"

Serena tittered. "Don't bet any money on that one."

Their conversation downshifted into small talk until they

pulled off the highway, rolled past an emptying Dayton Mall, and parked on a sparsely lit, tree-lined residential block a mile down the road. Serena sat in silence as Tony climbed from the car and walked around to her door. As he opened it for her, he reached a hand forward. "Walk with me?"

As they strolled hand in hand, their hips close but far apart enough to look respectable, Tony smiled in Serena's direction. "Okay, so tell me exactly why you called from out of the blue *now*."

"Tony, we talked about this before we went to the club. Don't make me rehash Jamie's mess, please."

Biting his lower lip and grinning, he said, "I'm not asking a thing about Jamie. I'm asking about you." He came to a stop, clasped both her hands, and peered into her oddly shy gaze. "Are you manic right now, Serena?" When she tried to tick away from his line of fire, he cupped her chin lightly. "Maybe just a little bit?"

The question made Serena's spine itch, but she was shocked by the warmth suddenly coating the pit of her stomach. *He knows*, she thought. *Senses, at least*. In the days of their youthful romance, her mania had reared its head a few specific times, including one that resulted in her hospitalization. Tony had seen her through that crisis, visiting as much as was allowed and moving her in with him for the first few nights after she was released from the hospital. She had always waited for him to finally grow tired and dump her over the depression, and to this day she wondered whether that had been a factor in the end of their relationship.

He was still looking at her, calm but concerned. "I won't judge you. I need to know if you're with me tonight for the right reasons, that's all."

"Trust me," Serena whispered, leaning her head against his chest. "I'm here because I've wanted to be right here since I saw you at the wedding. Honest." She patted his lean stomach for a minute, inhaled his woodsy cologne, the pomade brushed into his hair. "But, yes, I'm a little manic. I haven't taken my lithium in a few days. I guess I've let Jamie get to me again."

Given that she'd held Jamie's most recent confession so close, spilling it to Tony sounded strange to Serena's own ears. She watched her ex-lover's face twist with disgust at the news of Jamie's betrayal, and knew again that she had chosen poorly on the day of her wedding.

"That's enough," Tony said finally, laying a finger to her lips as she recounted another litany of Jamie's infidelities. "He's really beside the point. The question is whether you want to get back at him through me, or whether you want to eventually be with me."

Chewing over his words, Serena felt some of her own mental fog lift. "You may have a point, Mr. Gooden, but for the record why would I want to jump right from Jamie to you? Like I said at the wedding—Kym's wedding, that is—it's no coincidence that you're still single. If you wanted the dream a woman like me wants—the spouse, the kids, the white picket fence—you'd have found someone to discover it with by now."

"Interesting theory," Tony replied, languidly resuming their trek but keeping his eyes on Serena's. "So there's no chance a man like me is single because he's carrying a torch for that one special someone?"

"Oh, I've known men for whom that might be true," Serena said, "but you're nothing like them. They were all the sort of guys who only get so many cracks at the women of their so-called dreams."

"And I'm the type who can just land a superwoman whenever I want one?"

Serena sliced him with another stare. "Don't act like I don't have a memory, brother. You and I were always fighting off folk trying to get between us. We were both in demand."

Hands in his pockets, Tony shrugged. "I don't get your point, Serena."

"How's this? I'll bet you've ended every relationship since me, just as it got serious."

Tony peered heavenward, did some quick calculations. "You'd be right about eighty percent of the time. I have had my heart broken since you, believe it or not. That's proof that my heart's generally in the right place." Her name had been Juanita, and the pain had lasted roughly seven and a half weeks, if he recalled correctly. By comparison, the clock on the pain Serena inflicted ten years earlier was still running, but he didn't mention that.

As they continued past one brick ranch home after another, Tony and Serena's discussion continued this way, rising and falling, alternating between playful conversations about their adult lives and heated discussions over the meaning of this very night.

"What drew you to Cincinnati, really—me or the Rowan Academy?" Serena crossed her arms, getting to the point as they circled back toward Tony's car.

He took a slight step away from her, as if sensing the importance of his answer. "I believe in what Rowan does, don't doubt that," he said. "And it was Larry Whitaker's call, months ago, that first got me thinking of moving here. Would I have moved here if you lived somewhere else, though?" Tony paused, took a few quick strokes on his beard. "I'll let you make that call." A small part of him feared that the truth would eventually lead to a stalking charge.

They were there in the dark, staring at each other and standing not fifty yards from the Passat, when a police cruiser pulled up with silent lights, its orbs and flashes placing the couple in an unwelcome spotlight.

The next few minutes proceeded in the exact way that Tony's father had warned him of from a young age. "When you're in *their* neighborhoods," Wayne had first told him when he turned thirteen, "you have to accept that you're on enemy territory. You're not welcome, least of all after dark and even more so if you're in an odd car—either one that's a junk heap, or one that's nicer than most of the residents can afford." When the pair of officers, both of them around Tony and Serena's age, climbed from the car, Tony heard his father's voice whispering inside his head. As the heavier officer's greeting question—"You two live around here?" delivered in an inappropriately skeptical and threatening tone—hit his ears, Tony acquiesced to Wayne Gooden's teachings.

With one officer in his face and the other one leering disre-

spectfully in Serena's direction, Tony spoke calmly and respectfully, carefully explaining exactly why he and his lady friend had
traveled thirty miles up the interstate to hang out in this precious,
alien neighborhood. He even ignored the taller officer's knowing
crack about their left hands—Serena's wedding ring, his complete
lack of one. He was pissed off at their nerve, craving the chance to
suggest they get real jobs fighting crime in an urban area. He realized, though, that he had to look out for Serena's immediate welfare as well as his own. As a result, Tony did what the responsible
black man occasionally must do: eat it.

Back in the car, hurtling back down I-75, Tony's grip on the
steering wheel didn't lift until Serena grazed his shoulder. "You
gonna make me ride all the way back in silence?"

"Got to get you home," Tony said, forcing a brittle smile. The
sober end to the night had reminded him that Serena had a family waiting on her. "You need to be rested when your mom brings
the girls back in the morning."

"That may be true," Serena replied, "but that doesn't mean you
have to drive. I think you need a little rest, Tony. Why don't you
pull off at the next exit. We'll get some coffee; then I'll drive the rest
of the way while you cool off from those assholes' harassment."

Releasing the knots in his brow, he was unable to argue with
her logic. "All right, you have a deal this time." His guard down,
he took an exit three miles later and made a right turn off the
ramp.

That's when she signaled her intentions, a warning that came
too late given her quick touch. "You remember what we used to
call our 'rest stops' back in the day?" His mouth had barely
formed an "o" meant to ward her off when Tony felt Serena's
hand running from his right knee up the middle of his thigh.

Shuddering involuntarily, he looked at her, feeling a cocktail
of pleading and hunger within. "Now look, w-we talked about
this."

"I know," Serena said, leaning over as Tony involuntarily followed her every navigation. Up ahead lay a Super Wal-Mart just
shutting down for the night, its lot empty save the cars of em-

ployees finishing the night's close. "Go straight, then we'll hook around to the back lot," she whispered, her voice the coo of a young mother.

When he had pulled into a space in the lot's dark, deserted corner, Tony sighed before leaning over and kissing Serena lightly. "I mean it," he said as he pulled away, knowing in reality that she had him wide open.

"Oh, I know you mean it," Serena said, pulling Tony's chin back toward hers. "We've talked about plenty tonight. Enough with the tell, Tony; I'm ready to *show*."

17

When he awoke the next morning in his hotel room, Tony was alone but in no ways lonely. Wiping his eyes and yawning with contentment, he felt a rise in his spirits as he smelled Serena's perfume, still thick in the air. Running a hand over a pillow matted with squiggly strands of her hair, he inhaled deeply as an image from the night before hit him.

Seated in his car's passenger seat, he had braced himself as she hiked her skirt, lowered her panties, and straddled him. Momentarily freed of the pain in his leg, he'd let years of experience and his dormant familiarity with her body take over. With each stroke, lick, and tickle, the truth in his heart rang with added clarity. *I'm home.*

He was now too much of a gentleman to dwell on it, of course, but it wasn't lost on him that he'd stepped up to the plate quite well for a brother who'd kept it in his pants for five months. There with Serena, parked in the corporate shadows of the Super Wal-Mart, he'd come off the bench and nearly matched their teenage glory days.

He didn't believe for a second that this was an accident; no, this was meant to be. Those who loved him most thought he was out of his mind, and for his first two months in Cincinnati it seemed they might be right. Against all odds, Tony told himself the past twelve hours proved them wrong.

Rising from the bed, he grabbed his silk boxer shorts from the floor and stepped into them, drawing the undies up over his narrow hips. Quickly, he searched the apartment for any hopeful sign Serena's absence might be temporary. Seeing no such evidence in the bathroom, front room, or kitchenette, he shrugged confidently. She'd be back. She did have a family to tend to.

Returning to the bathroom, he went to the sink and drew back the mirror covering his medicine chest. That was where he saw Serena's handiwork.

Propped in front of his can of aloe shaving cream was a card in a red-and-white envelope. It was a sign of just how dull his senses were that his immediate reaction was joy. Snaring the card between a thumb and forefinger, he smiled sheepishly, wondering what creative words she'd used to praise his performance last night. When his smile faded, it disappeared in small bits and pieces as he interpreted the hastily scrawled words.

I love you, but I can't promise ANYTHING .

18

Lucky for Serena, she'd always been a light sleeper. Her eyes popped open at the slight squeak caused by the turn of a key in her front door. As her vision came into focus, she stared first at the eggshell-colored ceiling overhead, then lowered her gaze to the disheveled clothing covering her exhausted body.

"Uhh." Propping herself up on her elbows, she looked over her shoulder to see her purse and heels lying on the floor a few inches away. Rolling her tongue around the inside of her mouth, she tasted the residue of cigarette smoke and instantly knew she'd relapsed. From the way she was sprawled out in her living room, it had clearly been one of those nights where you did well to find your own home, get the key to work properly, and collapse just inside the door.

As her ears filled with the creaking of the front door, Serena began a ritual she'd hoped to leave behind: cleaning up after a manic episode. Her doctor always stressed that her episodes were really hypomanias, far milder than those experienced by most of his patients, but that was a small comfort. It did, however, mean that Serena more quickly recognized the wreckage she left in her own wake, and that was why she was ready now to cover her tracks.

"Hello!" The giggling of the girls in the background, her mother's voice echoed through the house as Serena hopped to her feet and crept up the back staircase. "Serena! Your babies are here!"

Nearly at the top, Serena hustled up the steps and rounded the corner. She didn't say a word until she'd crossed the doorway of her master bedroom. "Hey!" Gripping the bedroom door and swinging it halfway shut, she leaned through the opening. "I was just about to get in the shower! Be right down!"

Slamming the door behind herself, she bit her lower lip and tried to catch her breath. Already she could hear Sydney's light footsteps flitting up the stairs. Turning the lock, Serena jogged into her dressing room and began stripping off the very clothes Tony had pushed past hours earlier. The very thought rewound her to the first moment when he entered her, to the exultant, thrilled look in his eyes. The purity of his desire for her was intoxicating, intensifying the heat flooding her body as they rocked that poor Passat in a way Volkswagen never intended. She'd lost count of how many times she'd slammed her palms against the car's ceiling, her hands flailing in uncontrollable ecstasy.

"Mommy!" Sydney tapped eagerly at the door. "We're home! Let me in."

In nothing but bra and panties, Serena stared into a mirror as she hastily removed her earrings. "Give me a minute, baby. I just came out of the bathroom."

Sydney's tapping turned into solid knocks. "Mommy! Come on, I want to show you what Granny bought me. I helped pick it out!"

Serena stared over her shoulder, smiling at her little girl's loving impatience. "Okay, baby, here I come—" Turning her head away from the mirror, she was cut short by the sight of a scar on her neck. Distracted, she asked out loud, "What is that?" Leaning closer toward the mirror, her heart dropped as she realized this was no scar. It was a pure, undeniable passion mark, the sort little Willie Johnson always left behind after their junior high make-out sessions. In his fevered state, Tony had left an oval-shaped hickey inches below her left ear. "Oh, God," she whispered.

Sydney's knocking hadn't slowed yet. "Mommy!" Her voice took on a distant quality, as if she were shouting back over her shoulder. "Granny! Mommy's not answering me!"

"Sydney!" Serena hustled to the other side of her door, leaned against it. "I'm coming, baby. Just be patient." As the words spilled from her, she hopped over to her dresser and yanked out a thin red turtleneck. *Lord Jesus, it's high school all over again.*

When Serena finally flung her bedroom door open, well concealed beneath the turtleneck and a matching pair of nylon sweatpants, Sydney jumped into her arms before taking a step back to strike a pose. Her movements showed the grace her ballet instructors had been drilling into Sydney for the past year. Clad in a pretty blue-and-white-striped jumper, the child was stylin' and proud of it. "See?" She asked, beaming.

"Ooh, Sydney, look at you." Serena placed her hands against her hips and frowned playfully. "You trying to match your momma or something, looking so good? You didn't really pick that out all by yourself, did you?"

"Granny will tell you she helped me," Sydney replied, winking confidentially, "but it was really all me. She just paid for it."

"Oh, child, listen at you." Jan snuck up from behind Sydney, peeking her head into the bedroom but staying at the threshold. She raised her eyebrows at Sydney before smiling at Serena. "She did find it first, though. I guess she gets her fashion sense from you. I'd have her and Dawn dressed like schoolmarms if it was my call."

"Mark that on the record," Serena replied, chuckling and feeling the sweat on her brow dry. "You said it this time, not me."

"Well, that doesn't mean you get a pass on saying it again," Jan said, crossing her arms. Her smile faded slightly as she asked, "Sleep well last night? You must have been knocked out when I called you. Both times."

Serena drew Sydney up against her and played lovingly with her baby's long locks of hair. "I went out for a few hours," she said. There'd been a time when she would have taken her mother's invitation to lie and accepted it with open arms. She was a grown woman now, so she decided to take a pass on that. She might be picky about how much truth she'd share, but she wouldn't tell outright stories.

Jan shut her eyes momentarily, then looked at Sydney. "Will you go get your sister for a minute? I need to talk with your mother about big-girl stuff."

As Sydney strode past Jan, Dawn's name on her lips, Serena felt as if she was losing a protective shield. She tried to smile without straining herself. "So, is this going to be a grand inquisition?"

Jan adjusted the fit of her wire-rimmed glasses against her narrow nose. "I'm just sensing an evasive spirit, Serena." She crossed the threshold and came to within a couple of inches of her daughter. "You've suffered a stressful event, honey, learning about Jamie's child. Any woman would have a difficult time handling that."

Serena stepped around Jan and reached for the bedroom door, which she shut with carefully restrained force. Turning back toward her mother, she didn't blink back the tears forming. "And if 'any' woman would have a tough time, certainly a nut with my issues would, is that it, Mommy? You think I'm manic, again, don't you?"

"Serena, don't start trying to make me feel guilty for asking." A bead of sweat rolled off of Jan's nose as she crossed her arms again. "Don't forget I have walked a few miles in your shoes." The best explanation Serena had for her own depression was her mother's experience with what today would be called postpartum episodes. "You can handle *anything* if you do the right thing about your medication," Jan said. "You *are* still on it, aren't you?"

"Of course." The rattle in Serena's voice traveled down her throat into the pit of her stomach, and she swore to herself that she'd get back on the lithium this very morning. She felt as if her mother had X-ray glasses and could see through her turtleneck and sweatpants, as if Jan was well aware of the passion mark and even the DNA Tony had left inside and outside her body. The guilt pushed her to make another internal resolution; Monday morning she'd call Dr. Kristos and schedule an appointment to confess her relapse.

Jan reached a hand forward, a familiar look of loving pity rising in her eyes. "Serena, honey, let me—"

Serena turned away, her hands on her hips. "I said I was fine, Mommy." She raised a hand, waving anxiously. "Thank you for watching the girls, but I'm fine now."

Silence filled the room and Serena could feel her mother calculating the right reaction. "I'm here when you want to talk," Jan said finally. "You know we love you very, very much."

Still unable to face her mother, Serena waved a hand again. "I love you, too, Mommy. Bye."

Serena spent the rest of the morning and afternoon attempting to atone for her wild night. She was too thrown off her regular schedule to get to church with the girls, but after taking her medicine and napping for an hour she fixed them lunch and then suggested they play outside. As the only nonathlete in the family, playing any sport with her daughters was Serena's ultimate sacrifice. Whether in tennis, volleyball, or kickball, Dawn and Sydney had become her superior by the respective ages of four and six. That wasn't even getting into basketball, the sport Dawn most excelled at and one Sydney was strong in in her own right.

As humiliating as the experience was, Serena stayed out on the family's driveway basketball court for nearly an hour. As she missed one shot after another and watched her girls sink the majority of theirs, a pinch of her morning unease wore off. The physical activity focused her mind unexpectedly; as she ran in panting pursuit of her daughters, the foolishness of her escapade with Tony slammed home. It wasn't even about loyalty to Jamie. It had nothing to do with him, really. She'd earned the right to relieve herself with someone else, in exactly the way he'd done for years.

No, it was all about the girls and her parents. None of them deserved the humiliation that would come with Serena's impulsively taking up with an old boyfriend. First, the girls would suffer the traumas of a broken home; then both they and Serena's parents would have to endure all the "told you so" comments from people who'd looked down on her back in the day. For people who defined Serena Height by her years of boozing, drugging, and just plain being "common," the disintegration of her ten-year marriage would fit right in. She wouldn't give them the satisfaction.

The rising determination in Serena's spirit powered her as their game of twenty-one drew to a close. She guarded Dawn as closely as she could, matching her taller daughter's pace and keeping her from getting a clear shot off.

"Ah, you think you bad now, huh, Mom?" Laughing and pulling her hair back into a tighter ponytail, Dawn backed up to the edge of the court. "You can't handle this."

"Maybe not," Serena laughed, awaiting Dawn's next move on the balls of her feet. "I'll die trying to, though, so come on with it." They had gone at it with this snappy patter all afternoon, and it felt so good. Dawn's attitude about everything had brightened in the days since she'd been enrolled at Rowan. Serena's optimism about the school had only increased after her opening conference with Audrey Jacobs, the school principal. As long as she could keep Tony from getting in the midst of things, Serena was confident she'd made the right decision.

As Dawn scored a three-pointer over her outstretched arms, Serena looked over her shoulder and saw a gleaming black Acura pull into their long driveway. The waning beams of sunlight bouncing off the car's front windshield, she couldn't make out the driver. Leaving the girls to take each other on for a minute, she walked out toward the front of the driveway. When she got a better look at the driver, she crossed her arms defensively.

Fritz X's car rolled to a stop. As Serena glared toward him, he gave a curt head nod before opening his car door and stepping onto the pavement. Short and skinny—more similar to Serena in build than to Jamie—her husband's best friend had apparently come straight from the local mosque. He had removed his bow tie, but otherwise Fritz was still clean enough in his white shirt, gray single-breasted suit, and black wingtips to sell *The Final Call*s on the nearest corner.

"Sister Serena," he said, nodding his head ever so slightly in veiled deference. She and Fritz had talked many times about her distaste for the false modesty she felt the brothers in the Nation showed women, and Fritz knew to go lightly with her. "You look like you're trying to ball something serious today."

"You know me, Fritz," Serena said, frowning playfully but staying rooted where she was, a good twenty yards from Fritz's car. "I'm just getting myself spanked out here, but a girl can use the exercise."

"Well, that's a mature attitude," Fritz replied, swinging his car door shut and strolling toward her. His hands clasped respectfully in front of him, he looked at her with smiling eyes. "What's new?"

Forgive me, father, for I have sinned. Serena didn't know why, but even though she didn't buy into an ounce of the Nation's theology, she always felt like she was in the presence of God when Fritz was around. A childhood friend of Jamie's and a former hanger-on who'd followed her husband to Cincinnati years ago, Fritz had converted to the Nation in the mid-nineties, while serving time for a drunk driving charge. The little fella had always been oddly cool and calm, but stripped of his most obvious bad habits he radiated a Zenlike calm. Serena didn't know anyone who was more patient, more open, or more apparently thoughtful.

"Serena?" By the time she realized she had never answered his question, Fritz was nearly whispering her own name into her ear. "Are you okay, sister?"

"Oh. I'm sorry, Fritz." Serena cleared her throat and took a step back, reminding herself she had every right to show some 'tude right now, even to Fritz. "As you of all people should know, I've had a lot on my mind this week."

"I understand," Fritz replied, placing a gentle hand to her shoulder before waving to the girls, who shouted respectful greetings as they bounced the ball between them. He turned his gaze back to Serena. "You have every right to be unhappy about seeing me right now, dear sis. I'm not here for my health, though. I'm here to support my friend."

Serena glanced over her shoulder at the girls, who continued playing obliviously. "Let's continue this in my office, please."

Once she'd welcomed Fritz into the kitchen and locked the back door to avoid any surprise eavesdropping, she walked to the refrigerator. "Okay, what do I have that a black Muslim can eat?"

Fritz waved a hand. "I have no needs." He slid into a chair at the kitchen table and ran both hands over his freshly shaved head. "Just news you should hear."

"What's that?" Serena slammed the refrigerator door and turned back toward the table. "Jamie has *two* kids by other women, not just one?"

Fritz bunched his lips together and began polishing his glasses with a handkerchief. "Petty," he whispered. "Let's resist that urge, sister. Hear me out."

"Look, Fritz, don't you tell me—"

"He's on his way home, Serena."

Her shoulders jumped with disbelief. "Please, that whoremonger just left. Jamie's in Italy for another eight weeks."

"Not so. I spent last night on the phone with him." Fritz cleared his throat patiently, as if it was an art requiring concentration. "When he told me about his confession to you—a confession I've been on him to share for months, for the record—I told him it was irresponsible to drop such a bomb and leave the country."

"Oh," Serena replied, laughing sarcastically, "so I have you to thank for my beloved's return."

"Serena," Fritz said, his hand outstretched as if to halt the insults poised on the tip of her tongue. "There is so much Jamie has not told you."

Serena knew she was wrong but didn't stop the words. "Uh, yeah, no shit, Fritz."

Fritz bunched his lips again and shut his eyes. "Such language is beneath you, sis, but I guess you've earned the right." His hands clasped, he met her hard stare. "Your husband is ready to be a real man, a real father, and a real husband," he said, "because he is finally ready to submit to Allah."

Serena failed to stifle a chuckle. "You *do* know he tells you what he thinks you want to hear, right?" Fritz was too bright to keep falling for Jamie's half-ass claims of converting to Islam. Serena had long ago given up on otherworldly help of any type for her husband's indiscretions.

"I know my boy," Fritz replied, his eyes bright and his gaze steady, "and I know that I heard a sincerity in his voice I have never heard before. Serena, do you realize what it will mean when Jamie gets on that plane headed home tomorrow?"

Serena shook her head, not sure she could believe she was having this conversation. "He'll be fired." Jamie's league didn't mess around; foreign players' visits home were carefully restricted and managed, and several of Jamie's teammates had been dropped for missing a week's worth of practice, much less the months it would take Jamie to patch up their marriage.

Her eyes transfixed to Fritz's confident stare, Serena found herself fumbling for words. "Fritz, I don't . . . I mean, what would make him change now?"

Finally satisfied with the polish on his glasses, Fritz returned them to his nose and patted the seat across from him. "Come," he said, clearing his throat. "We have much to discuss, sis, starting with what Jamie told you about his mother's boyfriend. The fights?" He paused and his eye contact faltered for the first time Serena ever remembered. "Jamie wishes that was all that man did to him."

19

*T*wo weeks after his rendezvous with Serena—two silent weeks without so much as a hiccup from her in response to three messages left on her office phone—Tony took his twin mentees on a field trip to his windy hometown. As they drove toward the Oak Lawn branch of Gino's East pizzeria, he probed them about their recent midterm reports cards, as well as their studies for the upcoming PSAT. For more than two months he'd shared his wisdom with them, but he had yet to break through the last of each kid's protective layer, the false fronts common to most young males.

On the plane Saturday morning they'd mainly engaged in small talk, so as they cruised down Ninety-fifth Street he took a minute to dig a little deeper. "You guys heard from your brothers or sister lately?" The twins were their mother's youngest children; two brothers and a sister in their late twenties were scattered across Ohio.

Ben, who sat next to Tony in the passenger seat, gazed out his own window. "I'll let Glenn answer that one."

"Mr. Gooden," Glenn said, piping up from the backseat, "you may as well know. Our ma was a pretty trifling trick for a while; still is, really. Hell, back in the day social workers took everyone from her except us. By the time we came along, she learned how to hoodwink the system."

Ben turned suddenly in his seat, his right hand balling into a fist. "That's enough, Glenn."

"What?" Glenn glared back at his brother's daring stance, rising to the challenge. "You got a problem, little brother?"

Collecting himself as Tony cast a stern glance his way, Ben shifted in his seat, facing forward again. "You don't even have to say it, sir." He looked out the front window, clasped his hands. "I'm not going to disrespect you or your car by setting him straight now."

From the backseat, Glenn chortled with abandon. "Bring it on, sucker."

Tony rolled his eyes but kept them on the road. "Glenn, take it from a man with a little experience in this department. If you drew a short straw when God handed out moms, or dads for that matter, that's only the beginning of your story."

Coming to a stop for a red light, he looked over his shoulder. "It damn sure isn't the end." He turned back toward the dashboard but searched for the boy's eyes in his rearview mirror. "It hasn't been perfect, fellas, but my mother abandoned my ass when I was an infant, and I've lived a very nice life. I've had dinner with two U.S. presidents and four other heads of state, romanced supermodels and actresses, and helped pass legislation that improved the lives of poor kids in Chicago's worst neighborhoods, all by the age of thirty. So don't waste time hating on your mom; trust me, there's better things to do with your time." *Damn right*, Tony thought. *Use the time you'll save to hate on women who grab your heart, use you for a night, then pretend you don't exist.*

They rode in silence for the next several minutes. Glenn sat still, seemingly struck mute, while Ben sat nodding in wordless agreement with Tony's counseling. For his part, Tony couldn't quite believe the words that had just tumbled from his mouth. Not that they weren't true; as much bitterness as he harbored toward Zora's mother, he had come this far in life by refusing to waste time on it.

No, the surprise was that he'd immediately shared a forbidden secret with these two young cats, dudes he'd known for a matter of weeks. Dozens of women with intimate knowledge of Tony's genitalia still thought Stephanie was his biological mother; even lifelong friends like Mitchell and Trey had barely known the truth for a year.

By the time they pulled into the lot at Gino's, conversation was back in full swing. After sharing more of his own family history, Tony had coaxed the twins into sharing details of their mother's alcoholism, her convictions for money laundering, the ailing but loving aunt who enrolled them in Rowan, and the specifics of their daily weight-lifting routine, which they'd challenged Tony to take up with them.

"Please, no weight-pressing for this brother," he replied, laughing as they climbed from his rental car. "The ladies like me long and lean, fellas. Can't mess with success."

Three inches taller than his mentor, Glenn looked down at Tony as Ben flanked him on the other side. "Long, huh?"

"Okay, young buck, you're out of line now," Tony replied, chuckling as he elbowed both brothers. As they stepped into the lobby, Tony took a quick survey of the crowd. "Doesn't look like my boys are here yet," he said when he saw no sign of Trey or O.J.

"Gonna hit the men's room," Ben said.

"Cool," Tony replied. "We'll be here."

"Mr. Gooden," Glenn whispered, his words sounding like a question.

"Yeah, Glenn?"

"Were you for real in the car before, about your mom?" A skeptical spirit invaded the boy's stare. "I can't picture a silver-spoon brother like you being put up for adoption. You just wanted to shame me for dissin' my ma, didn't you?"

Eyebrows arched, Tony felt his cheeks rise with a smile. "Kid," he said, "I think I'm insulted. I look like a guidance counselor or a shrink to you? I'm just a brother living life, trying to share any tidbits I've picked up that'll help you and your bro. I'm not here to make you feel good, so when I tell you something, you can take it to the bank."

"Who is that *handsome* man there?" Though his eyes were still on Glenn's, Tony knew the wisecrack flying through the air had come from his boy O.J.'s mouth. Pivoting, he reached out and matched his friend's vigorous handshake.

By the time Ben emerged from the bathroom, Trey had trailed into the lobby as well and Tony made introductions all around. Taking their seats, Tony and his friends spent an hour stuffing themselves with Chicago-style pizza and trading wisecracks amongst each other and Tony's young guests. Just when Tony thought he might escape for the night without anyone bringing up the "S" word, Trey turned to the twins.

"Yo, you fellas into any of those video games they got up front?"

"Well, since you asked, sir," Ben said, cocking his head toward the front of the pizzeria, "they do have a couple of games I'm pretty skilled at, stuff I could whip up on my brother on without breaking a sweat. Didn't want to be rude, but—"

"Nothin' rude about that," Trey replied, flashing a toothy grin and plunking five one-dollar bills onto the table. "Why don't you two go and knock yourselves out for a few, get away from us old farts for a second."

"While we're at it," Glenn said, sliding out from his side of the booth, "I may make a detour, to, uh, lay a little rap on that fine Latina hostess."

"How about you go play the video game and stay out of trouble," Tony said, looking up at the twins. "I'm not trying to have to go back to Cincy explaining to your mom why you're stuck here in prison for harassing some girl."

Chuckling, Glenn rolled his eyes. "Like she'd really care, but whatever," he said as Ben punched him in the shoulder.

When they were gone, Tony looked at Trey, hoping his pupils communicated the depth of his scorn. "Funny I see you here, but never when you're in my town." Even though Trey visited Cincinnati every couple of weeks to see Serena's girl Jade, Tony saw more of his so-called friend on these trips home. For one, Jade wasn't exactly interested in seeing Tony now that he was "stalking" Serena. On top of that, Tony had little desire to bother with Trey anyway; if his so-called friend hadn't told Zora and his father about Serena, he'd at least be suffering her rejection in private.

Clearly sensing his boy's animosity, Trey stared at the half-eaten slice of pizza on his plate. O.J. responded instead. "Be cool, Gooden." He and Tony had talked several times since Tony's move, but of course Tony had never let on about Serena to him. "Let's just get all the bad news on the table, my friend. In addition to ratting you out to your sis and your pop, Trey has told me about your misadventures with the old flame."

"Breathe, my friend, breathe deep." Sensing Tony's anger, O.J. placed a hand on his friend's shoulder before he could bolt from his seat. Eyes laughing, he said, "Don't fight it, man. Just tell ole O.J. the ugly truth, from the ground up."

"I don't have anything to explain," Tony said, his words snapping aggressively, his eyes flashing heat. "I'm not the fu–" He paused, remembering his hospital pledge to clean up his language. Within reason. "I'm not the damn traitor, O.J."

"T, come on." Seated directly across from him, Trey was close enough for Tony to see the wounded look in his eyes. "I told your pop and Zora about Serena 'cause I was worried about you. I mean, you ain't never tell me, Mitchell, or O.J. a thing about why you really moved to Cincy. I had to find out from Jade."

Tony slammed a fist against the table. "Who is Jade, Trey?" He glared at his friend as he sat there, head drooping with shame. "What does Jade know about me, really? She's some girl who knew me in passing, a decade ago! You take her word over mine about why I moved away, then pass her slander on to my family?" It took that long for Tony to realize his upper lip was twitching. He bit at it, then looked back at Trey. "You can roll, for all I care."

After clearing his throat, O.J. sighed. "Gooden, let's forget Trey for a minute, all right?" He leaned toward his friend. "Lower your voice, and start the story from point A. Why'd you really move to Cincinnati?"

The truth dribbled from Tony in coaxed, spastic bits of revelation, until he replayed—at a respectable bird's-eye view—his recent night with Serena. "That's it," he said, collapsing against his bench, his expression stone cold and emotionless.

O.J. tented his fingers, searching the tabletop respectfully. "You haven't heard a word from her since you hit that, am I right?"

Tony occupied himself with his menu. "Let's see, maybe I'll get a dessert . . ."

"Okay. Asked and answered," O.J. replied, grinning and shaking his head. "Now look here. You got a point, I'm not gonna lie to you. Trey was out of line telling your family about this Serena lady. Wasn't his place." He leaned closer. "Does that make *you* right? Hardly. You're still wrong as two left shoes. You need to lay off that woman. Getting dissed ain't proved that to you yet?"

Trey snorted, looking away from Tony as he spoke. "Nah, there's always hope, O.J. Maybe she lost his number."

"Trey, kiss my black ass—"

"Uh-uh," O.J. said, slicing a finger across his neck. "No profanities around these newly ordained ears, please." Having just completed his church's requirements, O.J. had preached his inaugural sermon the prior weekend. "Truth is, I have no business being out with you heathens on a Saturday night, when I should be home with my wife and babies. But I love y'all, so here I am."

As the night wore on, O.J. saw to it that Tony wasn't on the hot seat the entire time. The conversation hopped from one arena to another—the happenings with their friend Mitchell, whose pregnant wife Nikki was on bed rest, the politics at WHOT, their former workplace, and the latest political news. Before they called it a night, O.J. pressed the point Trey could never have attempted.

"Uh, Gooden, is there a chance you need to move back here, now that you know you'll never score Ms. Serena for good?"

"You obviously haven't been listening," Tony replied, finishing off his latest beer. "I love my job, O.J. That was part of why I moved to Cincy, and that's why I'm staying." Tony stared at his friend with a muddled certainty. In a sense, every word was true. Serena's refusal to return his calls had been neatly offset by weeks of significant achievements at work. With his boss Larry and the esteemed Arthur Champion at his side, Tony had crisscrossed the country pitching major donors, politicians, newspaper editors, and parents' groups on Rowan Academy's successes and why every city needed a Rowan of its own. The numbers spoke for themselves: not only had his presentations been highly praised and well received, they had already won twice the level of planned funding and political support.

"Okay," O.J. replied, scooting out of his bench after Trey had slid out of his way. "So all's right with the world, Big Man, is that it? The fact you got hard-core dissed by homegirl? No issues with that, right?"

Tony would soon pay a price for his dismissive answer. "O.J., please. A few months ago I nearly *died*." He touched a hand to his chest, looking down at his shorter friend. "You saw my battered ass in the hospital, remember? You think I'm gonna come through that and sweat a woman with a boatload of her own issues? I'm out, man." Without even bothering to acknowledge Trey, he stalked off to find the twins.

20

Holding the foil condom wrapper between a thumb and forefinger, Serena took a deep breath as she swung Dawn's bedroom door closed behind her. As she hovered wordlessly over her daughter's bed, where Dawn lay reading a copy of *Vibe* magazine, Serena felt her soul pitch and rattle with indecision.

As the door clicked shut, Dawn raised her eyes, the lift of her eyebrows betraying her annoyance. "Yeah, Mom?"

Keeping the hand holding the condom behind her back, Serena cleared her throat. She hadn't felt this shy since the first time she slow-danced with a boy, nearly twenty years ago. It wasn't like she and Dawn hadn't had done the birds and the bees thing: she'd told her daughter how a sperm becomes a baby nearly three years earlier. Between Serena's counseling and a traditional sex ed class at school, Serena had known for years that her daughter had the owner's manual to her body. As she stood fingering the rubber, though, Serena realized she'd never guided her child about when to put that knowledge to use. God, she prayed she wasn't too late.

Distracted from a lazy Sunday's reading, Dawn didn't seem to appreciate Serena's deep contemplation. "Uh, Mom? Can I help you?"

Too shook up to choose the right words, Serena stepped forward and plopped the condom onto her daughter's lap.

Dawn's eyes ticked down toward her lap; then she raised her chin and stared into her mother's eyes. "You and Poppa Jamie still using these?" she said, a daring tone matching the arching of her back. "No wonder I only have one sister."

"You know good and well where I found this," Serena replied, leaning over her daughter and fighting to keep her voice down. She pointed toward her daughter's lap, as if she needed to remind Dawn of the evidence at hand.

Dawn blinked as if confused. "What were you doing in my purse anyway?"

"I locked my keys in the car when I got home," Serena said, "and I remembered I made you a copy of the keys when we got your driver's permit." She put her hands against her hips. "Not that I have to explain it to you. Talk to me, Dawn, quickly."

Serena knew her daughter's rebellious nature was at work as Dawn shut her eyes, and she appreciated her child's attempt to be respectful. To show it, she took a seat on the bed as Dawn tried to form a response.

"Glenn bought them for me," she said, her voice just above a whisper, eyes still closed.

In the face of her daughter's serenity, Serena felt her spirits cool. "Glenn, hmm? Is this the boy you've been on the phone with so much since you started at Rowan? The football star?" Just saying the phrase "football star" pissed Serena off. As cute as Dawn was, she knew her child would quickly attract the interest of Rowan's few jocks and other members of the in crowd. She also knew from her own youth that such attention usually led to nothing but an early bun in the oven, an unwelcome addiction, or just plain hurt feelings.

Eyes still closed, Dawn pressed a hand to her own neck. "He's more than just a jock, Mom."

Serena frowned. "Of course. I'm sure he'll end world hunger some day." She knew her cynicism was a little stubborn; when she'd first coaxed the name of Dawn's new boyfriend from her, she quickly screened him via a confidential call to Audrey, Rowan's principal. According to her, this Glenn had a roughneck style and wasn't exactly a 4.0 student but also had no prison record and was on track to attend college with or without a football scholarship. Of course from her perspective as Dawn's mother, that meant nothing unless the boy was also impotent and infertile.

"I gave you an honest answer. I got it from Glenn, okay?" Dawn opened her eyes, which were weighted with the sobriety of the embarrassed. "We've been talking about getting together, Mom. We haven't done nothing yet, though. I swear."

"Baby," Dawn said, scooting closer to her child and taking her hand, "why are you two already talking about sex? You haven't been at Rowan a full two months. You can't possibly know this Glenn well enough to give him all you have to offer, not this soon."

"Mom, I didn't say *when* we'd do anything," Dawn replied, shaking her head at her mother's apparently low IQ. "Besides, there's girls at Rowan and my old school who sleep with boys after a few hours, forget a few weeks."

Serena shook her inhibitions suddenly, rearing back and letting loose with a hearty laugh. "Oh, really? Well, bless my virgin ears." As Dawn stared at her with arms crossed, Serena rubbed her daughter's shoulder. "You think you're telling me something I don't know, child? Baby, not only do I work in a school system, hearing all the scary anecdotes about you and your classmates, I've lived this thang." She slowed her words, let the laughter fade from her tone. "Dawn, I'm not saying you should wait until marriage. I'm not even saying you should only sleep with one or two men before marriage, necessarily. But I sure don't want you to fall into the same holes that captured me."

Dawn shook her head slowly. "You turned out okay, Mom."

"Really, now?" Serena tapped her arm playfully. "Have you forgotten that your grandparents had to raise you the first five years of life? Or maybe you didn't notice when your stepfather packed his stuff and rolled out last month?" Though Jamie had returned from Italy, just as Fritz promised, he'd immediately moved in with Fritz, saying he needed to earn his way back into Serena's good graces before returning home. He got no fight from her.

"Life's rough, Mom," Dawn replied, laying back against her trio of fat pillows. "If my daddy hadn't been killed, he'd have helped you raise me and everything would have been okay. And as far as Poppa Jamie goes, even I know he's a trip when it comes to other women. That's not on you either. Glenn says that's just how men are, regardless of age."

Serena licked her lips, reaching for a pinch of patience. This Glenn was sounding like a great influence. Not to mention she was already well aware that, at sixteen, he was a full year older than her baby. "Dawn, my point is that I've been through more than you need to know, at least for now." She placed a pleading hand to her daughter's arm again. "Just trust me, please? In another year or two, when you're a little more mature, you'll have plenty of time to embrace your sexuality."

"Mom, please." Dawn's gaze wandered and she bit at a fingernail. "Let's not turn this into some after-school special."

"Uhh," Serena said, literally thinking out loud as she pressed the back of a hand to her forehead. "This is so not fun. Maybe I should have your granny talk to you—it didn't work, but she gave me a hell of an abstinence talk when I was your age."

"Oh. My. God." Dawn's mouth was a gate ajar, her shock was so great. "I can't have Granny know I'm even *thinking* about this, Mom. Are you crazy?"

Serena patted Dawn's hand. "You realize, right, that your Granny had to have sex in order to bring me into this world?"

"Duh," Dawn replied. "I also know I don't want my granny even thinking about me doing anything sexual. Ooh! The thought makes my skin crawl."

Serena raised an eyebrow. "You saying if I warn your granny that you're thinking about sex, it'll spoil the appeal of getting your little underdeveloped groove on?"

Dawn's complexion was suddenly ashen, her horror was so

great. "Mom, if you tell her one word of what we talked about, I'm done with you. Really. Done."

"Take it easy, take it easy." Serena patted her child's arm this time and tried to collect herself. "I won't tell her anything, I promise, as long as you hear me out and don't rush into anything."

"You want me to hold off?" Dawn's eyes brightened with a challenging flourish and she crossed her arms. "You gotta tell me some of these things you've been through, Mom. Give a girl a reason to be square, at least."

"Dawn—" Serena's eyes darted down out of embarrassment. It would be so easy. *You want a reason, huh, do you? How about this? Six weeks ago your momma bum-rushed her old boyfriend like a two-bit whore. Rode him half the night and whipped it on him like a twenty-year-old. And now, just as your Poppa Jamie's trying to do right by all of us, I can't even appreciate it like I should.*

She didn't take it there, of course. Instead, she clasped her hands and shared something less earth-shattering. "Well, I've told you about my problems with drunk driving," she began, "but there was more. I was fourteen when I smoked my first joint—"

Footsteps scampered down the hallway and ceased outside Dawn's door. "Mommy!" Sydney's yell was followed by eager knocks at the closed door. "Daddy's home! Daddy's home!"

Looking over her shoulder after checking her watch, Serena realized Jamie was actually right on schedule. After a two-hour phone conversation three nights ago, Fritz had convinced her that Jamie was ready to move back into the house. Serena hadn't promised to be a welcoming host, but agreed to give it a try.

She turned back toward Dawn but yelled over her shoulder. "We'll be right out, Sydney!"

"No, Mom, it's cool," Dawn said, pivoting and swinging her long legs over the side of the bed. "We can pick this up later." She nodded suddenly. "And so we're clear, this conversation stays between us, right?"

"As long as you agree we're not finished."

Dawn shrugged. "Whatever."

Serena reached out and quickly pinched the skin in the center of Dawn's right hand. "Whatever, huh? Count on this conversation being continued, missie."

By the time she emerged from Dawn's room, Jamie was already in the master suite, an open suitcase before him on their bed. Or what had been their bed. Standing in the threshold of the doorway, Serena crossed her arms but took the edge off of her tone. "Hello."

"How are you?" Jamie turned and stared at her, clearly wishing he could cross the distance between them and greet her properly. Long arms hanging at his side, his posture was solid but meek. The new humility still seemed like the lingering effect of Jamie's belated sharing of the childhood abuse he'd suffered. He had first sent Fritz to Serena with the most sordid details, but a week after his return from Italy he had come by to fill in the gaps. "I was just too proud," he kept saying. "No real man wants to be identified with that type of abuse." Serena still couldn't believe the way he had cried in her arms, finally unleashing the pains that send many to an early grave.

"I'm sorry if I interrupted a private moment between you and Dawn," Jamie said now, facing her. "I thought we agreed on five o'clock."

"We did," Serena replied without moving an inch. "Um, why are you unpacking in here?"

Jamie, who had started to turn back toward the bed, whipped around again. "What do you mean?"

Serena touched a hand to her throat but kept her eyes fixed to her husband's. "I don't feel comfortable with you sleeping in here, Jamie. Not yet."

"No?" His shoulders rotated as he processed her words. "I–I didn't know that was an issue. I guess I thought after all we've been through the past few weeks–"

Serena raised a hand, as lovingly as she could. "Jamie, this doesn't take away from what we've been through. Really, I respect everything you've shown me since you came back." This was the naked truth. Fritz's revelation about the sexual abuse Jamie suffered in his teens had convinced Serena to give him a second chance. While she didn't excuse his years of infidelity, she did feel she better understood them now.

In the month since he'd returned from Italy and retired from basketball, Jamie had done nothing but reward her decision to give him the benefit of the doubt. Not only had he subjected himself to Fritz's calming influence, he was in the process of formally converting to the Nation. At any given moment, Serena knew Jamie was either at the mosque, at Fritz's, or at his new job: teaching chemistry at Princeton High School, where the principal had convinced him to also serve as an assistant basketball coach. With his newly found inner peace, Jamie was much more comfortable than he'd been in his previous life as a substitute teacher.

If he wasn't in one of those three places in recent weeks, Jamie was out with the girls—taking Sydney and Dawn shopping, to plays, or attending their after-school activities. He and Serena had even gone out on a weekly date night, taking time to soberly discuss secrets they'd withheld and weighing the price of forgiveness. After their last "date," he'd presented her with a trinket she knew she'd cherish regardless of what the future held: a locket with an enclosed picture of her, Jamie, and the girls from the year Sydney was born. Reliving days that had been so full of hope and promise was painful on one level but invigorating on another, a reminder of the good things life had to offer. In moments when she was tempted to skip another dose of her lithium, she found that a glimpse at the locket quickly fortified her.

They had covered considerable ground in a short time, but as Serena pictured herself climbing back into bed with this man, she knew an unwelcome guest would be joining them, and after just a few weeks she wasn't quite ready to face Tony Gooden. If she wasn't ready to face him, Jamie certainly wasn't.

"I can't be intimate with you, not yet," she said as Jamie impatiently crammed clothing back into his suitcase. "You breached my trust in a major way, remember." Serena caught her breath as her lungs filled with desire: the desire to save her marriage, to prove her maturity, to make her parents proud. "I will be ready eventually, okay? I just can't turn it off and immediately turn it on again, that's all."

"The guest bed's fine," Jamie said, his lips pressed flat, his words barely audible. Turning back toward her, he grabbed the suitcase and tried to smile. "This is all my fault, after all." Striding past, he paused long enough to say, "I do love you, Serena."

Standing just inside the bedroom, her husband's energy still surrounding her, Serena found herself gasping for air. He didn't know it, but Jamie's declaration was alcohol to the open wounds of her guilt.

21

As he began his first work week in Cincinnati after spending the previous two in Atlanta and then Phoenix, Tony ignored his better judgment and tuned in to his usual morning programming. In his heart he knew it was a perilous move, but by the time he roused himself from a worthless night's sleep he was too tired to face that. Habit took hold and before he'd pulled out of the Extended Stay's driveway he had punched the programming button for The Wiz, the FM station carrying O.J.'s syndicated radio show.

As Tony guided his Passat toward I-75, he limply sang along with the closing notes of Usher's "Confessions" and smiled as his friend's familiar voice filled the car. "Twenty-two before the hour," O.J. said, still chuckling at a secret jibe he'd apparently shared with Liz, his cohost. "That was Usher, of course, who I understand is headed to our fair city on the lake next month. Interested in some free tickets? Stay tuned for your opportunity to get included in a drawing, ladies! Men, too, if any of y'all are actually interested, that is. All right, Liz, let's get some more folk on the line with the morning's question. Here it goes: Do you have 'one that got away' in your life? You know, the one you still compare every date to, the one you would have worked things out with, *if only*.

"It's like this. I came up with this question after talking with one of my boys a couple of weeks ago. Now, this cat is a hard-core player, understand? I mean, my bachelor days pale in comparison to this man's history. Turns out, Liz, that even my boy, this player-mack, has 'one that got away' in his life. And his nose is *open!*"

A chorus of other studio jokesters laughing in the background, Liz chuckled before trying to focus her boss. "His nose is open, O.J.? What's he done that makes you say that?"

His foot growing heavier on his accelerator, Tony felt his blood pressure rise as O.J. described the mysterious friend's actions. They were very familiar, of course: the poor fool had followed a woman to a new city, tried to get her to work at his company, jumped headfirst into a one-night stand, then suffered the humiliation of her complete silence in the weeks since.

"Can you believe this?" O.J. hadn't stopped laughing. "Now I love this brother, but really. I want to hear some calls from folk with sense, people who can help my boy *pull up*. Hit the lines now, while you can!"

"O.J., you trifling . . ." The DJ hadn't named any names, but, damn, their argument that night had been private. In a flash, Tony reached for his cell phone, ready to punch in the 800 number at O.J.'s station. He was ready to show his boy up on national radio; the little fool had knowingly exaggerated all over the place. *For one, I haven't exactly put down roots; this is just, uh, an experiment—yeah, that's all.* He wasn't that far gone—if he was, he'd have gone through with buying that house in Avondale that caught his eye the week before he and Serena hooked up. Since her very thorough dis, he'd ignored every message from the realtor who'd shown him the property.

The line at O.J.'s station was still ringing when Tony hung up. *What are you, crazy?* Like he hadn't been embarrassed enough. *Just take it,* he told himself, suppressing the boil of his blood pressure. *Take an asshole for a friend, you get your own hole plugged on national radio.*

Arriving at the Whitaker Holdings tower, Tony converted his anger and humiliation into fuel for a day's work. As usual, there was plenty to distract his attention from Serena's silences and his loved ones' ridicule. Press releases to proof, journalists to sweet-talk, politicians to pressure, donors to hand-hold, budgets to review. By the time he left the office to head over to the academy, where he was due to pick up Ben and Glenn from school, he had nearly wiped his mind clear of the inconvenient realities in his own life. It was the right move, given that the twins had plenty of inconveniences of their own.

Their mother, Evelyn, the same woman who'd allowed Tony to take them to Chicago despite being "too busy" to meet with him and get acquainted first, had run up against the law once again. This time it involved several ounces of heroine found in her pocketbook when the car she was riding in was stopped in Over the Rhine after zooming through a red light. Although Glenn refused to miss a football practice in order to attend her arraignment, Ben had asked Tony to accompany him. If the sister was convicted this time, she'd finally have a good reason for never being home when the boys arrived there each night. As self–sufficient as they had become, even the twins seemed concerned about what the upcoming days might bring.

Plotting strategies to help the boys find a family member to take them in, Tony stepped into the school's empty front hall. As if she had a tracking mechanism taped to his thigh, Audrey appeared suddenly from around the corner. "Hey," she said, smiling and waving with a flirtatious verve he hoped she hid from students. "You are right on time, thank God."

"Don't look so excited," Tony replied, rolling up to her and smiling lazily. "Cheese any wider and your skin will split wide open, girl. What, you didn't think I'd actually come?"

Audrey fought back a playful grin, gripping her clipboard to her full chest. "I knew you wouldn't blow the guys off," she said. "I know this latest news can't be easy, though. They're really going to need your positive influence, given Evelyn's legal issues."

"I'm right here for them," Tony said, pounding his chest. "For better or worse, I guess I kind of like these young cats."

"Well, I know you weren't too excited about mentoring at first, so I guess I felt a little guilty about talking you into it, now that things are getting more complex."

Tony narrowed his eyes playfully, tipped his chin up. "Thought you knew me better than that," he said finally. "Sounds like you need a personal course on my character, with me as the instructor."

Audrey's eyes warmed as she glanced over her shoulder and stepped forward. When she finally stopped, she was deep in the pocket of Tony's personal space—the zone appropriate for no one but trusted friends, or of course lovers. "If that's a challenge, I accept."

What are you doing? Before Tony could answer the question, the school bell rang deep and long through the hallway and the air erupted with the sound of excited, restless youth. As shouts and chatter surrounded them, Audrey hugged her clipboard to her chest again and took three reluctant steps back. Whipping around to face the first wave of students chugging toward them, she picked them off in ones and twos, engaging them in conversation and building the crucial rapport between student and principal.

Settling back into a corner near the school's trophy case, Tony watched Audrey with admiration and considered whether to answer the question floating through his mind. He was still toying with it when Glenn rolled alongside and nearly caved his back in with a friendly slap. "What's up, Mr. G."

"Glenn." Biting his lip and fighting back the tear lodged in his right eye, Tony denied the pain and exchanged a brisk handshake with the youngster. "Was it a good day today?"

"It was cool," Glenn replied, nodding confidently. Despite his streetwise manner, the boy's intelligence and ambition were unmistakable. "Found out I got an A on my first trigonometry test." He placed a finger to his lips, smiling. "That's between you and me, though, sir."

Tony shook his head. "Don't tell me you still have classmates who say it's 'white' to get As? We all work overtime to break you of that idea here, you know that."

"Mr. G," Glenn replied, a solemn hand to his chest now, "it's nice that you all bring these VIPs and celebrities to the school every month, telling us there's no shame in getting good grades. I suppose it helps, on a certain level. But at the end of the day, y'all don't have to live among the knuckleheads who don't get it. I mean, if those fools know that you get good grades, they work overtime to paint you as a nerd. I prefer to handle my business in secret—that way I get my props from my teachers, and someday I'll get it from the colleges and employers. But, sir, when I'm with the 'people,' I ain't trying to take unnecessary mess."

Tony shook his head again. "It's just shameful. And our people wonder why we can't get ahead."

"We're not all ashamed, sir." Ben stood just behind Tony, a gym bag slung over his shoulder. "Don't let my inferior half let you think he speaks for all Rowan kids."

"Yeah, that's right," Glenn said, huffing playfully as Tony exchanged handshakes with Ben. "That's why you always getting picked with, too."

Tony raised his hands, refereeing good-naturedly. "Let's not get into a brother fight right now, okay, gentlemen?" He glanced at Ben's gym bag. "Ben, I was hoping you had your suit for tonight and your brother's." Tony had decided to mix a night of sober talk—helping the boys prepare for the intrusions of Children's Services into their lives—with an educational night on the town. Their conversation would take place at none other than La Maisonette, the country's longest running five-star restaurant and a jewel in Cincinnati's crown. That meant the boys had to be as sharp tonight as Tony tried to be every day. "You got your suits balled up in that bag?"

"Nah, they're in our lockers," Glenn said nonchalantly. "Why don't we grab 'em and meet you at your car, out front?"

"That's a plan, fellas," Tony said, checking his watch. "I'll be in the red Passat—"

Tony was interrupted by a sudden burst from a passing student. Bouncing between him and Glenn, she playfully slapped the twin's chest. "What's *uuup*?" Tall, trim, and leggy, the young lady had cinnamon brown skin and wore her auburn-colored hair in a freshly trimmed pageboy. She faced Tony and the twins with her hands on her hips. "Glenn? I said, what's *up*?" She glanced at Tony. "This y'alls' daddy?"

Realizing suddenly that he'd seen the girl before–the day when Zora and his father had visited him at Rowan–Tony choked back a laugh, realizing he was too old for her question to be a stupid one. "I'm Mr. Gooden," he said as the twins shuffled in place uneasily. As hard as Tony tried to probe at times, the boys largely preferred to be vague with him about who they were dating, and exactly what "dating" meant. "I'm Glenn and Ben's mentor. You're a relatively new student here, right?"

"Yes, sir. I'm a sophomore, but just transferred a few weeks ago," the girl replied, her hazel eyes glinting as she nodded toward Tony respectfully. "My name's Dawn Kincaid."

"Yes," Ben said, the first of the twins to recover from their silent condition. "Glenn's been helping Dawn learn her way around."

Dawn . . . Kincaid. The base of Tony's neck warmed suddenly and he recalled the flash of recognition that had crossed his mind that first day he'd met the girl. Serena wouldn't enroll her child here at Rowan, would she, not as an officer of the city schools? As counterintuitive as that would seem, Tony looked again at the child's luminescent eyes and smooth cheekbones and knew something was very wrong.

Stifling a spike of panic, he plowed forward with the conversation. He cast a playful sideways glance at Glenn. "Good old Glenn, he's just an unselfish soul, isn't he?" Tony didn't need things spelled out for him: take a girl this cute, drop her into a relatively small school like Rowan, and she was bound to wind up with a star jock like Glenn, at least for a hot minute.

"I only knew three people my first day here." Dawn had sidled up against Glenn and had an arm lazily draped around his shoulder. "Glenn's opened a lot of doors for me since. I love it here, all thanks to my man."

Tony's response caught in his throat. "Your–" The smile she'd flashed as she settled into Glenn's hug did it. *Dawn. Kincaid. The eyes, the nose* . . .He was staring at Serena's daughter, and the realization was a brass knuckle to Tony's balls. The sensations rippling through him–the clammy brow, the sudden urge to get the hell away–confirmed it was her. He needed no birth certificate, no DNA mouth swab. Serena's baby stood before him, womanhood tumbling upon her like a relentless waterfall.

He was still trying to believe it when Glenn kissed the top of Dawn's head and let her out from under his arm. "We gotta run."

"All right, then." Dawn popped Glenn's shoulder, stuck out her tongue. "But I want my football jersey back tomorrow, that's what I sleep in. You know that."

Tony longed for a pair of earplugs. In Bizarro World, he could easily be Dawn's stepfather. As much as he cared for young Glenn, his relationship with the young buck might be headed for a rocky adjustment period.

He realized suddenly that Dawn was speaking to him. "See you around, Mr. Gooden?"

"P-Probably, Dawn." Looking into her eyes, Tony felt momentarily trapped, on the verge of breaking down and begging the child to carry a message to Serena for him. He resisted as he waved toward her. "Take care now."

Ben tapped Tony's shoulder before following Glenn back down the hallway. "See you in a couple of minutes, Mr. Gooden."

Tony heard his mentee's words but didn't respond. Standing alone in the now-empty front hall, he stood rooted in place, watching Dawn saunter out the front door and into the middle of a trio of female classmates. He hadn't seen her since she was three years old, and now she was probably weeks from tasting some of the passions, pains, and rejection her mother faced at the same age. Time's unforgiving passage hit Tony, and he struggled with a bitter reality. He didn't have time to wait around, not for Serena or anyone else.

22

Serena had kept her condom discussion with Dawn confidential for two weeks and two days when Jade picked her up for an evening trip to the gym. They had each worked a long day, but had agreed that a good workout session would be a nice break in the middle of the week. Once Serena had picked the girls up from school, made a stop to grab some Chinese takeout, and zoomed home to get her clothes changed, she had taken a restful seat in her front room. As the sound of Dawn and Sydney's dinner conversation wafted in from the kitchen, she had looked out her bay window onto the street below until Jade pulled up in her newly purchased Nissan Maxima.

The first few minutes of their conversation, as had been the case for the past month, focused wholly on Tony. "You still haven't returned any of the brother's calls?" Jade had *tsk-tsk* written all over her tone. "You know I'm not a fan of what you two did, Serena, but the only way to get rid of the boy is to answer just one of his calls. Tell him there's no hope whatsoever, that you and Jamie are giving things a sincere go."

Serena shook her head. "Spoken just like a woman who's never been in love, at least not with the right brother."

"Ohh," Jade replied, voice rising. "So because I've never gone

Boo-Boo the Fool over a brother, let him convince me to make an ass out of myself, I don't know what real love is?"

"I'm just saying you always manage to draw a bright line between your heart and your body," Serena said, her eyes pleading for a cool head on Jade's part. "That's not easy for most of us women. A girl like me, I know what it is to face a man who knows how to *work* you, one who convinces you that what you thought was wrong is just about right."

"So what's your point?"

"My point," Serena replied, snapping her plaid hand towel as if backing Jade off, "is that I'm not even giving Tony the opportunity to talk me out of giving Jamie one more chance. A girl's got to respect her weaknesses."

Her hands sliding over her steering wheel with a right turn, Jade harumphed. "Meanwhile, Tony keeps hanging around town, confident he'll eventually break you down. You're that afraid to talk to him, sounds like his hunch is right."

Serena turned toward her friend, her left jaw quivering. "How about some free advice?"

Jade waved a hand. "I know, I know—"

"Just drive."

Once they had turned onto the next block, Serena punctured the creeping silence before it overwhelmed them both. "So, speaking of your dating expertise, what's the latest with you and the wigger?"

"The wigger, huh?" Jade grumbled defiantly. "Not very mature language, my sister. If you're referring to your recycled boyfriend's partner in crime, whose name happens to be Trey, I can answer your question."

"Well, then?"

"I'm trying to decide whether to go see him, girl," Jade said in a confessional tone.

"I thought he booked you on a flight to Chicago for the end of the month?"

"He did," Jade replied, her teeth sinking into her bottom lip. "The question is whether I'll go. I mean, Serena, I've enjoyed his visits here and all—"

"Based on your stories, I'd say so," Serena said, grinning. Jade had sheepishly admitted that one of her more enthusiastic nights with Trey earned complaints from her upstairs, downstairs, and next-door neighbors.

"I'm just not sure I'm up for visiting his world, though," Jade continued. "I mean, just meeting all his kids would take up the entire weekend."

"Now I told you up front you were wasting his time and yours if you can't deal with the fact he has kids."

"It's not the kids," said Jade. "It's the baby mamas."

"Yeah, not to mention the sexual math tables you have to do, on him and the baby mamas."

"Huh, you better know the one thing I've made sure of is to make that brother stay swathed in latex before we do *anything*. Speaking of which, girl, did you hear about Lacy Turner?"

Serena's eyebrows rose with concern. Lacy had been one of their study buddies at Northwestern, and a sorority sister as well. She and Jade had lost touch with Lacy around the time she married a doctor and moved out to Denver. When Jade dropped the news—HIV, apparently inflicted from Lacy's husband, who had admitted to covert drug use and was widely believed to have had a homosexual affair—Serena's stomach clenched.

As they continued toward the gym, the two friends mourned for Lacy's plight, recounted hopeful news about advances in fighting HIV, and even said a quick prayer for their old classmate. By the time they pulled into the health club's lot, though, Lacy had been replaced in Serena's thoughts by someone far more crucial to her: Dawn.

Reminded of her promise to keep Dawn's secret as well as the heavy stakes involved, Serena stirred in her seat as Jade opened her own door. A foot on the pavement, she peered at Serena with concern. "You okay? Let's go."

"You go ahead," Serena said, her voice sounding far away to her own ears. "I need to make a quick phone call about something. Be right in."

"All right, cool."

The slam of Jade's door ringing in her ears, Serena rehearsed her justification for Dawn. *I'm your mother, and I'm not doing anything to risk your winding up with HIV. And that's what I'd be doing if I didn't let your grandmother have a crack at talking sense into you.* With that, she pulled up her mother's number on her cell phone and punched DIAL.

23

*T*ony was in the air when he got the news about Serena and Jamie. Shifting away from from Audrey, who sat next to him with an eager hand in his lap, he typed an angry response into his BlackBerry:

Trey, I thought Jamie was back in Italy.

Trey's reply hit the right apologetic tone:

Just heard about this, dude, let's not get too excited about it. Jade doesn't sound convinced it will work out. But then, she's kinda biased against Muslims anyway.

Chewing on his lower lip, Tony tossed the BlackBerry onto the meal tray to his left. Along with Audrey, Larry, and three other Rowan Academy employees, he was aboard a chartered plane. The team was returning from Washington, D.C., where they'd spent three days wining and dining the Congressional Black Caucus and members of the District's city council. With Tony's leadership, they'd made such impressive progress that Larry was confident they'd be breaking ground on a D.C. Rowan Academy within six months.

That was all well and good, but the news he'd just received was a big distraction. Worse yet, the unrest stirring within just reminded him that Zora had been right. During his last visit to Chicago, when he'd taken the twins over to meet her on Loyola's campus, his sister had resurrected the intervention she and Wayne had attempted during their visit to Rowan.

"I just think you need some type of help, Tony," she'd said, "because I know if I hadn't gotten any after what we went through that night, I couldn't get through each day."

He had argued with her plenty, insisted on his ability to weather the occasional fear of crowds and the infrequent nightmare without professional help.

"What about Millie, then?" Her formal use of their mother's first name still sounded funny to Tony; she'd started using it only after Tony shared the many ways in which Millie had ignored the few overtures he'd made to her when he was a young, dumb preteen. "I don't think you're in touch with your emotions toward her."

"And no stranger can help me with that."

His response had been aimed at shutting her down, but it only served to rev his sister's engines. "You're in denial about all this, Tony. Really, you need to . . ."

Tony's recall of their argument blurred as he shook his head at the buzzwords Zora had learned from her own therapy. Focusing on the present, he set his BlackBerry aside. Trey probably didn't have any more information about Serena anyway. Feeling his mood sour, he laid his head against his bulbous traveler's pillow. It took Larry's voice, a forceful barrage from over his shoulder, to wake him up.

"I almost forgot to tell you, Tony," Larry said from the comfort of his roomy leather seat, where he sat flanked by Art and Tina, Rowan's parent and police liaisons. "I got that contact information for you, my friend who's with Children's Services? She can walk you through the entire foster parent application process."

Tony turned around in his seat, nodding gratefully. "They don't say you're the man for nothing. I really appreciate it, Larry." He still couldn't believe he'd embarked on this challenge, but after his recent visit with the twins' ailing aunt Carrie, who'd be burdened with them the very minute Evelyn reported for her "unfortunate incarceration," he knew someone had to step up. He'd already called the county office of Children's Services, and an information packet was on the way.

"She said you're right, by the way," Larry continued. "Sounds like getting approved will be harder since you're new to the Cincy area. But she says as long as your background check's clean, you'll still get a fair shot. You will need to get a real address, though. Living at Extended Stay's not exactly a sign of long-term stability."

Tony nodded and gave a dry chuckle. Just that quick, he had a reason to commit to some local real estate.

"Bottom line," Larry said, "if the court is convinced the boys' only choices are being dumped into the foster system or being directly placed with a friend of the family, they'll look at you favorably."

"All right," Tony replied, raising a fist in satisfaction. "Sounds like I owe you, boss."

"Huh, don't go there quite yet," Larry replied, nodding toward Audrey. "You've seen what some of these foster parents go through to get approved, haven't you?"

Audrey's smile dimmed. "I've warned Tony about the pitfalls, how tough the process can be." She'd delivered her cautionary but loving lecture over a romantic dinner a few days earlier; Tony was grateful she left that out.

"Not to freak you out," Larry said, "but my girl at Children's Services says you should prepare to have your life turned inside out, upside down. Sounds like it's harder to be a foster parent than to just squeeze out a crumb-snatcher of your own."

"Yeah, I know," Tony replied. "This'll be as much fun as a colonoscopy, before it's all said and done."

Once they had traded horror stories about the unfit parents overwhelming the system with neglected and abused children, the plane quieted down and Tony again shut his eyes, eager to forget the unsettling news about Serena and Jamie. His respite was brief; in seconds he felt the warm dance of fingers near his zipper.

"Need help staying awake?" Audrey, who had a thin blanket stretched over both their laps, let her fingers graze one sensitive spot after another. She looked over her shoulder, where Larry, Art, and Tina were engaged in their own conversation. With the two seats facing them vacant, Audrey's eyes flickered with joy at having Tony all to herself.

When her hands hit their mark, sending a heated rush through his groin, Tony felt his eyes pop open. "Whoa, whoa," he whispered, a pleasured smile on his face even as he playfully scolded her. "Girl, if your students could see you now."

Audrey cupped his chin, leaning in close. "Look, we have a lot in common, don't try to deny it. You got where you are by knowing what you want and going for it. I'm no different." She pulled his chin closer, pecked a kiss onto his cheek. "I've been trying to send nonverbal signals forever. You gonna make me bore you with a speech before you make your move?"

"Audrey . . ." Tony chuckled to lighten the mood but turned away, staring out the window. *Well, self,* he reflected, *you got yourself between a rock and a hard dick right about now.* His much-neglected penis stirred into action by Audrey's onslaught, his slacks were tented for the whole world to see. One wrong shift and he'd soil his boxers with rapid-fire squeezes of DNA.

He wanted Audrey; there was no sidestepping the reality. This was different from those weeks in Ghana, when visions of Serena distracted him from Ama and the other women who'd propositioned him. His heart still burned with a longing for the one that got away, but at this point the celibacy routine had lost its appeal. In light of the phone calls she refused to return, the rumors of her sudden reunion with Jamie's trifling ass, and the loneliness of his daily routine, Tony was tired of sacrificing for this unrequited love. So why couldn't he make that final leap, the one necessary to meet Audrey on the other side?

"You have some other woman back in Chicago?" Audrey's voice was low and her hand was no longer in his lap, but she was still halfway into his seat. "I mean, as hard as you work you can't have a woman here, or I'd hear about it. Cincy's only so big, unless you're dating a white girl."

"It's not about me being with anyone, Audrey," Tony admitted, crossing his legs with care. Relieved that little Tony didn't discharge an unplanned load, he folded his hands soberly. "I have no one, but that's how it should stay. Simply put, I've got issues."

Audrey seemed to take his admission as a challenge. "And who doesn't? Have you heard a word I've said the past few weeks?" As their friendship had grown, especially during the three recent outings they'd enjoyed with Ben and Glenn over the Thanksgiving break, Audrey had talked much more frankly about her past than Tony had. Ambitious and unselfish, her professional wisdom hadn't carried over to her love life. To hear her tell it, she'd had only a handful of lovers, but each had been a typical scoundrel: unfaithful, abusive, underemployed, sometimes all three. For years she'd attempted to save an on-again, off-again relationship with her first boyfriend, a whorish, alcoholic banker who was clearly beneath her.

Tony scratched nervously at his right ear. "Audrey, nobody's perfect, but just trust me. If you're looking to break your losing streak with men, you might want to keep walking."

Audrey grinned, turning away for a second. "I think you're still beating yourself up for old sins," she replied. "I'm betting that the man I see now, Tony, has come a long way from the shallow little player you were back in the day." She reached for his cheek, pinching at a dimple that popped up as he smiled against his will. "Let your new self come out to play."

He looked at her with heavy eyes but didn't remove her hand from his cheek. "That man can't be trusted."

"You won't know until you let him try out a real relationship," Audrey said, stroking his cheek and returning to his chin again. "I'm not asking you to marry me. I just want to be friends, and if that leads to anything more, well, we play it by ear." She pulled him close again and whispered into his ear. "I'm a big girl, Tony. You won't break me."

24

When Serena pulled into her reserved parking space at work, the fire red Passat sat in the far left corner of the administration building's parking lot.

Even with a blanket of snow flurries testing her vision, Serena recognized the car on sight, and her heartbeat immediately began to race.

Mouth growing dry, she took a deep breath, shut off her car's ignition and stepped from the driver's side door. Slamming it shut and activating her alarm, she searched in vain for Mr. Brewster, the lot's security guard. Any other day he'd be out here as employees pulled into the lot, directing them into specific spaces and prodding them for opinions about the day's news as they headed toward the back entrance.

Not today. With the early morning's dusky skies brightening slowly, the Passat's headlights were still noticeable as they blinked off and the driver opened his door. As Tony's black leather shoes hit the dusty white pavement, he closed his door forcefully and slid his hands into the pockets of his beige cashmere overcoat. Though he was a good hundred yards away, Serena heard his voice as clearly as if he was next to her. "Good morning."

With still no other cars pulling in behind her, Serena gripped her purse and began striding purposefully toward the main entrance. Stepping around the occasional patch of ice, the clack of her heels against the blacktop ringing in her ears, she cursed her inability to move faster. Tony, meanwhile, closed in fast, his limp doing little to slow him down. "All I need is one minute, Serena," he said, his voice growing louder as he approached. "I just want to close the loop."

As Serena arrived at the door, she felt him on her heels and turned to take him on. "I was wrong, Tony." Her right arm jutting out like a spear, she felt her voice shake but knew her face was a mask of resolve. "I wasn't in my right mind that night, but I used you. It's that simple." She stayed rooted even as he inched closer, his desire radiating like fumes. "I'm really no better than I was when you caught me with Jamie those years ago. Just forgive me and forget me, okay?"

Standing on the balls of his feet, Tony reached out and slowly slid his hands up and down Serena's stiff arms. Massaging them until her defensive posture softened, he let his words dribble out. "I should ask you . . . to forgive me," he said, "but this was the only way I could get your attention. Answer one question, and we don't need ever need to speak again. Do you really want Jamie back, or would you rather rebuild your life with someone new—whether that's me or a complete stranger?"

Serena heard the question, felt the true answer rock her soul, and knew she could never share it. "It doesn't matter. Whatever the answer, you wouldn't be on my list of new people—first, you're not new, and second, I used you that night for nothing but a sex high. I was manic, Tony! I'd been spotty with my meds for weeks when we hooked up." She regained her composure, lowering her voice to a whisper. "I was with you that night for all the wrong reasons. My fault, not yours."

Pulling her close, he smiled nervously. "We talked about all that," he said. "But I know you sought me out based on real emotions; you wanna know how? I'll bet my life you weren't manic the night of Devon and Kym's wedding. *You* called me that night, Serena, not the other way around."

Tony's benign accusation sinking in, Serena knew he was right, and knew she couldn't acknowledge that inconvenient fact. "I have to go . . ."

Realizing she was pulling away, Tony gave in to the desperation gripping him. "Please, we need to talk this out. We can do it in a public place, wherever you're comfortable—"

A car's brakes squealed behind them and they both involuntarily turned toward it. After lurching into a nearby parking spot, the yellow Mustang's driver's side door flew open. As he stepped from the car, adjusting the fit of his woolly scarf, Levi Little's eyes shot toward Tony and Serena. Serena saw the flash in his gaze, recalled the security director's infatuation with her, and knew immediately she wanted out of this whole situation.

They stood, mute, as Levi strolled toward them. "Good morning, Serena," he said, tipping his leather cap in her direction before glancing at Tony. "Good morning, brother." He stopped suddenly, took another glance at the stress etched into Serena's brow. "Everything okay here?"

Tony had his hands in the pockets of his overcoat and his eyes aimed at the snowy sky, but his tone showed no fear of the larger man. "Mind your business, brother. Mind your business and keep moving."

Serena grabbed at the elbow of Levi's overcoat as he turned toward Tony. "Levi, everything's fine. Get inside, away from all this cold." As Levi huffed and spun back around toward the building's back entrance, Serena scolded Tony with her eyes.

"I'm going inside," she said, stepping away after the door had shut behind Levi. "If I see your car from the window when I reach my office, I will call that brother or one of his guards." Biting her lower lip to keep any tears at bay, she looked back toward him. "God, Tony, I am so sorry. Please go, just forget me."

"Serena," Tony replied, his chest heaving, the corners of his eyes stinging, "you walk away now, that's it." Audrey's invitation from the night before rang in his ears, and for the first time he felt her presence as a comfort, a salve for the constant pain of this woman's rejection. "There's another lady in the picture, one I won't hurt by starting something only to float back to you."

One hand on the back door's handle, Serena resisted the swelling urge to learn more about this mystery woman. Instead, she turned away from Tony, hoping the strength in her tone was an effective mask. "Give her a chance, Tony. Maybe she'll be blessed by what I missed."

25

When Serena opened her eyes that morning, she nearly jumped when Jamie shifted in place. For more than three months she'd had the bed to herself, and she'd realized at bedtime last night that the initial loneliness that caused had quickly morphed into a comforting sense of liberation. Now that Jamie had earned the right to return to their bedroom, she realized his presence would feel like an intrusion for the first few days.

She was turning away when she felt him stir again. In seconds she felt his warm breath on her neck, followed by a quick hit-and-run kiss to her cheek. Her body tensed as if awaiting a blow, she shut her eyes in relief when he pulled away and flopped onto his back.

"Good morning," Jamie said, his voice low and respectful as if he was in church. When she didn't rush to reply, he continued. "I feel very blessed this morning, Serena, just being here with you. And I'm really excited about the program tonight; it'll be our first family outing in forever." Sydney's school had its Christmas program—which of course now had to be called a "holiday" program—and for better or worse, it would be the Kincaid family's first reemergence into the social scene. "And," Jamie continued, "you should know, there's no rush, no specific timetable about anything else."

Serena gave a friendly-sounding grunt and fought the urge to shake her head. As much as she respected Jamie's ongoing meta-morphosis, she knew good and well what his words meant. *I'm horny as hell, babe. Haven't gone this long without it in years, but I'll give you a few more days to get back to breaking me off regular.* He was only human, after all.

Letting her husband back inside of her, however, presented new problems all their own. As long as she kept Jamie at arm's length, Serena had found it surprisingly easy to hide the fact that her sex life consisted largely of reliving her one night with Tony. While her recent appointments with her psychiatrist and her lithium regimen had bolstered her ability to turn him away when he showed up at her job, the memory of him that day—the long-ing etched into his brow, the soulful plea in his eyes—intensified their rendezvous in her mind. In a way, it was as if she'd returned to her teens, when bad boys ruled her world, and Jamie and Tony had traded places. Where Tony was a bearded, limping mystery, the husband who'd let her down so many times had become a tee-totaling, devout Muslim. Or at least he was trying to be one.

Serena knew that her years of cheating, of taking numerous lovers at the same time, were too far in the past for her to go back. The very thought of sleeping with Jamie, without first confessing what she'd done with Tony, made her gag with nausea. She'd tried to explain it all to Jade the day before, when she'd panicked as bedtime neared.

Jade, who never missed a chance to disapprove of what her girl had done, bore down on her like a sumo wrestler. "You and I both know that you don't *have* to tell Jamie what you did," she said as they sat on her front porch. "Let's be real, girl. After all the fun Jamie's had on the side, it's really not his business if you fi-nally lost it one time and went buck wild." Pouring herself another glass of red wine, she'd shot a sudden glance toward her friend. "Of course, that's only true if you never see Tony again."

Serena circled the rim of her wineglass with an index finger. "I haven't done anything to keep in contact with him. You know that."

"You know what I mean," Jade replied. The corners of her

small mouth dove into a frown. "Are you holding Jamie off because you're afraid to admit you cheated, or because you just want out of your marriage?"

Shocked, Serena sat still for a moment before shaking her head slowly. "Where do you get that idea? He's the one that cheated on me all along, remember? He's the one that had a kid by someone else. If I wanted out of the marriage, I'd have never let him back in the house, okay?"

"I don't know," Jade had replied, eyes averted as if embarrassed to speak her mind. "I think you've convinced yourself that the only way to make the marriage work is to confess about Tony, because you know once you do that Jamie will step. Then you'll be free to hook up with Tony."

Climbing from her bed, Jamie's new snores buzzing in the background, Serena considered calling Jade to tell her off. In the moment, she'd sat back and let Jade's loving accusations hang in the air before changing the subject, but her mind was full of rebuttals now. The only problem was they all rang false.

After going to Sydney's room and waking her younger daughter, reminding her they had to move fast in order to get to her basketball practice on time, she went to the kitchen and began setting out breakfast items. That was when she remembered to check in on Dawn.

Between her unsettling confrontation with Tony and her struggle to integrate Jamie back into her life, Serena had nearly blocked out Wednesday night's knock-down-drag-out with her older daughter. That was the night she invited her mother to stop by and broach the sensitive topic of Dawn's budding sexuality. Even though Dawn had sworn her to secrecy, Serena had been confident that her child would respond positively to her grandmother's loving counsel about abstaining from "fornication."

It may have been her most disastrous parental calculation to date. The minute the word "sex" passed Jan's lips, Dawn's eyes rolled back into her head and her mouth went slack. "This isn't happening, this isn't happening," she began saying to herself in a tight whisper. She had leaned forward, her elbows on her knees, her chin resting against her lower neck. "Granny, I promise I'll keep my legs closed if you don't talk to me about this."

Jan had scooted closer to her granddaughter on the couch, rested a hand against the child's shoulder. "Dawn, honey, there's nothing to be ashamed of in having certain feelings. The question is what you do about them."

Dawn shook her head, seemingly unable to process the combined stimuli—her grandmother and the topic of sex. "I don't have any feelings, okay? I'm gonna be a nun, even! I swear!"

"Dawn," Jan replied, her nose twitching at the sound of her granddaughter's tone, "watch your language now."

"You lied, Mom! Straight-up lied!" Dawn was on her feet before Serena or Jan realized it, an index finger pointed toward Serena like a rapper's nine-millimeter. "Why'd you do that?" The words barely escaped Dawn's mouth before a bubble of her tears and spit covered it. "Why?"

Serena still wasn't sure how she and her mother finally got Dawn calmed down, but by the time Dawn went to bed Serena had apologized for breaking her daughter's confidence. Hoping to smooth things over some, she had even agreed to Dawn's request to attend a Friday night sleepover at the home of Celia, a former classmate of hers from Western Hill. Serena hadn't initially liked the idea of letting her sexually curious child out of her sight for that long, but had decided to show some trust and hope it would be rewarded.

When she dialed Dawn's cell phone and got voice mail, Serena grabbed her Pocket PC and looked up Celia's home number. "Hello, Jenny," she said when Celia's mother answered the phone. "I can tell you've got a very quiet house right now. The girls were probably up until a few minutes ago, I suppose."

"Oh, you better know that," Jenny replied, laughing heartily. Serena had always liked Jenny, a divorced fund-raiser for the local Urban League. The lady had her hands full raising two girls and a son by herself, but never seemed down or full of complaints. "You must be trying to find your young lady."

"Well," Serena replied, chuckling softly, "she talks me into buying her a cell phone on the basis it'll be easier for me to keep track of her, then never answers the darn thing."

"Honey," Jenny said, her voice humming with amusement, "she never answers the darn thing when she sees *your* number on the caller ID. In a weak moment, mine admitted she treats me the same sorry way."

Serena's shoulders vibrated with laughter, and she savored the light moment. "No respect for the mommas, huh?"

"Uh-uh. Hold on while I go downstairs and pick through the crowd of bodies in sleeping bags."

Nibbling on a fingernail, Serena cradled her phone on one shoulder and set up her frying pan for bacon and a griddle for pancakes. By the time she began stirring flour and eggs in a bowl, she was wondering whether Jenny had accidentally hung up on her. Just as she prepared to punch the FLASH button and call back, a breathless voice greeted her from the other end. "Uh, Serena?"

"Yes?"

Her tone uncertain, Jenny's words dribbled out. "I don't know where Dawn is, exactly. She and another girl aren't in the house." She paused, and Serena pictured Jenny biting a lip. "I've searched everywhere."

The news sinking in, Serena did all the right things, questioning Jenny and then young Celia with the precision of a prosecutor. As she continued her inquisitions, though, Serena's fears of foul play were dwarfed by a gnawing, dimming resignation: the cycle had begun. After Serena's lectures and every other blood, sweat, and tear, Dawn was pissing on it all, taking off on the very trail of tears her mother had warned her about.

"I'll find her, but I'll find you, too, Glenn," Serena whispered under her breath after hanging up, visions of that condom from a few weeks ago filling her head. "You won't do her the way they did me."

26

From a distance, he recognized them both and was immediately stunned. Though he'd never met her in person, Tony recognized Zora's mother—his mother—even from a distance. As Zora and the petite brown-skinned woman at her side approached from the other end of the airport's baggage claim carousel, he marveled at their resemblance. The similarity in their postures, in the way their hands circled the air in broad gestures, down to their matching profiles, advertised their shared bloodline. His heart aflame, Tony coughed uncontrollably, several times, and doubled over, his hands clamped to his knees.

The jumbled emotions traveling through him left him nearly senseless. He heard voices surrounding him but couldn't perceive their meaning. His mouth went dry and pasty, and his vision blurred as if he'd slipped on a pair of his grandfather's jacked-up bifocals.

She loves me.
Who is she to bring her ass here like this?
Mommy!
What the hell does she want?
She's here for Zora, to show her love for both of us.
Told Zora not to try this; she wasn't my sister, she'd get her ass kicked.

"Tony?"

Zora's voice rose above the crowd, nearly tapping him on the shoulder as he pondered whether to stay or to go. His hands balling into fists, clenching and releasing, he shut his eyes before turning around. "Damn," he whispered under his breath.

When he opened his eyes, Zora and the woman he'd loved to hate stood before him, each with a small overnight bag in hand, each wearing a perfectly phony smile. Zora's was at least offset by the mischievous, earnest glint in her eyes. "What's up?"

The overhead lights in the carousel began to flicker on and off, making Tony feel as if his eyes were in a constant blinking motion. Trying to fix Zora in his sights, he heard his voice drag like a record played at the wrong speed. "I told you not to bring her here."

Lights flashing on and off, Zora stared up at Tony, her eyes growing empty and clueless. "Why wouldn't you want to see Mommy, Tony?" she said. "What's wrong?"

His response was a deep, guttural roar. "What did I tell you!" He looked toward his mother, who still looked something like the photos Zora had shown him, with the exception of a few stray moles, and raised a hand. "I'm not ready!" As Zora and his mother drew back in horror, the lights snapped off again, and the room went pitch-black.

His own heavy breathing filling his ears, Tony at first ignored the ring tone purring just underneath the sound of his breath. When it didn't go away, when it in fact intensified to a point he couldn't ignore, his eyes snapped open and he realized he lay in his own bed, still dressed in a wrinkled dress shirt and slacks. *As if,* he thought. A dream was the only place his mother would ever come looking for him.

After wiping some butter from his eyes, he reached around two empty Bud Light bottles on his nightstand before punching the SPEAKER function on his phone. "Hello?"

A feisty woman's voice snapped across the line. "Is this Tony Gooden?"

His protective instincts stirred, Tony matched her attitude. "Who is this?"

"Who said you can raise my boys better than my own damn family?"

Grabbing up the beer bottles and removing his tie, Tony finally caught the voice. "Wait a minute, this isn't Evelyn, is it? Glenn and Ben's mom?"

"That's right," she replied, still sounding ready to challenge Tony to a duel. They'd had exactly two conversations in the three months that he had mentored her boys, and the twins had pretty much tied Evelyn to her couch to coordinate those. As sad as her recent prison sentence was, especially for what it meant for the twins, a part of Tony whispered, *Good riddance.*

Headed for jail or not, Evelyn wasn't through marking her territory. "I'm these boys' momma," she said, her tongue sounding a bit heavy. "And you can call me Ms. Hampton, dammit. You ain't my *friend.*"

Sighing, Tony chucked his beer bottles into his kitchen's recycling bin. "Yeah, God forbid I should offend you, *Ms.* Hampton."

"You tryin' to be smart? You know, I ain't got to consent to letting you spend time with my sons. I'll call Principal Jacobs and get your ass barred from the school."

Tony laughed long and loud, though he stopped short of mentioning that he was probably days away from sexing the principal. "How about we cease with empty threats, *Ms.* Hampton, and you just tell me what's the matter?" Sarcasm welling up in his throat, he raised his arms overhead. "I've simply offered to help the boys get through this difficult time, this pain of being separated from you."

"They are disrespecting me, damn you," Evelyn replied, the words popping out forcefully but with a measured strength. Tony sensed, as he had during their other brief meeting, that Evelyn Hampton had the raw material to be at a completely different level of society, save for a few wrong turns through the years. "Now, look, I may have let my kids down, especially this latest time, but I've never laid a hand on 'em in anger. They got me ready to break that pledge."

Smiling at her candor, Tony began stroking his beard. "Why don't you put one of them on the phone, Evelyn? I mean, *Ms.* Hampton."

"Just so you know, I don't appreciate having to do this shit," she replied, the words dripping out tersely. "They had the nerve to say they wouldn't obey me unless *you* said they should. Like you already their foster father."

"Ma'am," Tony said, "if the twins have told you that I've ever suggested they disrespect you, then they misunderstood me."

"Whatever," she said, huffing. "Here's one now."

Tony caught Ben's voice immediately. "Hey, Mr. Gooden."

"What's going on, man?"

"It's a little complicated, sir," he replied. The boy cleared his throat. "Would you, uh, mind coming by, as soon as you could?"

Tony checked his watch: not even eight a.m. yet on a Sunday morning, his rare chance to sleep in before a late morning meeting with his realtor, to put together an offer on the house he'd thought he didn't need. It occurred to him that taking on the challenge of foster parenting was going to quickly cramp his style, what little bit of it he had left. His next words escaped with the reluctance of air hissing from a balloon. "Let me get cleaned up, okay?"

27

As Tony drove into the city, his mind was less on the twins than on Audrey. She was away for the weekend, visiting friends from graduate school in Philadelphia, but on Friday he'd courageously left a message on her home voice mail.

"Hey," he'd said after her machine beeped, "it's me." They had talked on the phone enough the past few weeks that he knew no further introduction was necessary. Ever since her midair invitation, where she'd made it clear he didn't have to marry her in order to lie down with her, Tony had bounced back and forth like a tennis ball between Venus and Serena. He'd never been so indecisive.

He'd definitely moved the line separating him from Audrey. Technically platonic, they were undeniably sliding toward some form of intimacy. Hands had been held, lips had touched, brushed, and bonded, but the line hadn't faded completely. Four times in three weeks she'd had him at the foot of her bed, and each time she'd beckoned him forward, her hands drawn out in coaxing fashion.

Serena, of course, still hung in the air; as a result he'd been too torn to take that last familiar step with Audrey, the same one he'd taken with dozens of women of all races, nationalities, and zip codes. As half-dressed as she was—not to mention his zipper being distressed by a nearly painful bulge—he'd pulled away each time. By the third time, this past Thursday night, Audrey had simply sunk to the bed, pulled back her covers, and climbed in as he gathered his things and slipped off.

"Look," he said to her machine while biting his lower lip. "You were right. I have to stop holding back. Not just with you, but in life itself. I mean, I guess I'm realizing that with grudges, and with some relationships, you just have to let 'em go. Okay, I'm rambling, so just call me when you get home Sunday night. I need to see you before I go home for Christmas."

He'd definitely had warmer greetings. "You better handle your business, Mr. Mentor." Evelyn's dark stare pinned Tony where he stood, just outside the threshold of her tiny walk-up apartment. "If you'd taken another minute getting here, a set of twin heads was about to get bashed up, real good."

"Now, we can't have that," Tony replied, shrugging nonchalantly. His years working at the elbow of the mayor had schooled him in the art of conflict management, and the first rule was that the more emotional the other person got, the cooler you had to be. Anything else just fanned the flames. He extended a respectful hand, which he would have otherwise used to cover his nose from the pungent, greasy odor in the hallway. "You mind if I come in?"

Swinging around, Evelyn trudged down her narrow hallway with Tony in obedient pursuit. Still ignoring him, she slapped her hands to her hips as they stepped onto the brown linoleum tile lining her cramped kitchen floor. "He's here, you ingrates. Let's deal with this mess—now!"

Engaged in animated conversation, the twins sat at a low, square wooden table shoved into a corner. Both were sprawled across their seats with the lazy posture of teens, but Tony noticed that they not only stopped talking upon seeing him, but each sat up a bit.

Glenn spoke first, his mouth in a mischievous grin. "Mr. Gooden, what's up?"

His eyes smiling, Tony frowned. "What's up? How about *I'm* up, instead of enjoying a lazy morning's sleep, thanks to you." Stepping forward, he popped fists with Glenn and shook hands with Ben. Standing over the table, he glanced from one brother to the other. "Not to mention I've still got my Christmas shopping to finish, so I don't have all day. Who's going to explain why I'm here?"

"I'll tell you the deal," Evelyn said, stepping up to the table, hands still cemented to her hips. "I come home this morning to find some hoochie-ass whore sleeping in my bed, and it was clear she did more than sleep on my bed with one of these two last night." She waved a finger between her sons as if Tony didn't know who they were. "So I tell the little tramp to clean up after herself and never trespass on my property again." She flicked a long finger toward Glenn. "That's when this one laid a hand on me," she continued, her eyes growing into enraged saucers of disbelief.

Glenn snorted and threw his hands into the air. "Ben, you were there. You were there. Did I harm Ma at all, huh? Did I?"

Ben, who was clearly more anxious than his twin, fiddled with his hands and spoke into his chest. "You just eased her out of the bedroom, before she could do any more damage." He looked up at Tony, his eyes asking for help. "I mean, Ma basically slugged homegirl."

Tony pulled out the third kitchen table chair and offered it to Evelyn. When she flashed him a look of disgust, he flipped it backward and plopped down onto the crooked, prickly wooden seat. "This true, Ms. Hampton?"

"I was defending myself," Evelyn replied, stomping a foot as her neck muscles bulged. "That was between me and the little whore. Glenn had no business puttin' his hands on me."

Tony had heard enough about Evelyn's antics that the next question fell easily from his lips. "When you came at this girl, were you sober?"

Tapping a foot rapidly, she responded to Tony but kept her gaze firmly over his head. "I'm their momma, they ain't got no right to judge my sobriety or anything else. This is my house."

"It ain't nothing but your apartment," Glenn said, nearly under his breath. "You pay rent, Ma. It ain't nobody's property but the landlord's." Though he stayed slumped in his seat, he actually flinched when Evelyn feinted toward him with a raised fist.

"See what I deal with?" She asked Tony as she backed away from the table.

As Tony tried to fashion a response, Ben cleared his throat. "Ma, why don't you tell Mr. Gooden what's really up with you? Why you're really mad."

Evelyn retreated farther from them, until she was leaning against her off-white, dust-caked refrigerator. Her arms crossed, she looked heavenward. "It's a separate issue, Gooden, but it's like this. I don't want you trying to raise my boys. We don't hardly know you, it ain't right."

"Evelyn, we both know your aunt can't take on the responsibility." Tony kept his tone respectful but raised his voice. "I've talked with her myself, and she's submitted a statement to Children's Services, too. For God's sake, the woman is in and out of the hospital as it is."

"So?" Evelyn hunched her shoulders, frowning. "These boys good as grown, big enough to take care of themselves anyway. If anything, they'll help her."

Tony looked at the boys, ran a hand through his hair. "Evelyn, it's probably best if we continue this conversation woman to man."

"Whatever," she said, crossing her arms. "Once you all get that little tramp out of my house, then we can talk about something else."

Tony did a double take before staring the twins down with a furrowed brow. "This girl's still here?" He'd pulled plenty of mess in his day with babes from Martin Luther King High School, but Tony had never let a girl be caught in the act by his parents. This poor girl had not only been harassed by Evelyn, she was still cowering back in that bedroom? "Whoever brought her over here better make sure she's dressed. Evelyn, you and I should drive her home."

Standing now, Glenn smacked one fist into the opposite palm. "Uh, Mr. G, she's not gonna be comfortable riding with Ma."

"Oh, really?" Evelyn's grin was wide and wicked. "She was comfortable letting you break her back out, but too good to ride—"

Tony sensed Glenn's anger and shot an arm out just in time, holding the youngster in place as he glared at his mother. "Evelyn," Tony said, "you don't know exactly what this girl did with either of your sons. Let's all get ahold of ourselves." Wincing at the pain in his left leg, he put a hand on Glenn's shoulder. "When we take this young lady home, guys, it'll look better if your mother's with me than if you or Ben are. Trust me."

Ben hopped from his seat. "Mr. Gooden, I'll stay here with Ma. You two go get Glenn's girl out of there."

Glenn's girl. It took a second to realize why, but Ben's simple words chilled the pit of Tony's stomach, and he desperately wanted to stay right where he was. Life had been so crazy lately, he'd managed to momentarily forget who Glenn's main girl was.

When he turned and saw the football star enter the kitchen with the girl at his side, he knew it would be young Dawn Kincaid. Hair matted, clothing rumpled, a black scar below her right eye, she was nowhere near as frazzled as a girl with good judgment should be. Gum popping, mouth wide with a smile, she looked Tony dead in the eye. "What's up, Mr. G?"

28

Going on noon and still no word from Dawn, who hadn't answered her cell phone any of the dozen times Serena had dialed her number this morning. After her last try, Serena looked up from the phone in her hand and stared into Jamie's watchful eyes. Leaning forward, his elbows on his knees, he took her hands into his. "What do you want me to do, Dee?"

Serena tugged absentmindedly at her slacks, balling the fabric inside of a fist. "I don't know what to do. Should I call my mother? She has firsthand experience with foolish, rebellious daughters."

"Serena, baby, stop it." Jamie stood, then took a spot next to her on their love seat, settling in close but keeping his arms to himself. "This isn't about you or your past; this is about Dawn doing something stupid. We'll get her through it. In the meantime, we just need to pray for her safe return. And after we pray, you give me the names of every friend and potential boyfriend she could be with, and we'll make some damn house calls until someone leads us to her."

Eyes blurred with tears and shoulders shaking, Serena was humiliated by her rare inability to hide the shame and fear within. "I could have done more!" The words shrieked from somewhere down deep, but she didn't believe they were hers. She couldn't fall apart like this, not this early in Dawn's disappearance and not when she was still hiding so much from Jamie. To depend on him now wouldn't be right. . . .

"Mommy?" Sydney's voice snapped Serena out of her pain. She looked up to see her baby daughter enter the family room, a hand stretched toward her mother's cheek. "Why are you crying?"

As if sensing Serena's fragility, Jamie reached forward and grabbed Sydney into a bear hug. "Hey puddin'," he whispered. "Mommy's going to be fine, she's just a little sad right now."

Taking a seat on Jamie's lap, Sydney laid a hand against her father's chest but looked toward Serena. "Why is she sad, Daddy? You're not leaving us again, are you?"

"Daddy's not going anywhere," Jamie said, his voice still low as he kissed Sydney's forehead. "I promise you, honey, when Dawn gets home later today, your mommy won't be crying, okay? And I'm taking everyone out for dinner tonight." Jamie looked toward Serena, his gaze patient but insistent. "We'll have a good talk with Dawn, figure out how to help her, but we're having some real family time tonight, Dee."

Resting against her father's expansive body, Sydney lay back and smiled at Serena. "Mommy, I'm glad Daddy's back," she said, a look of relief lighting her face. "I don't ever want him to leave again. I love you both too much."

"Baby," Serena said, reaching over and touching a hand to her daughter's lips, "I love you, too." Wiping her eyes, she stood, kissed both her husband and daughter on the cheek, and stared at Jamie. "I'm going to take you up on your offer. I'll go get my Pocket PC and make a list of her friends' addresses, starting with that Glenn character." She glanced at Sydney. "You mind spending the afternoon with Granny and Poppy?"

As Sydney shrugged her approval, Serena walked to the family room's bay window, which looked out over the home's front porch. Stepping to the side of her recently decorated Christmas tree, she noticed that a car had come to a stop at her front curb.

A fire red Passat.

29

*T*he temperature outside was twenty-four degrees, but it felt sub-zero inside Tony's car. With Evelyn stewing in the passenger seat and a newly submissive Dawn in his backseat, Tony may as well have been by himself.

"In, uh, two lights you'll come to River Bend." A new stick of gum popping busily, Dawn provided halfhearted directions in a muted voice, as if hoping her humility would avoid a repeat of her earlier beat-down at Evelyn's hands.

As he leaned his Passat into a right turn, passing a cluster of University of Cincinnati buildings, Tony hoped no one could hear the increasingly frantic beat of his heart. With each passing block, each ticking second, his brow grew hotter and his mouth grew moister with saliva. He wasn't proud of it, but after everything that had transpired between them, the thought of seeing Serena's home, seeing Serena herself, was monumental.

But this wasn't about that, he reminded himself as Dawn's directions brought him to a coasting stop in front of a three-story brick home with a stone porch and a long, steep front lawn. Peering up the hill, Tony gathered his will. Fate had thrust him into an embarrassing intersection, but he knew if he ever became a parent, he would want someone in his shoes to look out for his child, too.

He'd opened his door and stepped up on the curb when he realized Dawn was still sitting in the car. Evelyn had sprung out before he had and stood on the sidewalk with a toe tapping impatiently, but the teenager was still in her seat, whittling her fingernails into nubs with chattering teeth.

"Young lady," Tony said, extending an arm after opening the back door. He leaned into the car, keeping his tone firm but calm. "Come on, Dawn. I know this is embarrassing, but I'm willing to bet your parents have been so worried where you were, they'll just be relieved to see you."

Her eyes rolling in annoyance, Dawn turned away from him. "Mr. G, don't kid a kidder. I know I'm about to get read the riot act."

Rubbing his hands against the cold and realizing he'd lost his gloves, Tony cracked a smile. "It won't be that bad. Trust me."

"Whoo." From just over Tony's shoulder, Evelyn's exclamation whistled through the air. "Mr. Sweet Talker think he can sell *anything*." As Tony led Dawn from the car, turning to face her, Evelyn crossed her arms and grinned. "Look at this neighborhood, this house. And you say the girl's momma is an officer with the school system? Please, she's gonna be so shamed by her hoochie daughter, she'll work her over more than I would—"

"Evelyn, chill," Tony said, keeping himself between her and the cowering Dawn. "I asked you to come along so this wouldn't all look too weird. I'm not trying to be mistaken for some pervert who's kidnapped these folks' child." He wasn't even thinking of revealing his relationship with Serena to either Evelyn or Dawn; that would have to take care of itself.

He laid a gentle hand on Evelyn's shoulder. "Will you work with me here, just help make this a peaceful handoff so Dawn learns not to pull this again?"

"Fine," Evelyn replied dismissively, shrugging off his hand and adjusting the fit of her wool winter cap. "Let's roll, man. I got places to be today."

"Dawn!" Even Evelyn went quiet when the deep bass voice cut through the air, echoing from the home's porch. Tony's eyes followed Evelyn's and Dawn's up the hill, where a tall, bald brother wearing only black slacks and white shirtsleeves stood with his back tensed and his eyes narrowed. His words flowing aggressively, Jamie Kincaid burst down the porch's stone steps, a cougar advancing on his prey. "Get up here. Your mother's been a basket case all morning!"

That's when Tony heard it, the sudden gasp in Dawn's throat. Her stepfather closing in, the child reflexively slid behind Tony, placing him directly in Jamie's line of fire. Being in his way wasn't what frightened Tony. No, what took him by surprise was the angry pride taking root in his soul, the vengeful spirit cackling with glee at the shock slowly spreading across his rival's face as he neared.

That's right, bitch, said the voice inside Tony's head. *I'm back.*

30

At the sight of Tony's car, Serena did the only thing she could: get Sydney away from the hell about to break loose. Without knowing what Tony had in mind, the only thing she knew was that she didn't want Sydney in the middle of it. In a swift motion, she'd coolly turned back toward her daughter and insisted she come upstairs so they could pick out a nice outfit for her to wear to her grandparents' house. They were halfway up the steps when she heard Jamie's angry gulp. "Serena, that's Dawn out there!"

Once she'd ordered Sydney into her bedroom, Serena sprang back down the stairs, knowing she could hide no more. After shrugging on a goose-feather jacket, she rushed onto the porch but froze as Jamie barreled down the steps toward Dawn, some strange woman, and Tony Gooden.

When she first saw him, she actually pivoted and placed a hand on the handle of her front door. Her hand only lingered for a second, though, before she gathered the will to turn back and flit down the steps after her husband. She was simply too old to keep running. She quickly covered the dozen steps between her and everyone else, but by the time she reached them Jamie and Tony were already in each other's face.

With Dawn loitering a few inches behind Tony, Jamie stood

with a long finger pointed in the smaller man's face. "What are you doing with my *daughter*, Gooden?" The meaning was clear: *Thought it was my wife you wanted.*

"Jamie." Serena edged up onto her husband's heels, tugging at the waistline of his slacks. "Let's not make a scene. What matters is that Dawn's home now."

With Jamie towering over him, Tony's eye contact didn't waver. Matching the intensity of Jamie's angry stare, he acted as if Serena weren't even there. "Mr. and Mrs. Kincaid," he said finally, nodding formally and placing a hand on the back of the scraggly woman at his side, "this is Ms. Evelyn Hampton. I've been mentoring her sons, Ben and Glenn. They're classmates of Dawn's." Shifting his weight between legs, struggling a bit to keep his balance, he glanced at the woman. "Mr. and Mrs. Kincaid know me from my official role working for the academy," he said, switching his gaze to Jamie and then Serena. "Our past interactions have been a little, uh, strained."

"Oh, yes," Jamie replied, offering his hand to Evelyn clumsily. "You could definitely say that." Serena wondered if it was the Nation's influence that enabled him to cool down so quickly, or the simple desire not to embarrass himself in front of a stranger. Either way she'd take it.

Tony's expression was still calm but growing grimmer by the minute. "Do you two have a minute? I think we can help explain where Dawn's been the past twelve hours."

Serena cleared her throat, then motioned Dawn toward her. "Come here." When her daughter took the tentative steps that brought her within reach, Serena pulled her close in a hug but whispered into her ear. "Fifteen or not, I *will* be whipping that ass." She raised her voice then. "Get in the house." She'd ask where the child got her black eye later.

"Mr. Gooden," Serena continued once she had sent her daughter on her way, "I think it's best if we discuss things right here. Given the past, that's most appropriate, don't you think?"

"This is pretty private stuff," Tony replied, his eyebrows jumping in concern.

"There's a lot of space between these houses," Jamie said, his gaze daring Tony to keep pressing his luck. "No one will hear anything. Now what was my daughter doing with you all night?"

Tony sighed. "She wasn't with me," he said impatiently. "You were aware that Dawn's dating Evelyn's son Glenn, right?"

"I do know something about my daughter's social life, yes." The weight of Jamie's accusing stare on her, Serena braved a glance into Tony's eyes. The minute she did, their argument that cold morning outside her office began replaying in her head. What had she told him about their night together? *I wasn't in my right mind.* Shaken, she looked toward the ground, then asked, "Dawn was with Glenn last night, wasn't she?"

"Yes," Tony said, his voice oddly low and confessional. "She, uh, spent the night at Evelyn's."

Evelyn nudged Tony suddenly, her languid gaze mocking Serena. "Finish the story, brother. Tell 'em why I had to chase the girl out of my *own* bed—"

Not that she hadn't already expected the worst, but as she put the pieces together Serena's throat filled involuntarily with bile. She pushed past Tony, took Evelyn by the shoulder. "Cut to the chase, okay, sister? What, did your son fuck my daughter?"

Serena couldn't tear her angry stare away from Evelyn, but she felt another hand on her shoulder. "It'll be okay," Tony whispered. "Just take it easy—"

Jamie nearly roared as he slapped Tony's hand away from Serena. "Keep your damn hands to yourself!"

After shooting an amused glance at Serena, Evelyn raised her eyebrows at the two men. "Uh, look, you don't need to be touchin' me, for starters. Second of all, you got no call to make it sound like my boy raped your daughter or any crazy shit like that. Glenn doesn't mess with any hoochie what doesn't first throw her stuff at him. So anything he did, that little hot tamale of yours asked for."

"This isn't helpful," Tony said, his voice pleading but insistent. "None of us here saw who did whom, dammit. But as the guy caught in the middle, I thought you two as Dawn's parents should know that she's . . . behaving like a woman now. I'd hate to have her and Glenn have an accident and wind up being parents too early, or worse."

"Or worse?" Evelyn's face twisted into a frown. "What, like she's some virgin my Glenn's gonna infect with a virus or some shit? Please. I taught that boy and his brother how to wrap themselves tight when they hit thirteen. My boys are *clean*."

Tony was leaking patience like a ship wrecked against boulders. He couldn't say a thing to make anybody happy. "Will you all stop fighting over whose kid is the least guilty here? I just wanted the truth aired." He shot an exasperated glare at Evelyn. "Let's go, my job's done here."

Still trying to process her daughter's foolishness, Serena found herself staring into Tony's penetrating gaze, her plea from their last argument stinging her insides. *I wasn't in my right mind.* For some reason, the trauma of Dawn's betrayal had kicked loose something inside her, a realization she'd fled for weeks. Her words to Tony had been a lie. She'd been off her meds, yes, but her affair with Tony had been driven first and foremost by the chemistry that sparkled between them that afternoon at Devon and Kym's wedding. Jamie's infidelity had just given her the final chance to explore it.

Serena was so twisted up with her conflicting desires—a healed marriage, a second chance at happiness with her first love—that she was caught flat-footed when Jamie shot a long arm out, snaring Tony where he stood. "Why don't you go wait for Mr. Gooden at his car, Evelyn," he said, his voice a calm growl.

Still immobilized by Jamie's grip, Tony chucked his car keys to the woman. "Go ahead." As Evelyn rolled her eyes and turned toward the car, he looked up into Jamie's sneer. "What you need, man?"

Jamie tightened his grip, yanked Tony so close the crown of the smaller man's head brushed up against Jamie's chin. "You got real balls, waltzing up on my family like this."

His jaw set, Tony kept his eyes fixed on Jamie's. "I've explained myself, Jamie. This is only as personal as you make it."

Jamie flashed an odd smile, the type that usually precedes violence. "I'm going to be praying for you, Gooden. Praying that you find whatever it is you think you'd find if you could get my wife back. But if you ever step foot onto my property again, if I ever hear you've come anywhere near Dawn or Serena, no amount of help from Allah will save you."

"Jamie," Serena whispered, edging up to her husband and avoiding Tony's serene gaze. "He was just doing the right thing, for Dawn's sake. He's not worried about me, okay? I'm here with you, baby, even after all the turmoil. Tony's no threat to you."

Looking at her arm on his, Jamie turned slowly toward Serena and let her pull him into a hug. As he leaned down, allowing her to reach up and rub the back of his head, Serena shut her eyes tight. She heard Tony's footsteps as he headed back to his car, heard his car's ignition turn over, heard his Passat roar away from the curb.

Tears filling her eyes, tears she hoped her husband would believe were for him, she comforted herself with the thought of her girls, especially the joy on Sydney's face when she'd talked earlier about her love for Jamie. The last thing her baby needed was the same "daddy" issues that probably inspired Dawn's latest rebellion.

Even with that assurance, Serena had to bury her head deep into Jamie's chest. She couldn't watch Tony go; if she did, the truth was bound to burst from her. *I lied about that night, she thought. With or without my meds, in my right mind or not, I would have done the exact same thing.*

31

When she first heard the news, Zora raised both eyebrows at her brother. "Tony, this isn't funny." Seated across from him in a booth at a Caribou Coffee near her apartment, she kicked him under the table. "Now tell me what you've *really* been up to."

Taking a sip from his mug of Kahlúa-sweetened coffee, Tony cast his gaze on the streetlamps outside, which had kicked into gear as the skies darkened. "I just told you, sis."

Zora leaned forward, blowing air through her lips. "You know I love you, right? So don't make me say what's on my mind. Just admit you're playing with me."

He grinned mischievously. "What's on my baby sister's mind? The thought that her brother's lost his?" He had just revealed his attempt to become the twins' foster father, right after bringing her up to speed on the house he'd finally purchased. He had introduced the boys to her and to his father back in the fall, but had kept the foster thing quiet until recently passing the first stage of the application process. It had helped that he'd finally won over Evelyn, who had formally asked the court to place the boys with him. Coming as it had the day after New Year's, it felt like a belated Christmas present.

Zora was still processing everything. "Tony, I just can't believe you're taking on this challenge, with all the other things going on in your life."

He leaned back against his seat, his arms spread wide in opposite directions. "I've got a new job, in a new city, all because I'm a new man. Would the old Tony Gooden have been willing to mentor two knucklehead teens? Hell, no. The new me took that first step, Zora, and now I'm in too deep to turn back."

Her brow knitted, her hands clasped together in concern, Zora leveled a precise stare toward her brother. "They don't have anyone else to watch over them, no other family?"

The memory of Evelyn's court hearing two days earlier, the one where she'd been sentenced to another six months of prison, sobered Tony up, and he felt his grin vanish. "There's an aunt who's provided financial help through the years, but she's got health problems of her own." He reached forward, tapping Zora's clasped hands. "Trust me, sis, if Glenn and Ben are gonna have some good direction in their lives, not to mention the positive influence of a male role model, someone's got to step in."

Her nose scrunched up, Zora offset the anxiety in her voice with a weak smile. "Is this really the time for you to serve as a role model?"

His pride pricked, Tony focused his eyes on the store's front register. "You're worried about my situation with Serena, aren't you? Why don't you spend your time in a more productive fashion, kid? Don't you have a big-ass speech to write?" In a culmination of some of Tony's wildest dreams for his sister, Zora had founded an activist group of female rappers, writers, and poets who were scheduling local rallies in a dozen cities across the country, all aimed at encouraging a female boycott of all hip-hop that disrespected women. After unwittingly finding herself in the midst of the hip-hop cultural wars, Zora had decided to embrace the battle and choose sides.

"Never mind my speech," she quipped with a playful roll of the neck. "Now about you and Serena. Why shouldn't I be worried?"

Tony sat back in his seat but began punctuating his words

with gestures, his hands slicing through the air. "Z, all that's over. I've accepted that Serena is part of my past, not my future." The funny thing was, he actually believed the second half of what he was saying. After his confrontation with the Kincaid family, he'd come away convinced that Serena had more things on her mind than recreating some college crush.

What had he been thinking, anyway, fantasizing about starting his life over with her? While he was free to reinvent himself at will, Serena didn't have those liberties. Little Sydney was still eight years away from getting out of the house, and damn if Dawn wasn't in the most vulnerable phase of a child's life. The more he thought about it, he wasn't sure he could respect a woman who would place her own happiness over that of her children. He'd sensed at their house that she was committed to saving her marriage, and with all that in mind it was hard to argue with.

He tolerated Zora's probing questions until she finally pushed her pie plate aside. "You should know, I'm proud of you, big brother. I mean, I could never do anything as unselfish as what you're trying, but I admire your courage." She patted his outstretched hand. "You're gonna have to keep me updated on this."

Tony was surprised by the swelling pride his sister's words stirred. "Of course."

She smiled, patting his hand again. "Just one suggestion as you get going. Wouldn't this time—embarking on becoming a parent—be the perfect opportunity to seek Millie out, to make her meet with you at least once?"

"As my boy Jack Nicholson once said, go sell crazy someplace else, please."

"But Tony—"

"Sis." He slid his hand out from under Zora's, reaching over with his left hand and enclosing her hand in both of his. "It's not gonna happen. You lived with her for eighteen years; why's it taking you longer to figure her out than it took me?"

Zora raised her free hand and covered Tony's. "Well, until she comes to her senses, you could go ahead and handle business on your end. Therapy would be good for you, trust me."

Tony drew back, sliding his wallet out of his suit jacket. "It's getting late. I have to meet my colleagues downtown at eight-thirty. Will twenty cover the bill?"

Zora snagged the money from his hand, frowning playfully. "There'll be change, but I'll keep it to get you back for ignoring me."

He smiled. "Don't be like that, Z. I mean, you can have the change, but I really have to run. You never know how long it'll take to hail a cab in this neighborhood, and if I'm late for this dinner I arranged, my ass is grass." Although Chicago had initially been excluded from the list of cities targeted for new branches of Rowan Academy—the city's legendary political machine intimidated both Larry and Arthur Champion—Tony had finally convinced them to conduct this scouting trip to the city. For tonight's dinner he had invited every area politician, bureaucrat, and journalist he knew. It was his best chance to open doors for Rowan in his hometown.

Sliding out of the booth and standing, Tony leaned over his sister. "I wasn't ignoring you, Z." He gave her a quick peck on the cheek. "I give. I'll schedule my head for a good shrinking, okay?"

32

"Y ou d-did what?" Eyes suddenly vacant, his mouth wide as his lower lip and chin plunged toward the bed, Jamie jerked as if he'd been shot through the heart. Still as naked as the day God brought him forth from the womb, he reared back in shock at his wife's words, losing his balance until he tumbled onto his back, his quickly shrinking penis now a shadow of itself.

There had been several motivations, but it was Serena's libido that had finally forced her to come clean. Raging, long-neglected hormones, combined with her sincere respect for the compromises they'd made to reach this point, meant she couldn't make love to Jamie without putting everything on the table. As Jamie had straddled her, his hands rediscovering her body, his tongue hanging out in eager anticipation, she shut her eyes and let the truth flow.

"I won't lie anymore, Jamie. I spent—I spent a night with Tony."

According to the clock on Serena's nightstand, it was now 6:34 p.m., meaning three entire minutes had passed since her husband had tumbled onto his ass. Shifting, Serena turned onto her right elbow as Jamie sat at the end of the bed, motionless. For a moment, she couldn't figure whether his silence was involuntary shock or calculated punishment. She was ready to hear something, anything from him in response. Staring across the darkened room into the abyss of her husband's pain, Serena longed for the comfortable cover of the past few weeks, the time she'd spent acting as if that night with Tony never happened.

Maybe she'd have never brought this up, if not for Jade. She and Serena had been at the gym a week ago, preparing for aerobics class, when her friend challenged her. "So, when you gonna pay the piper?"

Once she finished playing stupid, Serena had leaned against her locker and swept her eyes around, making sure no one else was in earshot. "Jamie and I have had a lot to deal with, Jade. We've done more team parenting the past two weeks than we'd probably done the past two years, okay?" In the time since Tony had brought Dawn home from her little sex sleepover with Glenn, the Kincaids had tried their best to put her under lock and key. At every minute of the day, either Serena or Jamie monitored Dawn's movements in some manner—calling teachers to confirm her attendance in classes, picking her up immediately after school and confining her to house arrest until the next morning, even limiting her weekend outings to family activities.

Oddly enough, their daughter hadn't fought back nearly as much as expected. Apparently Glenn's ghetto momma, Evelyn, had struck enough fear of God into the child that she found her own parents quite reasonable by comparison. Even more odd, while Dawn was tolerating Serena, she'd taken to nearly fawning over Jamie. Her stepfather had earned the adoration; not only had he aggressively assured Dawn that her rebellious sexuality was normal and was more of a bump in the road than a big deal, he'd publicly put Glenn on notice, interrupting a phone call between him and Dawn one night. "You lay up with my daughter like that again, letting her get clowned by your ignorant mother," Jamie had said into the phone, his eyes glinting with caged bravado, "and you and I will need to meet face-to-face, like men." Dawn had protested, but only after watching Jamie with something bordering on awe.

That didn't mean the child was through with Glenn, of course. In the course of forbidding her to see him anymore, Serena had been disappointed to learn that the young buck handled his business in the bedroom. Her daughter held no apparent pangs of regret at surrendering her virginity; like her mother before her, Dawn felt her "first" had opened the door to a world of pleasure and excitement she'd only heard of before. In return, for the next several months and possibly beyond, Serena knew good and well that Glenn Hampton would be welcome to Dawn Kincaid's body whenever and wherever he wanted it.

If he got past her and Jamie, of course.

That day at the gym, Jade hadn't been impressed with Jamie and Serena's successful partnership. "I know you're both busy, and I know you've already come a long way," she said. "But that doesn't mean you can just keep on without bringing the truth into the open." Jade took a seat beside her friend on the locker room bench. "Why have a sword of hidden secrets hanging over your head, girl? It's not like Jamie's a babe in the woods. He'll understand. Eventually."

"Real reassuring, sis," Serena replied, rolling her eyes but keeping her head down. "I'm already tied up in knots about this. Until I decide I'm ready to take Jamie back into my bed, I just don't think it's worth springing the news on him."

A crooked grin invaded Jade's face, a nervous twitch Serena recognized in her old friend. "Come on, Serena. Are you trying to tell me Jamie doesn't already have suspicions? I *know* he's said more to you about the way Tony showed up at your house with Dawn."

"We had harsh words that night," Serena admitted, sniffing nervously. "But that was it. I told him there was always a risk Tony would cross our paths when we enrolled Dawn at Rowan. I reminded him that he was the one who wanted Dawn there, and that we both felt, her dumb-ass recent move notwithstanding, that it was a smart move. He backed off the whole subject when I stood my ground."

Jade frowned. "How'd you feel, lying to him like that?"

Serena turned narrowed eyes toward her friend. "Excuse me, but that was no lie. As far as I know, it was pure coincidence that Tony wound up mentoring Dawn's boyfriend."

"Please," Jade sighed. "You know what I mean, girl." She put a hand to Serena's shoulder. "There was a time, sis, when we played games and did dirt, let the brothers we were dating think they were the only one and all that." Her voice quieted as she turned away and said, "I thought we'd outgrown those days."

That little guilt-inducing sentence had perched in Serena's subconscious ever since, and as she awaited her husband's reaction she realized its role in her outburst. What was done was done, though.

Soft beeps prickled Serena's ears and she realized that Jamie, who now sat with his back to her, had dialed a number into their cordless phone. "Fritz," he said, his voice low and morose when his friend answered. "That space on your couch? I need that for myself this time. I'm coming back, but I'll have Sydney with me. She'll need to use your guest bedroom."

Keeping his back to Serena, a still-naked Jamie stood, his butt cheeks flexing as he waved a hand dismissively. "Nothing to discuss or cool down about, brother. I can't tell you the details right now, 'cause if I do Allah will lose control of me, and my wife might wind up in an ambulance. Just give me an hour to gather my things and Sydney's, okay?"

Much the same way she'd been paralyzed when Jamie first confessed his own adultery, Serena felt she was watching a movie of a stranger's life. *Isn't that a trip,* she thought. *Woman's husband done lost his damn mind, trying to punish her by walking off with her baby.*

"What are you looking at?" Jamie had turned and faced her now. Still buck naked, he embraced his naturally bowlegged posture, rays of aggression shimmering forth.

When Serena heard her own voice, she was surprised at how deceptively calm she sounded. "Jamie, you're talking crazy."

"Did I ask for your opinion?" Jamie scowled as he opened a drawer full of boxer shorts. "I'm trying to be restrained about this, woman—don't press me. I'm gonna get dressed." He snapped a fresh pair of boxers in the air, then stared into her eyes. "Go pack a few days' worth of Sydney's clothes. I'll pick her up on my way over to Fritz's." Along with Dawn, Sydney was spending the afternoon with Serena's parents.

Serena reached toward her nightstand, grabbing the pair of panties lying there. "I know this was hard to hear, okay? But you don't have any legal right to take Sydney with you, Jamie. Why don't you let me finish explaining—"

"There's nothing to explain," he said, hiking his boxers up his legs and over his equipment until they were secured in place.

"Jamie," Serena replied, suddenly feeling too shamed to throw off her covers and confront her husband on her feet. "I wasn't in my right mind that night. After you told me about everything going on with you, I stopped taking my medicine for a while and—"

"Save it," he replied, his menacing stare piercing her. "You haven't had a real relapse since Sydney was born, so I'm not buying that you conveniently had one after finding out about Angelita and Andrea. What you did was revenge. You took a squat over my attempts to clean up my life, and pissed all over them."

His eyes a raging fire, his voice a slowly heating oven, Jamie aimed a long index finger toward his wife. "For months now I've been celibate, studying at the mosque, doing all the right things by you and by the girls, and you respond by hiding your own sin, the very one I feared months ago."

Serena couldn't look her husband in the eye, but her mouth still worked. "Jamie, this didn't happen in a vacuum—"

"I don't want to hear it!" His yell echoing through the house, he glanced at her with eyes struggling to conceal the pain within, then turned toward their bathroom. "I'm not telling you again," he said, his voice no longer a shout but no less insistent. "Go pack Sydney's clothes before this gets out of hand."

As desperately as she wanted to fight him, Serena knew she had no choice. As the rush of running water crept from the bathroom, she darted inside long enough to grab a house robe.

As she advanced on Sydney's bedroom, her steps uneasy and uncertain as if walking in inky darkness, Serena coached herself. *Take your medicine, girl.* Many women who'd admitted to what she just had might be lying dead, half strangled, or severely beaten by an abusive husband right now. If the worst Jamie had in mind was to deprive her of his and Sydney's company for a few days, that was a blessing by comparison.

As much as she wanted to believe that, it didn't stop the choked sob that rushed up her throat when she reached her daughter's closet. More than anything, she found herself haunted by that afternoon that Tony brought Dawn home, when Sydney sat on Jamie's lap and thanked her parents for staying together. What had she said? *I don't ever want Daddy to leave again.* Not only was her nightmare coming true, this time Sydney was leaving with him.

Her eyes burned, but after the turmoil of the past months, Serena wasn't surprised when tears refused to come; she figured she was out of them by now. "Oh, Sydney," she whispered, her words muffled as she hugged her daughter's favorite plaid sweater close. "Please forgive me. I tried. I really, really tried."

33

*B*y midnight the crowd at the Westin Michigan Avenue had finally thinned. Standing at the entranceway to the private ballroom they had reserved, Tony stood shoulder to shoulder with Larry, Audrey, and Arthur Champion. A small crowd of local VIPs surrounded each of them. Just about every one had been bowled over by Rowan Academy's success, with most now promising to help bring the Rowan "magic" to the Windy City.

By the time the three younger executives' crowds had disappeared, a throng of well-wishers and ass-kissers still surrounded Champion. As their in-house celebrity continued with the handshaking and backslapping, Tony collapsed into a chair at the nearby table where Larry and Audrey had settled.

"Damn, Gooden," Larry roared, popping Tony's back. "You proved me wrong tonight. I never would have expected this type of reaction, not here. Figured folk here had already seen what a place like Rowan has to offer."

"What did I tell you?" Tony shook his head playfully and grinned at Audrey, who sat on the other side of Larry. "This man's sold me short since day one, hasn't he? You remember when he hated on me for turning down his first job offer?"

Audrey chuckled, then wiggled an index finger toward Tony. "Come here, fella. Need to ask you something."

Tony met Larry's curious glance, then crossed his legs coolly before smiling at Audrey. "Why don't you ask me now? Why I gotta move?"

"Never mind," Audrey replied, her voice a breathy sigh. "I guess it's not important."

Tony knew the exact question on her mind: *Why you sitting all the way over there?* It was a fair question, considering that he and Audrey had technically been dating for nearly a month now. They hadn't done the old pound-pound with each other yet, weren't yet fully intimate, but platonic friendship was definitely in the rearview mirror. Whatever you could call what they had, though, it was still under the radar. While his boss had been the first one to point him toward their fellow colleague, Tony wasn't ready to hip Larry to things quite yet.

Before Tony could recover from Audrey's scolding, Larry clapped his hands together. "All right, good people," he said, scanning his employees' weary faces. "Doesn't look like Arthur's gonna be freed up anytime soon. You all want a nightcap? We head back to the hotel right now, I'll treat on a couple more drinks." While the Westin had offered the best deal on facilities and catering for tonight's dinner, Tony had convinced Larry to put everyone up at the Hilton Garden Inn, a black-owned property a few blocks down Michigan.

Saying their good nights to Champion, the three of them piled into a cab. Back at the Hilton's bar they knocked back adult beverages for another half hour before riding the elevator to the floor they all shared.

As Audrey stepped off, heading right as the men turned left, she looked over her shoulder. "Good night, guys." She addressed them both, but her eyes rested solely on Tony.

As Larry grunted a weary good night, Tony opted for silence but kept his eyes glued first to Audrey's luminous gaze, then to her voluptuous form as she strode down the opposite hallway.

Five minutes later he stood outside her room. She answered

just as his knuckles hit the door, as if she'd had him timed to the second. As she pulled the door back, Tony's eyes swelled in their sockets. Already attired in something a little more comfortable, she stood draped in a white silk robe, one whose plunging neckline revealed a full, unrestrained bosom.

"Oh," she said, her tongue flicking playfully between her teeth, "you want to be around me now, do you?"

As he shut the door behind himself, he stood toe-to-toe with her. Nearly swaggering with pride in her seductive abilities, she brushed closer to him. "Oh, you're still uncomfortable. Tony, I know you don't want to move too fast, but I don't get it. I know you want me, you just don't *want* to want me."

Standing there engulfed in Audrey's beauty, her scent, Tony felt freer than he had in years. The weights holding him back from her these past months had lost their hold on him. Maybe he'd never be happy about missing his chance with Serena, but that didn't mean he didn't have other sources of joy in his life.

Without using a word to defend himself, he pulled Audrey up against him and began tracing a hand over her face, taking time to appreciate every curve, every faint scar, the very warmth of the blood vessels beneath her skin. As she let her robe fall to the floor, he took the same liberty with her neck, her breasts, her stomach, her legs. By the time they began kissing and maneuvering toward her bed, Tony was more levelheaded than he'd ever been before sex.

The night was endless, kinetic. He was still rusty and "completed his mission" too quickly in the first two rounds, but the simple fact that he recovered three additional times more than made up for it. For her part, Audrey was more quiet than Tony had preferred in the old days—nothing fed the ego more than a lover's unrestrained gasp or curse word—but by the third round the frenzied looks on her face made up for it.

It was five minutes after three when they collapsed against each other into a sweat-soaked sleep. His body worn, his brain fuzzy, Tony heard Audrey's soft snores—thank God they were soft; he didn't need an excuse to question his decision—and asked himself what he'd been running from since the day they'd met.

What more do I need? At thirty-two, he was closer to forty than to twenty, barreling toward middle age, and lying next to him was a woman of beauty, wit, intelligence, and ambition who had the spirit of a compassionate warrior. He hadn't come to the decision formally, but as he clicked off the lamp on his side of the bed, he knew that he'd slept with Audrey only after deciding to give things a go. A few more weeks at this pace, and he might be ready to unveil their romance, and not just to Larry. He was ready for a relationship, one that might put him on the path to marriage, kids, and the type of future he'd once scorned. Only one obstacle to that gateway remained.

Throwing back the covers, he slipped out of bed and felt his way through the dark room until he came to the pile of clothes heaped outside Audrey's bathroom. Grabbing his suit jacket, he slid inside the restroom and shut the door behind him. With the overhead light on, he rustled through the jacket's pockets until he'd retrieved his cell phone. "Not exactly a convenient time to call," he said to the empty room, "but if not now, when?" Scrolling through his phone's address book, Tony fought every indication of nerves, denying the warmth of his brow, the sandy taste in his mouth, the queasiness leaking into his stomach. For years he'd laughed at, even pitied men who subjected themselves to psychiatrists, psychologists, and psychotherapists. His promise to Zora on his mind, his bubbling adoration of Audrey feeding him, he left a curt voice mail for the therapist his sister had suggested.

34

On Serena's first night apart from Dawn since she'd once again become a single parent, a stranger knocked on her door at five minutes to midnight.

Unable to sleep well in the weeks since Jamie had stormed out with Sydney in tow, Serena had been wide awake, in the midst of reading J. California Cooper's new novel. When she heard the stranger's knuckles beat against the door of her hotel room, she quizzically threw back her covers and stepped to the peephole. When she saw Levi Little, one of her dozen fellow colleagues on this work retreat, a growl stirred Serena's throat.

Her boss, Dr. Kellogg, had sequestered his top executives and the school board at Hueston Woods State Park for the next two days, all in the name of hashing out the upcoming year's strategic plan. Serena had pretty much sleepwalked her way through today's sessions, including the one she led. She didn't have it in her to present a false face these days; she was doing well just to show up.

For every one of the sixteen nights since Jamie and Sydney had moved in with Fritz, her wearying bedtime routine consisted of two nearly schizophrenic activities: boxing (usually just verbally) with Dawn, followed by a bedtime phone call devoted to soothing poor Sydney's rattled nerves.

Although Dawn's grade point average had increased and her teachers praised her for an improved attitude, the child had taken careful note of her parents' distress and was happily exploiting it for her own sake. With each day her requests for "freedom" grew more indignant. Serena had nearly put her into a headlock after last night's jibe: "Mom, why don't you worry about me when you get your own act straight, okay?" She was considering buying a book she'd heard about, something about ways to discipline your kid without leaving a mark.

Tempted as she was, Serena knew she couldn't react to her older child's taunts with anything more than stern words and cringe-inducing, strategically placed pinches. On top of her father and sister's relocation, another inescapable shake-up overshadowed Dawn's world: Glenn was getting ready to dump her.

It wasn't official yet. The two still talked on the phone almost daily and planned to attend an upcoming Sadie Hawkins dance at school. With all that going on, though, Dawn was convinced her lockdown status was a poor match for Glenn's needs. While Glenn's freedom under his new foster father—Tony—was more limited than it had ever been before, the boy still had roving time every day, from the hour when school let out until Tony picked him up from football practice. With Dawn sidelined, Serena couldn't deny her daughter's logic: it was just a matter of time before Glenn would move on to the next hook-up, some girl whose single parent (or guardian, weary grandparent, or foster parent) didn't care enough to restrict his access to her.

Although she felt it was for the best, Serena knew Dawn was hurting and would suffer the pain for a good while; her child was a rebel, but that didn't make her callous enough to be unfazed by the impending loss of her first lover. When Glenn dropped the final bomb, Serena would be prepared. If she was anything like her momma, Dawn would lash out while struggling to absorb the blow.

Sydney, for her part, was confused and full of a quivering sense of betrayal. Every night she hit Serena with the same questions: "When will Daddy and I get to come back home?" "What happened *this* time, Mommy?" "Why can't we all just be happy?" Night after night, Serena would patiently explain things in terms her baby could process, then bite her lip as Sydney whimpered on the other end of the line before dropping off to sleep.

With all that riding her back, Serena didn't have the energy to finesse her reaction to Levi. Her lithium and a constant regimen of good sleep, a nutritious diet, and regular exercise had held her hypomanias at bay, but with the pressures of her crumbling marriage she struggled at times to keep her spirits up. *This nigga,* she thought, weighing what to do with her unwelcome visitor. She'd thought the admittedly handsome security director had forgotten all about her. His daily visits to her office had pretty much trickled down to monthly occurrences until last week, when he'd suddenly come sniffing around again. And now he was here, at an hour too inappropriate for words. She placed a palm against her side of the door, considered just going to bed and shutting off the lights, but a sudden anger ripped through her and she unbolted the door, whipping it open. "What?"

The stretch velour of his Adidas sweat suit lying nicely atop his muscled, athletic build, Levi slid his hands into his pants pockets. After running his tongue across his top teeth, he cleared his throat and leaned forward, resting a hand against her door frame. "You want me to go back to my room?" His voice was low, his tone a swirl of gruff assurance and passive sensitivity.

As a girl and as a single woman, Serena had experienced many of these moments: a dark hallway, a furtive visit from a confident brother poised to move in for the kill. There had been some unwelcome advances along the way, most of which she'd successfully stifled, but in most cases the brothers' confidence had been rewarded, and it was clear Levi Little believed his would, too.

Shaking her head, Serena stepped back from the door's threshold, the shame of the moment hitting her before she reminded herself that she'd never encouraged any of this. When an increasingly eager Levi actually crossed the threshold, a smug grin on his face, she let him follow her back toward her king-sized bed.

Behind her, she heard him click the door closed after himself.

"What we do here, Serena, will stay here," he was saying in a near-whisper. "I don't believe in airing a lady's dirty laundry—"

Her back to him, Serena arrived at the bed and dove forward. As she lay with her legs splayed, her hand groping toward the nightstand on the other side, she heard Levi's confident exhalation. "That's perfect," he said. "Don't move. Levi's coming right over."

"Well, hold on one second." Her cell phone secured in hand, Serena flipped onto her back and sat up just that quick, her legs crossed in front of her. She punched an option from her speed dial and held the receiver to her mouth. "I want to share your little unwelcome visit with Dr. Kellogg," she said, winking. "I bet he gets a real kick out of it, the security director showing up at midnight to get in my pants."

"Hey, hey, hold the hell on here!" As if she'd poked his naked genitals with hot coals, Levi danced and hopped back toward her doorway, his right hand extended as if fending off a knife. "Put the phone down, Serena," he shouted, his voice now sounding like Prince doing a falsetto. "Please!"

Serena snapped the phone shut just as Dr. Kellogg's voice mail greeting clicked on. "Do you get the message now, Levi?"

"You know," he said, licking his lips and grabbing the door handle, "all you had to do was tell me you weren't interested. Damn! Don't act like you haven't been checking me out since the day I started working downtown."

Serena stood, arms crossed. A small part of her felt guilty for being so harsh with Levi. "Even if that's true, it never meant I wanted you to come proposition me."

Hand still gripping the doorknob, Levi nearly grinned, though wounded anger was still deep in his eyes. "You thought about me every now and then, didn't you?"

Serena felt her eyes examine the floor's carpet fibers before replying, "Yes. But thinking was all I was ever going to do, Levi. Sexually, you were as real to me as Lil' Kim or Beyoncé is to you."

"Well, hell," Levi said, chuckling dryly. "On the occasional lonely night, those two ladies seem pretty damn real to me, for a few minutes at least."

Serena smiled, hoping to further diffuse the tension between them. "Too much information, my friend." She flashed a tentative smile. "Hear that term, 'friend'? I'd like to mean it the next time I refer to you. I do think you're cool people, if that means anything."

"I got plenty of friends with benefits, if you know what I mean," Levi replied, shrugging. "Won't kill me to have one who's strictly business. For the record," he said, lowering his eyes, "my timing tonight wasn't random. I figured after your boy's latest move, you'd be uniquely up for some company."

A wave of calm washed over Serena, with the exception of an intense tingling in the fingertips of her left hand. "Now, Levi, I'm all for being cool, but I'm definitely not ready to talk about my marital problems with you." She bit her lower lip, ready for him to get lost. She'd made a mistake lowering the tension before. She knew that the grapevine had probably circulated some distorted version of her latest separation from Jamie, but she had no interest in correcting the misinformation of gossips.

"I totally feel you," Levi said, turning back toward the door. His back still facing her, he inhaled before saying, "I'm just curious, tell me to go to hell if you don't want to answer, but I have to ask. How long did you know about your hubby's kid?"

Serena grabbed her cell phone again. "Damn, Levi. Do I have to call Kellogg again?"

Levi swung the door open. "Okay, message received."

Unable to fight the sudden rush of questions cascading inside her head, Serena snapped before she could stop herself. "Shut the door!"

Levi complied, then eased back around to face her, an eyebrow raised mischievously. "Second thoughts?"

Serena strode up to him, planted fists against her hips. "How the hell did you hear about his child?" The one thing she'd counted on was Jamie's discretion about Andrea and his mother. Although Angelita had come into town with Andrea several times the past few months, in search of the best medical treatment Jamie could afford for the little boy, Jamie had promised Serena he would limit any mention of them. It was the one way he could show respect for his wife and their two children. Serena had never stood in the way of providing for Andrea's health care—hell, she had actually lent Jamie nearly three thousand dollars for that very purpose—but she didn't care to be publicly embarrassed by the fruit of her husband's adultery. Her public dignity had taken yet another hit.

By now, Levi had backed himself up against the door, his hands raised as if Serena had told him to choose between his money or his life. "I'm a security professional, Serena! I make a living finding out things people don't want found out, or concealing the very same facts for others."

"That's not good enough," Serena said, reaching up and wadding the collar of his T-shirt between her right fist.

"Look," Levi said, a sympathetic look in his eyes, "I only asked how long you knew because you don't seem like the type of sister to take a brother fooling around on you. I mean, you have it all: brains, beauty, sass, self-confidence. I'd have expected you to kick him to the curb a long time ago."

Serena shook her head slowly, fighting off a snicker. "Boy, you really don't know me, do you?"

Sighing, Levi slid his hands back into his pockets, letting his shoulders slump with relief. "Here's all I know. Your husband apparently signed a lease to move the lady—Angelita—and the little boy into my sister's apartment building. She works in the management office, recognized Jamie's name on the application, started asking some questions, and . . . bingo."

When her interrogation of the now undersexed, humiliated security director was finished, Serena shut the door after him and returned to bed. Climbing back underneath the covers, she was determined to enjoy Ms. California Cooper's novel, but knew she was kidding herself. *I know this son of a bitch isn't moving his "family on the side" to Cincinnati, I just know he's not.* She didn't want to believe it, but Levi had been full of knowledge and details that rang true. The sad thing was, Serena realized she didn't know her husband well enough to even guess at his real motivation. Was this a sincere attempt to connect with Andrea, whose health had steadily improved in recent months? Or was it just mean-spirited payback for Serena's night with Tony?

Laying the novel aside and turning out the lights, she let a hand travel over her breasts, then down between her legs. She'd have plenty of time to discern the truth; in the meantime, if she was still paying for her night with Tony, she may as well milk it for all it was worth. The dark surrounding her, she closed her eyes and fantasized that Tony was here, and not just physically. No, as she slowly stirred herself to life, Serena invoked the very essence of her first love—the clear, slightly high-pitched tone of his voice, the smell of his favorite cinnamon gum on his breath, the scent of his Polo cologne, and the courageous confidence he filled her with every time they'd made love. Liquid heat bubbling deep within her center, Serena plunged into the world she wished she'd never left behind.

35

A female student in the third row of Tony's class raised her hand. "Mr. Gooden, I say you're just flat wrong."

Stepping away from the projector he'd hooked to his laptop computer, Tony eyed his seating chart. "Well, uh, Tanisha, why don't you explain exactly where you think I'm wrong." Four weeks into teaching a weekly seminar on political science, he'd spent today's class educating the kids on the nasty realities of political campaigning.

"I asked my uncle about the reading assignments you gave us," Tanisha said, her hands pressed together, her neck bobbing and weaving. Today's discussion had been based around a group of handouts Tony provided, all of them excerpts from books by or about the country's most successful political operatives: Lee Atwater, James Carville, Dick Morris, and Karl Rove. "My uncle," Tanisha continued, "he was a judge in the municipal court for years and worked with a lot of politicians. He says most of them are good people, trying to do the right things. He says you're too cynical about them."

"Really." Shutting off the projector and flicking on the classroom lights, Tony smiled at his student. "Well, I have to say, Tanisha, if that's really been your uncle's experience, you tell him he's found heaven on earth, because that's not how the real world works."

Tanisha was not deterred. "I just think you're too negative, sir," she replied, her head shaking. "How are you gonna convince any of us go into politics, when you make it sound so dirty?"

He stepped around his desk and took a seat on its front edge. He was good and tired of this child's naïve, starry-eyed views, but he reminded himself that she at least gave a damn about what he was teaching. Half the kids, while civil and polite, were clearly phoning it in.

"The reason I keep it real, Tanisha, is so that you can enter this field someday with your eyes wide open. How else can you help change things?" The hallway filled with the ring of the day's final bell, and Tony clapped his hands as the kids grabbed at their bags and coats. "Okay, your final will be coming up in two weeks, so make sure you read this week's assignment closely. And remember, my cell number is listed on the syllabus, so don't hesitate to call with questions!"

Once he'd tolerated a couple more of Tanisha's naïve stories about her uncle the saintly judge, Tony waved the girl good-bye, his classroom now empty. As he packed up his projector and laptop, he chuckled at what he'd turned into: Tony Gooden, Teacher. *This was never part of the plan.* As a money-hungry teen he'd pitied nearly every classroom instructor in his life, viewing them through the lens of the old saying "Those who can, do; those who can't, teach."

Despite his occasional clashes with overly idealistic students like Tanisha and the amiably apathetic kids surrounding her, Tony was glad he'd agreed to Audrey's suggestion that he lead this seminar. Now that he'd achieved Larry and Arthur Champion's financial goals for the year—he had raised a quarter million dollars more than required and paved the way for the establishment of four new Rowan Academies nationwide—his business trips were nearly a thing of the past, meaning it was easy to pop over to Rowan one afternoon a week. As a people person, too, Tony found he got more out of leading the classes than the kids likely got from his wealth of knowledge. He enjoyed the give and take, the opportunity to size up each student and experiment with ways to draw their interest. Sharing his talents with kids still seeking theirs was more rewarding than he'd imagined.

Though he was still trying to accept a life without Serena in it, he had accepted that he could have a very rich one, one richer than he'd ever had before, without her. After an exhaustive, sometimes insulting inspection process, the department of Children's Services had just certified him as Ben and Glenn's foster father. While adjusting to life as a full-time role model had its downsides—living with Glenn had brought the boy's roguish attitudes toward sex into full view, attitudes he recognized from his own youth—he had no regrets. The chance to guide two impressionable young men toward brighter futures was irresistible.

He had just zipped his laptop bag when he heard the knock at his door. Turning over his shoulder, he felt his shoulders jerk at the sight of Dawn Kincaid. Her hair having grown and now worn in shoulder-length curls, she stood dressed in a black leather skirt with a matching sweater and thigh-high boots. Not a Rowan Academy uniform; she'd clearly changed clothes as soon as the bell rang. A Coach bag over her shoulder, she crossed her arms and blew a bubble with her gum before saying, "What's up, Mr. G?"

Hoisting his laptop bag over his shoulder and buttoning his suede leather overcoat, Tony forced a smile. He hadn't seen Dawn in several weeks, not since running into her and Glenn in the school cafeteria during a rare unsupervised moment together. While he wasn't sure it was healthy, Tony had respected Serena and Jamie's decision to restrict Glenn's access to their daughter. Of course, even if he hadn't respected their choice, he wouldn't have done anything about it. He had decided to keep a wide berth from Jamie Kincaid; if the rumors in the wind were true, the dude knew that his suspicions about Tony and Serena had been well grounded, and frankly Tony was a bit amazed he hadn't come calling yet.

He walked toward the girl before she could step further into the room. "How's it going, Dawn? I have to run, got an urgent meeting back at the office." A bald-faced lie, but Tony had simply grown into a better man, not a saint.

"Mr. Gooden," Dawn replied, stepping forward suddenly. Her quick movements as well as her use of his formal name gave Tony pause, freezing him in place. "Please, I just need a moment of your time." She popped her left pinky into her mouth, began chewing. "I need you to talk to Glenn for me. It's serious."

They were both standing near the open door, and Tony crossed his arms before clearing his throat. "Okay, what's going on?"

Glancing at the open doorway, her eyes starting to mist, Dawn nodded. "Can we shut that? I don't want this getting out, at least not right away."

Better not be what I think it is . . . Tony stepped over to the door and slammed it shut. Turning back toward Dawn, he said, "Let's make this quick, honey." He gestured slowly toward her, trying to keep from getting too excited. "If you're pregnant, let's just get that out into the open now." He'd taken great pains to ensure both of the twins were versed in the art of condom management, and with Dawn specifically he had begged Glenn to find other girls to "express" himself with. If the boy had already made him a foster grandfather, somebody was gonna die, and it wouldn't be the baby.

"No, it's nothing like that," Dawn replied, slumping into a seat near the front of the class. She rested her head in her hands, sniffles punctuating her words. "I feel like Glenn's avoiding me." She looked up at Tony. "He said you told him to stay away from me." Her eyes betrayed fear, as if she didn't really want an honest answer to the question. "Is that true?"

His hands deep in the pockets of his suit pants, Tony stared at the ceiling, taking several silent beats. "Dawn, maybe what's important here is that you learn to realize when a boy's good for you and when he's not."

She whipped her neck toward him, her tears drying. "You saying Glenn's no good for me? I thought you loved him like a son?"

He slid into the seat next to the woman-child, struck by the great distance between her highly developed figure and her emotional immaturity. The injustice of young womanhood hit Tony between the eyes more squarely than ever. God allowed these girls to flower into targets for every man's lust well before they developed the smarts to cut through the haze of bad intentions.

For years he himself had abused that biological imbalance; as he stared into the girl's eyes, he forgot for a moment whose child she was. No, the thing most on his mind was that this was a chance to help balance the scales of justice, to help one jilted girl understand that it wasn't her fault.

"Glenn has his own set of problems," Tony said, his hands tented as he scooted his chair closer to Dawn's. "You have to understand, the fact that his mom's never been very attentive, the fact he's never had a real father figure, this makes it hard for him to really appreciate you right now."

Her eyes drying, Dawn stared at Tony and scooted her chair so close that their knees touched. "You sure it's not something I did? Or some grudge you hold against me, that I'm not a good enough girl 'cause I got caught sleeping with him?"

"No," Tony said, tapping Dawn's left hand lightly as a comfort. "Dawn, you're on your way to a great life if you make the right choices. You're smart, beautiful, and have two loving parents. Who knows? In a year or two, you and Glenn may both be mature enough to appreciate each other. Your story as a couple may end for the time being, but that doesn't mean it's over for good." He tapped her hand again. "Okay?"

Her head down now, Dawn flipped her hand over and reciprocated Tony's tap before taking his hand in hers. The merging of their warm flesh immediately felt wrong to Tony, but he resisted the instinctive urge to pull away. The child was hurting; the last thing she needed was to have him yank his hand away unceremoniously. He exhaled, certain she'd release his hand in a matter of seconds.

That was the very moment he felt a fingernail trail its way up the middle of his hand. Moving with swift, circular motions, Dawn applied something on the order of a hand massage, a type so out-of-bounds that Tony threw sensitivity to the wind. Jerking his hand back, staring at the child with contained concern, he began to stand. "Just remember what I said, okay? I–It's not about you." He couldn't get her out of this room fast enough.

As if anticipating his every move, Dawn rose from her seat as Tony did. "Can I ask you something else, Mr. G?" In a flash too quick for Tony to stifle, she undid the last two buttons on her sweater and slung it off, revealing a too-tight white turtleneck that barely contained her increasingly womanly breasts. "If I'm not good enough for Glenn, am I good enough for you?"

Looking away, Tony took the child by one arm, steering her toward the door. "I'm going to pretend I didn't hear that. Go home."

"No!" Her shout was loud enough that Tony just knew someone would come running. Before he could calculate what to do next, Dawn snaked her free arm out and grabbed the knot of his tie. "You know you want this, Mr. G," she said, lowering her voice now as if she didn't want them interrupted.

Tony slapped at her hand on his tie and missed, and the next thing he knew Dawn, who was nearly as tall as he was, had her face in his. Leaning into him, she opened her mouth and bit at his lips and his cheeks until Tony released her arm and used both hands to shove her away. It still wasn't enough; though her face was thrown back from his, the girl held tight to his tie, which had started to unravel in her hand. Eager to free himself from her grasp, Tony reached toward his own neck and undid the tie's knot until it flew free from his neck, the other end of it encased in Dawn's fist.

Staring back at him from her position near the closed door, Dawn twisted her lips into a snarl before grabbing her sweater. Still holding on to Tony's tie, she swung the door wide open. "Your loss, Mr. G," she shouted as she departed confidently, the *clickety-clack* of her heels filling the hallway.

His mind buzzing with blank energy, Tony sank into the nearest seat. Raising a shaky hand to his heated brow, he began coaching himself. He'd never make it to his car otherwise. *Nothing to report,* the voice told him. *You're Tony Gooden, after all. She's just one of many females overcome by your charms. You did the right thing, sent her away and drew a clear, bright line.*

Standing, he felt his legs finally stabilize beneath him. *I'll pretend this didn't happen, Serena,* he told himself, *but, God, have you got a handful in that one.*

36

As she rode the elevator to the top floor of the Whitaker Holdings office tower, Serena repeated the opening lines she had rehearsed. As ridiculous as she felt, she knew she was handling things in the only way that made sense, the only way that was true to the dilemma she faced.

"I'm here to see Tony Gooden, please," she said calmly when the receptionist greeted her. "Serena Kincaid." Standing before the young girl, a well-appointed twenty-something with a hairstyle that had probably set her back a few days' wages, Serena removed her gloves and wool overcoat as the receptionist rang Tony's line.

After speaking under her breath and pausing at whatever Tony's reaction had been, the young fashion plate cautiously turned her eyes back up to Serena. "What business are you here on, Ms. Kincaid?"

Folding her coat over her right arm, Serena smiled. "Oh, I should have specified that I'm treasurer of the Cincinnati school system."

"Oh." The girl's face brightened and she reached a hand forward. "Pleasure to meet you." She spoke back into her receiver. "She's with the school system, sir. Are you free now?" She looked back up at Serena. "Have a seat, please, ma'am. He'll be ready for you in a couple of minutes."

As she sat waiting on Tony, Serena practiced a public-speaking technique she'd learned years earlier. Taking deep breaths, she locked each hand's thumb and index finger together, drawing desperately on a sense of calm. Just a few more minutes, and she'd have this all behind her.

When she entered his office, Tony sat with his back to her, staring out his large window toward the Cincinnati skyline. Clearing her throat, Serena checked to see that the receptionist had closed the door behind her, then patiently took a seat across from his desk.

As he turned to face her, she saw two colliding emotions in her old lover's face. A peaceful, settled quality battled with a sense of trepidation, one made evident in his wavering eye contact and the occasional fiddling of his hands. Struck by this, she moved quickly to cut the tension crowding the air. "I'm here to apologize, Tony," she said. "And to explain myself."

Processing her words, Tony narrowed his eyes in what looked like surprised relief before walking around his desk and taking the chair adjacent to hers. Crossing his legs with controlled calm he said, "I guess I shouldn't complain about your choice of location."

Serena couldn't hold his gaze. "I figured we're both pretty busy in the evenings, with our families and all. And I didn't want to set up anything in advance, that would have just made us both nervous anticipating it."

Tony shifted in place, recrossing his legs. "Well, then." In a flash, he had decided to cast his bets on Dawn's silence about their run-in the day before. If Serena had come about that she'd have led with it; no way she'd waste time with small talk if she thought he'd made a pass at her baby.

Serena forced herself to look Tony in the eye this time. "I have loved you since the day you crashed my wedding," she said. "I think I loved you before that too, Tony, but, hell, what did I know about love? When you laid yourself bare like that, though, making a true fool of yourself in front of hundreds, including dozens of Northwestern folk you'd always tried to impress? I knew that was the type of love I wanted in my life."

His chest heaving, any fears about Dawn now knocked far

from his mind, Tony uncrossed his legs and scooted forward until his elbows were on his knees. His eyes on the floor, his voice warbling like a bad folk singer, he struggled to collect himself. "Do I ask the obvious question?"

"I was already pregnant with Jamie's child," she said, the words coming out in a biting staccato aimed at herself, not at him. "I was so driven by that. I had been such a screwup throughout my youth, making life hell on my parents, even forcing them to raise Dawn. When I knew Sydney was on the way, I had to make some practical choices in life, things that would give me some stability in my situation. And even though I knew how much you loved me, I still wasn't sure you could handle having to raise someone else's child."

Tony's lips formed an "O" as he exhaled, his chest nearly collapsing with the released tension. "And you were right to worry about that," he replied. "Serena, I know that I loved you, and you may as well know my intention was to raise Sydney as my own, or at least as a dear stepdaughter if Jamie would have insisted on being in her life. But at twenty-two, would I have backed up those noble intentions? God only knows."

"The reality is," Serena said, marshalling her resolve, "that everything you thought in moving here was correct. I did love you; in fact, I still do. I fantasize about being with you, Tony, about whether I could have been the woman to settle you down, about whether you could have helped me sharpen my ambitions even further. But it would have been so *risky*."

Tony sat silent and frozen in position, elbows still on his knees, eyes on the carpet. She was saying all the words he'd dreamed of hearing for years, but so much had changed in recent weeks. A selfish urge ripped through him and for a second he wished for a world with no twins, no Dawn, no Audrey, and—you better believe—no godforsaken Jamie Kincaid.

"I have to fight for my marriage," Serena said, the volume in her voice fading. "I can't say that I really want to, but I have to, for my children's sake and for my parents'. What type of example would I set for the girls, running off with you? Not to mention the embarrassment it would cause my parents, after they've spent years helping to raise my children."

Though he was starting to doubt her reasoning, Tony was not equipped to argue with Serena's bottom line. Hoping to make things easier for her, if not for himself, he scooted his chair closer to hers, and took one of her hands into his. "This is the right way to go," he said, reaching forward to wipe a tear from her eye. "Really. You remember the woman I told you about?"

Serena nodded soberly. "I know who she is, Tony. The grapevine in black Cincy is a bitch. Audrey Jacobs seems like a real catch. I–I'm happy for you."

"It's a relationship that deserves a shot," he replied, still holding lightly to Serena's hand. "Odds are I'll jack it up completely, but rest assured, your decision will help me and Audrey along."

Serena pulled her hand back, placed it over her mouth. "I hope you're happy, really I do. I just–I just have one request."

His breathless response was full of anticipation. "What?"

Serena couldn't look at him now, she had to just get the words out. "Why don't you move back to Chicago?" Stony silence hanging in the air, she clasped her hands and stared out his office window. "I know you've done some great things here, but didn't you really come here for me? If we're agreed that not's happening, do you really need to be here?"

Processing her request, Tony found himself truly speechless. The unspoken truth beneath her request—that she didn't want the temptation of him in such close proximity—was both flattering and heartbreaking. For nearly a minute, he grimaced, gestured, even began two separate false starts filled with "um" and "you see." What she was asking was incredibly self-centered, yet the underlying truth was undeniable. *You came here for me.*

In the days to come they would each construct their own memories of that moment, one they later recognized as a final chance to head off much heartbreak and destruction. As they sat there in his office, though, Tony and Serena stared blankly into each other's eyes, filled with a sense that if they could turn back time, they each knew the exact moment and place they would choose.

37

When Serena pulled into her garage that night, she still felt aftershocks in her soul from her confrontation with Tony. As of the moment she'd exited his office, he had left her request unanswered. She had no doubt that he was weighing it, though: the way his face morphed into a whipped child's the moment she'd asked him to leave, he'd clearly taken her seriously. Viewed through the lens of her ex's admirable accomplishments during his time in her hometown—securing Rowan's national expansion, taking on the twins, starting a meaningful relationship with a sister as thorough and respected as Audrey Jacobs—Serena felt about two feet tall asking him to abandon it all.

The animated confidence in his eyes had crumbled in slow motion, an incremental process that began the minute he heard her request. That sight haunted Serena throughout the afternoon and still hung in her memory as she shut her car door. Squelching a sob, she stepped around Jamie's Explorer, wondering what to make of the fact that he was even here. He had agreed to pick Dawn up from school so that she could work late, but she'd expected him to keep their older daughter at Fritz's for the night along with Sydney. Turning the key in the garage door's lock, she allowed herself a hopeful moment. Jamie couldn't keep their family separated forever.

Jamie, Dawn, and Sydney sat around the kitchen's marble-topped island, slices of LaRosa's pizza before each of them. Tapping the pizza box in the center of the island, Jamie turned cold eyes toward Serena as she set down her leather attaché. "Well, well, Mommy's here, girls. Pull up a chair and get something to eat. Once you do that, you and I need to talk before Sydney and I head back to Fritz's."

Serena wanted badly to let her shoulders slump, to give in to the fatigue hunting her, but she'd never do that in front of her girls, especially not when Jamie was acting an ass. "Fine, I can eat," she said flippantly, shrugging out of her suit jacket and rolling up the sleeves of her blouse.

Ignoring Jamie, she chatted Sydney up about school first, then probed around the edges for signs of life from Dawn, who sat nibbling listlessly on pizza crust. The girl's funky attitude was out for a jog this evening, her rolling eyes and recurring sighs informing the family she didn't care to be bothered. Based on the child's edginess, Serena sensed that the inevitable had finally happened: Glenn had forced her to walk the plank.

When they'd finished eating, Jamie sent Sydney upstairs. "Go get yourself a couple more outfits, baby," he said. "Choose 'em carefully so Mommy won't have to choose ones for you; then you can play on the computer for fifteen minutes. Okay?"

"All right, Daddy," Sydney replied, smiling wide. Serena knew her baby had already mentally fast-forwarded past the boring task of packing and was eager to log on to LizzieMcGuire.com or some comparable nonsense.

As Sydney rushed up the steps, Jamie snorted violently before turning to Serena and shoving a long finger toward Dawn. "When's the last time you had a real talk with this girl?"

She felt the judgment embedded in her husband's tone but paid it no mind. She rose from her stool, ready to wash the night's silverware. "You have a point you're trying to make, Jamie?"

"Sit down for once," he said, a red tinge invading the whites of his eyes. He cracked his knuckles, then crossed his arms as if applying a self-straitjacket. "I can't even raise this mess myself, Serena, I'm about to lose it as it is." He cast a sympathetic glance at Dawn. "Can you tell her?"

Dawn sat with her head over a plate piled high with abandoned crusts. Shoulders slumped, she at first seemed as tuned out as earlier, but as her cheeks caved in and her brow tightened, Serena saw her daughter fighting to suppress deep emotions.

"What is it, baby?" Serena leaned forward, a hand on Dawn's shoulder. When Dawn remained silent but her head began to vibrate from her effort to choke back a sob, Serena's eyes darted back to her husband. "Jamie, what's going on?"

When Jamie responded by angrily breaking eye contact and slamming a fist against the counter, Serena hopped off her stool and placed both arms around Dawn's shoulders. "Baby," she whispered into her ear, "it's Glenn, isn't it?"

"He's seeing, like, two other girls, Mom," Dawn replied, her shoulders shaking so hard Serena had to struggle to hang on. "He said—he said he can't wait around until you two let me 'grow up.' It's not fair!"

"Well, that's life, honey," Serena said, kissing the back of her daughter's head. "We'll get through this. I have plenty of experience with—"

"That's not it, Serena." Jamie softened his grimace as he looked in Dawn's direction. "Go ahead and finish, Dawn."

Dawn met Jamie's eyes, holding his gaze for a moment as if gathering strength from it, then turned to Serena. "Yesterday, I went to see Mr. Gooden at school. You know, Glenn's new foster father?"

Serena bristled in literal horror. "Baby, why the hell would you do that?" After the day he'd brought her home from Glenn and Ben's, Tony had promised to keep away from her family altogether. Now Dawn had sought *him* out? Serena realized right then that her request of Tony today hadn't been outrageous; it was the most sane idea she'd had in months.

Dawn had her hands clasped together, her face down as if embarrassed. "I only went to see Mr. Gooden 'cause I figured he could help me get Glenn to admit he really loves me. I thought

Mr. G was a good man, you know? I mean, Ben and Glenn really admire him, so I thought he could help reach them."

Serena sighed wearily, shooting an exasperated glance at Jamie and noting that he'd hardened his glare again. "Well, I'm sure Mr. Gooden told you that you and Glenn's breakup was none of his business."

"No, no," Dawn said, her head shaking but her eyes still on her plate. "He, uh, said that Glenn would come to his senses soon, that he'd realize what a great 'catch' I was. Said I was real pretty, smart, things like that."

"Oh." Serena felt her eyebrows raise, not sure what to make of Tony's generosity.

"Then he, uh, well, he uh–" Dawn gulped audibly and blinked away a tear. "He put his hands on my breasts."

Serena felt her neck snap and found herself asking Jamie a question with slitted eyes. *She didn't say what I think she just said, right?*

Both of Jamie's hands were coiled fists. "You heard her." One fist unfurled as he jammed a finger in her direction. "See what you've brought into our family?"

"Jamie, don't go there, damn you." A pool of moisture spreading across the tip of her nose, Serena turned her attention back to Dawn. "Baby, what are you saying? Mr. Gooden actually put his hands on you? Are you sure he didn't accidentally rub up against you or something?" Trying to grasp what she'd just heard, Serena wrestled with her own pride. She'd slept with her share of despicable human beings back in the day, but she didn't consider Tony to be one of them.

Dawn's shoulders were shaking again. "It was all a blur, Mom. All I know is he just kept coming at me, scooting closer, reaching out for me, saying how he could help me forget Glenn."

"I think you should stop with the inquisition," Jamie said, rushing from his stool and coming over to Dawn. Easing Serena aside, he took his stepdaughter in his arms and kissed her on the temple. Looking over at Serena, he shook his head. "It's bad enough she'll be interrogated every which way but loose when we report this. Not to mention, how are we gonna report this without going into all the nasty history?"

Still feeling like a figurine in a snow globe that had been flipped upside down, Serena waved her arms gently toward Jamie and Dawn, as if trying to cool a fire. "Just slow down, I'm still trying to understand how this happened. And, Dawn, why didn't you bring this up last night—"

Jamie's growl cut Serena short. "She may have stayed quiet if I hadn't come across this in her room." Reaching into his pocket, he emerged with a fistful of a wrinkled, slightly ripped red power tie. "She had to fight the son of a bitch off! Can you believe this? His tie came off in her hand, he was so aggressive." He hugged Dawn up against him one more time, looked into her eyes. "Why don't you go play with your sister? Your mom and I need a minute; we'll work this out."

When they were alone, Serena was still reeling, unable to find the right response to her husband's righteous anger and her own protective concern for her child. Jamie, on the other hand, was fully equipped and ready to go. Stepping closer to Serena, he slapped the tie's remains onto the counter and cupped her chin, raising her eyes to his. "I don't know what kind of game your boyfriend is playing, but you may as well know: his time is officially up."

38

As he chaired Rowan Academy's Monthly Business Review—a meeting in which school administrators, Whitaker Holdings executives, parent liaisons, and selected community leaders identified new challenges and solved old ones—Tony struggled to concentrate. As he completed his wrap-up of the major issues identified during the day's session, two things competed for his attention: an upcoming visit from Zora, who had agreed to come in and perform another reading and motivational speech, and his girlfriend's increasingly pissy vibe. Audrey had said barely a word during the morning's review, a frighteningly odd occurrence at work or at home.

Tony knew she was still digesting the many revelations he'd shared the night before. His showdown with Serena, as well as her dramatic request that he go back where he came from, had been too monumental to hide from a woman he was falling in love with. As he lay in bed with Audrey, relaxing in the warm afterglow of their lovemaking, he had opened up, hoping for a meaningful step in the growth of their relationship.

It was not to be. "You were with *Serena Kincaid*?" Flying forward in bed, Audrey had said his ex-lover's name with the reverence usually reserved for living legends. "God, that's depressing.

Here I land a man who seems perfect, and it turns out he's in love with a woman who's even more flawless." Climbing out of bed, she'd punched Tony's shoulder. "Damn, Tony, I've wanted to *be* Serena since I met her through Inroads, back in college. She doesn't just seem like the woman who has it all; she overcame some mess to get where she is." She'd crossed her arms before disappearing into the bathroom. "Tell me you're joking. Please."

It all seemed cute at the moment, but since then Audrey hadn't been herself. For one, she'd stayed in her bathroom so long that she was still in there when Tony had left to meet the twins at home; she hadn't even bothered to walk him to his car for the usual good-night kiss. To top it off, she hadn't delivered her usual early-morning, sexually profane wake-up call, either. He'd known he was screwed before he'd even left the house this morning.

With the monthly review over, he cut his conversation with Larry short and sprinted after Audrey as she headed out into the school's front hallway. "Hey," he said, falling into step but keeping his hands to himself. "Remember me?"

Her trusty clipboard held against her chest, Audrey kept her shoulders up and her back ramrod straight. Her eyes peered forward as if she barely sensed his presence. "I have a parent-teacher conference to supervise," she said as if speaking to herself. "The teacher is basically burnt out. If I leave him to his own devices either he or the mother's likely to go postal." She glanced toward him finally as she said, "And sorry, but this was so last minute, I'll be tied up when Zora gets here. I'll have to catch her on the next go-round."

She might as well have come to a sudden halt and hit him with an openhanded slap. Tony stood still for several seconds as Audrey continued her bustling pace toward her office. When he recovered, he followed behind until he reached her office doorway. Just inside the threshold, she had taken a seat at her conference table with a wild-haired woman, a skinny boy with eyes full of mischief, and an overweight, balding man who sat straightening his tie and wheezing with exasperation.

"Pardon me, good people," Tony said, knocking on Audrey's open door. "You'll have to excuse me and Ms. Jacobs for a second."

The balding man, who Tony guessed was the teacher, glared at him impatiently. "I don't know who you are, sir, but if you need Ms. Jacobs, I suggest you see her secretary to schedule an appointment."

"Rest assured, my brother," Tony replied, stepping all the way into the office and locking eyes with Audrey. "Ms. Jacobs knows *exactly* who I am." He stepped aside, extending an inviting hand toward the doorway. "If you'll excuse us and have a seat out in the reception area, I swear this will only take two minutes."

Audrey turned her head away from Tony, her lips pursed as she found herself oddly speechless. Tony knew her well enough by now; her desire to show strength by kicking him out competed tough with Audrey's desire to keep an orderly appearance, and he knew the second urge would ultimately win out. "I am so sorry," she said finally, a calm and earnest look washing over her face. "I forgot about an urgent matter Mr. Gooden, from our administrative office, needed help with. Please, do excuse us and I promise I'll be right with you."

When the mother had huffed her way out and the edgy teacher was through sliding Tony a series of looks that could kill, Audrey shut her door and stood in front of it, arms crossed. "I'm going to say this once, and one time only," she said, her voice low. "You have scared me senseless, Tony Gooden. Two reasons," she said, extending a matching number of fingers and shutting him up as he stepped forward. "First, like I said, I learn I'm being compared to Serena Kincaid. Second, I realize you withheld a pretty damn important part of your history from me."

Tony searched Audrey's face, feeling out the weight of the insecurities and anxieties filling her. "Well, you may as well know there's more to come. You can't freak out when I've only just started opening up."

"I know, I know," she said, rubbing a hand over her forehead before crossing her arms again. "I'm just processing all this, Tony— that's all, okay? We'll get through it—" A fist began banging her office door, and Audrey grimaced and turned toward the door as it nearly leapt from its hinges. "Okay, did they not hear me say I'd be right with them?"

"Yeah, they're trippin'," Tony said, chuckling. As the door rang anew with another set of fist-pounding, he stepped alongside Audrey and placed a hand against the small of her back. "This is my fault, anyway. I'll give you some space, call you later tonight." He leaned over and kissed her on the cheek. "Maybe we can do breakfast with Zora in the morning?"

Audrey smiled wearily, ignoring the insistent bangs on the door. "I'd like that." She let him draw her close for a quick peck on the lips, then stepped toward her desk. "Wave them in, please."

"No problem." Tony stepped to the door. "Calm down out there! I'm coming out now." He pulled the door open, still running his mouth. "Ms. Jacobs is all yours—" When he saw who was on the other side of the door, who had been doing the banging, Tony's words caught in his throat like a clump of peanut butter.

Jamie Kincaid stood there with Dawn close at his side. For a quick second Jamie looked as shocked to see Tony as Tony felt seeing him; Dawn, for her part, cowered behind her stepfather. Unlike their last meeting at Jamie's and Serena's, however, Tony's old nemesis recovered quickly this time. His neck still pivoting from a double take, Jamie rolled his shoulders and flexed both hands. "This is poetic justice, you being here," he said loudly. Smiling with satisfaction at the sudden attention he'd earned from the half dozen other people seated nearby, he whipped back toward Tony. "You've had this coming forever, you skinny-ass rat."

As Jamie drew back a fist, Tony heard Audrey's shriek, then felt his nose collapse in on itself as Jamie's punch pressed into his face. Nose and mouth dripping blood, Tony dropped to his knees. Grabbing at the nearest wall, he was vaguely aware of Audrey as she flew past him with a paperweight raised, shouting something defiant in Jamie's direction. Licking blood from around his mouth and gathering himself, he felt the pieces fall into place.

He wouldn't have Dawn here if this was about Serena. The previous day's events suddenly made sense, and Tony knew instantly

what was going down. He'd set up his share of the mayor's ene-
mies during his years in Chicago's city hall; this was more personal turf, but dirt was dirt and he knew it better than most. That
didn't quell the horror invading him, though, as he crawled toward Audrey and Jamie, who argued fiercely as a growing crowd
flooded into the office. Struggling to get onto his feet, Tony
wished against all reality that he could shut Audrey's ears against
Jamie's throaty accusations.

The white noise in his head relented and he heard Jamie's
words clearly as he jabbed a finger over Audrey's head. "I will sue
and shut this place down if I have to!" *Of course you will,* Tony
thought, though he found himself unable to speak the words. He
was in the perfect box, one with no escape hatch. *My word versus
hers.* For the first time since the moment of her request, Tony realized that Serena had been right. Only problem was, she'd been
too late.

39

Afabecter adjusting her sunglasses, Serena balanced her refilled popcorn tub and her second twenty-ounce Sprite. When she reached the blond-haired, pimple-faced movie attendant, he took her ticket for the 3:25 showing of Jude Law and Julia Roberts' *Closer* and chuckled. "Are you, like, planning to spend the whole day here, ma'am?"

Serena paused, looking the dumpy, four-eyed kid up and down. "It's a free country, son."

"E–Enjoy your show," he responded, clearly sensing he'd tread onto unwelcome territory.

None of his damn business why this is the third movie I've seen today, Serena told herself as she turned toward the appropriate theater. Not that the kid had asked why, but a part of her felt ready to explain herself.

In the forty-eight hours since Dawn's accusations against Tony had hit the local papers, spurring a healthy round of Rowan Academy demonizing, Serena had refused to face the music. She knew an element of her depression was at work, despite the fact she was just barely forcing herself to stay on her medication, but she only had so much fight left.

From the moment Dawn recounted Tony's attempted molestation, Serena had been plagued by nightmare visions of what would come next. Would the harassment she'd suffered push Dawn further along in her unhealthy sexual attitudes, maybe even drive her into the arms of a knucklehead who made Glenn look like a choirboy?

Was Dawn on her way to winding up like Serena at the same age, in part due to a man from her own past?

Whether or not Tony was innocent of the accusations, how long would it be before he'd try to use their affair as an explanation for Dawn's accusations?

Just what type of judgments would follow Tony's revelations? Would Serena lose the respect of Dr. Kellogg and her colleagues at work? Her parents? And, dear God, how would Dawn and Sydney process all this?

Struggling to process it herself, Serena had called in sick two days straight now. Yesterday she'd driven over to Indianapolis and spent the day shopping in precious anonymity. She had her cell phone on the entire time, had even forwarded her work phone to the cell number in case of emergency, but she knew she'd have lost it if she'd encased herself in her office. So yesterday, it had been shopping; today, movies at her favorite theater, the Showcase Cinemas in Springdale, enjoyed while productive people were at school or work.

Her hand was on the theater's door handle when she heard a familiar voice over her shoulder. "There you are! Serena, get over here, please."

Frowning, then sucking her teeth, Serena cursed under her breath. This was what she got for having a friend who knew all her habits—good, bad, and ugly. She turned back toward the entrance to the hallway and exhaled when she saw Jade standing on the other side of the attendant's outstretched hand.

"Look," Jade said, her arms crossed, her eyes scolding as Serena neared, "maybe I can't stop you from seeing a film you paid for, but the previews and trailers will last a good twenty minutes. Can I get ten?"

Her mouth twisted with annoyance, Serena ambled rebelliously past the geeky attendant and continued past her friend. "Have a seat in my office," she quipped before heading toward a low, round table near the main concession stand.

When they'd taken their seats, Jade reached for Serena's left hand. "I'm not here to beat up on you for hiding out here, okay? This is a crazy situation, girl." She sighed, resting her forehead against one palm. "I can't believe Jamie went public with this."

Scarfing down her popcorn as a distraction, speaking between crunches, Serena stared ahead blankly. "He said it was necessary, the only way to ensure Rowan doesn't just sweep Tony's alleged behavior under the rug."

Jade gripped her hand more tightly. "Well, if you both believe Dawn's side of the story, you should ensure Tony's prosecuted. Just having him fired wouldn't mean much, if he goes somewhere else and hooks up with other young girls." She drummed her fingers on the table nervously before saying, "Again, that's if you believe he actually did this."

Serena's upper lip curled as she yanked off her sunglasses and stared her friend down. "What's that supposed to mean?"

Jade removed her hand from Serena's and sat back in her seat. "Let's just be real here. Serena, from the first night you told me about all this, you've never told me how you reconcile Dawn's accusations with the Tony Gooden we knew back in the day. I never thought he was exactly husband material, but come on!"

An unspeakable frustration gripped Serena, and before she knew it, she'd flung her sunglasses across the table. When they landed yards away, skittering into a corner, Serena made no move to get them. "I have to go with what my daughter tells me."

"Have you asked Jamie what he really thinks? Maybe he can be a little more objective."

Annoyed, Serena raised an eyebrow. "How objective you think he was when he decided to press charges?"

Jade played with a loose curl of hair near the base of her neck. "Serena, I don't want to meddle, so I'm going to say this and then leave you to watch your movie. You know I'm not seeing him anymore, but Tony's boy Trey has been burning up my phone line since Dawn leveled these accusations. On top of that, he got word to Devon and Kym, too."

"And?" Sniffling, Serena popped a few more kernels of popcorn into her mouth. She knew good and well that Devon and Kym had heard; Kym had called twice the past three days, and Serena had let her go through to voice mail each time.

"No one in Tony's circle back in Chicago believes he's guilty of this," Jade said. "Devon is sick with anger, insisting somebody's lying on his boy. Everyone says Tony's always worked around attractive women, including young girls, since he worked in the mayor's office there. They swear this is not something he'd do."

Serena's chest burned with guilt as she replied. "Jade, how many of these people thought he was capable of what he's done the past few months? Moving to a new city, just to chase an old married woman like me?"

Jade took a second to let Serena's unfazed responses sink in, then shrugged. "I'm done," she said, her patience clearly shot. "I mean, for all I know Tony could actually be guilty of all this, and I don't want to help out a would-be molester. Enjoy your movie, girl."

"No, don't go." Serena clamped a hand to Jade's wrist, anchoring her in place. Her voice jumped two octaves as she asked, "Am I doing the right thing?"

Jade shook her head, confused. "How would I know? Do *you* even know what you're doing?"

Serena frowned. "I'm on my lithium, if that's what you mean."

"I know that," Jade replied. "Who reminds you every day to take it? I know you're in your right mind, girl, but that doesn't mean you're sure how to handle a situation as nuts as this one."

Serena held fast to Jade's wrist, the muscles in her neck straining. "I'm fighting to save my marriage, and to save my little girl's self-esteem. I have to stand by Dawn, and I have to back Jamie in his method of handling this. I owe him that much."

Jade inhaled and looked away before training her eyes back onto her friend. "Who says you owe Jamie anything? You know what I think? I think this is less about Jamie or Dawn than it is about you and your guilt."

"Okay, you can stop right there," Serena said, before pressing a hand to her mouth and letting the tears flow. "Dammit, Jade. I'm no fool, you don't have to analyze me. I've had plenty of time to do that myself these past few weeks. This is about me, you're right. It's about me stepping up and doing the hard work responsible people do every day to provide their children with two-parent homes, decent incomes, and a place that feels like home."

The corners of Jade's mouth turned up as she searched Serena's eyes. "You know something's not right with Dawn's story, don't you?"

Serena neatly folded her empty popcorn bag. "You think I'm a fool? I'd have to be lobotomized not to realize Dawn's word is no more reliable than your average teenage girl's, and that Jamie has every possible reason to take her accusations as gospel."

"But you don't care."

"Don't put words in my mouth," Serena replied. She pointed toward her bleary eyes, the tear tracks on her cheeks. "This look like the face of someone who doesn't care to you? I haven't returned any of Tony's calls since the day I asked him to leave town, precisely because I do care. Because if I let him tell me his side of the story, and I believe him—"

Her own eyes misting, Jade pressed a finger to her girl's lips. "You'd have to leave Jamie."

The truth hanging in the air, Serena sat with her best friend and had a good cry for the next fifteen minutes, right there in the midst of the growing crowd and the booms of the Dolby speakers surrounding them. By the time she and Jade left the cinema arm in arm, Serena had marshaled additional strength for the task she'd already assigned herself early this morning. After watching Jade pull away and into traffic, she drove out onto the road herself and headed back into the city.

When she pulled into the lot of the Nation's offices, Serena looked toward the gaggle of handsome, bow-tied brothers and began seeking her prey. Fritz stood amidst the crowd, barking orders and handing out stacks of *The Final Call*. When he saw her approaching, though, his features softened and he handed the papers to a taller brother standing nearby. Fastening the top button on his suit coat, he collected himself and strode over to meet her. "Sister Serena," he said, extending a gracious hand, "to what do I owe—"

"I need your help getting the one thing I'm not sure I want, Fritz," Serena replied, an odd peace overtaking her. "The truth."

40

Arthur Champion sat at Larry Whitaker's desk, staking his claim to Tony's boss's office. Sitting high in the massive leather chair, he swiveled toward Tony, his eyes simmering with judgmental rage. "Mr. Gooden, I'm a man worth hundreds of millions of dollars. I have employees, plants, and real estate on every continent. So, why do you think I'm here, in podunk Cincinnati, looking at your raggedy ass?"

Seated across from the desk, his ankles crossed and his hands in his lap, Tony arched his back. "I know exactly why you're here, Mr. Champion. Because Rowan's success is important to you."

"Damn right," Champion replied, glancing quickly to his left, where Larry stood at his office window with his chin in one hand. "I've already proven I can make any number of shareholders, including myself, wealthy. I'm into a new phase of legacy-building now, and proving I can make a difference in a field as crucial as education is the first step." Planting his feet suddenly and rolling closer to Tony, Champion leaned against the desk. "By jeopardizing Rowan's public image with these molestation charges, you're jeopardizing my legacy, do you understand?"

Turning back toward Champion and Tony, Larry took a step in their direction. "It's not yet been proven that Tony did anything," he said, his hands chopping the air for emphasis. "I agree this is a hell of a headache, Arthur, but let's be fair here. Something like this could just as easily have happened to me. There's every chance Tony's an innocent victim in this."

"Oh, certainly. Let's review just where we are, shall we?" Champion stood and grabbed a stack of papers from the desk, then tossed them into Tony's face.

Leaning over and grabbing up the magazines and newspaper sections, Tony scanned each one and quickly caught Champion's point. Dawn Kincaid's accusations against him—accusations for which the Cincinnati district attorney was preparing attempted molestation charges, while the family planned a separate civil suit—had given the national media a new hammer to use against Champion. *Newsweek,* the *New York Times,* even *Black Enterprise*: all had run stories using the charges to question whether Rowan's supposed successes were more illusory than real. The point: Champion's business success wasn't much help in his new role as a social do-gooder. The allegations rocking the school he'd joined forces with proved he ran a leaky ship, one so lax he couldn't even keep child molesters off his staff.

"You should be ashamed if this is your first time reading these," Champion said as Tony completed his skimming of the *Times* article. "I've found, Mr. Gooden, that most employees who cost me money and embarrassment bring trouble on themselves in some way." Rising, he stood over Tony, arms crossed. "What's your story?"

Tony leaned back in his seat so he could make eye contact with the tycoon. "Have you read my foster son's statement, sir?"

Champion stuck his hands into the pockets of his suit pants, grimacing. "Yes, very touching. He seemed to be saying this was his ex-girlfriend's way of getting back at him, by falsely accusing you of coming onto her? No one's buying that; the kid's obviously just looking out for you."

Larry strode back over to his desk but stayed on his feet as he searched Champion's eyes. "Why wouldn't there be some truth to that, Arthur? I suspect all of us here have broken our share of female hearts. You really wouldn't put this past a young girl reeling from a breakup?"

"Let me remind you of something." Champion matched stares with Larry, their respective egos filling the room. "I'm the investor here. I provide resources, and in return I get a say when you or your people screw up." He jerked a thumb toward Tony. "He screwed up. Why the hell was he alone in a classroom with that girl in the first place?"

The intercom on Larry's desk buzzed and he impatiently punched his speakerphone button. "I said I wasn't to be disturbed!"

"I—I understand, sir," his secretary said, only momentarily thrown off by her boss's heated response. "Principal Jacobs is here, though. She says there's an absolute emergency concerning the school, and she has to see you right now."

Larry cursed under his breath, then leaned back toward his intercom. "She's actually here?"

"Yes, sir."

"Send her in." He punched his speakerphone off and glared at both Tony and Champion. "How many things can go wrong at once?"

Audrey cracked Larry's office door open, peeking inside before opening it further and stepping across the threshold. "Good afternoon, gentlemen," she said, her face showing no signs of emotion, her voice cold and professional. Tony appreciated his girlfriend's acting skills; they had just been ready to go public with their relationship before Dawn's accusations, but with the disruptions that had followed, they'd agreed it was best to stay invisible a while longer.

Larry nodded toward Tony and Champion. "Can you discuss this emergency in front of these two?"

"Yes, I can." Stepping gracefully toward Champion, Audrey reached out and shook his hand respectfully. "Sir, I'm going to be straight with you. The only emergency is the one you're already here to discuss, but I had to get my say in regarding these allegations against Mr. Gooden."

The hairs on his neck tingling, his stomach growing warm, Tony turned over his shoulder and shot his lady a warning look. "That's really not necessary, Audrey. I can speak for myself."

Her arms hanging at her side, her back drawn tight, she gave Tony a brittle smile. "Well, I hope you've shared the full context of exactly who this girl and her family are. They have every possible motivation to set you up with lies."

Seeing the raised eyebrows of both men, Tony bolted from his seat. "You'll have to excuse us." Stepping quickly to Audrey, he took her by the elbow.

Champion bristled, focusing his sights on the way Tony had taken control of the young principal. "Excuse you? What gives you the right to shunt her out of the room?"

Tony shot the billionaire a look that said *back off.* "This won't take five minutes." He exchanged a more respectful glance with Larry as he led Audrey out the door and toward his own office.

Audrey slammed the door behind her as soon as they stepped inside. "Have you told them?" It was a shout, not a question.

Tony took a seat on the edge of his desk. "Told them what?"

She bounced in place as if ready to charge him. "Have you told them about your affair with Serena, about the fact her husband had every reason to tell Dawn to set you up!"

Tony crossed his arms, peered at the wood beams in his ceiling. "I don't see how that's relevant."

Audrey was pacing back and forth, clearly struggling to contain herself. "Not relevant? Tony, we have discussed this four separate times since this nightmare began. Now, correct me if I'm wrong, but don't you agree that Jamie probably put the child up to this?"

Tony rose and walked over to Audrey, placing an arm over her shoulder. "You need to have a seat, calm down."

Audrey let him lead her to a chair opposite his desk but wasn't finished yet. "Answer my question."

"Yes," Tony replied as he set Audrey down. "More likely than not, Jamie's behind this. I can't prove it, though. Besides, the minute I bring him into this, I bring Serena into it."

Audrey looked up at Tony, her eyes widening with surprise. "Why would that be so terrible? They've all brought you into this, shooting you full of specious accusations. My God, don't you understand your entire career in education is over if these charges stick? Even with that at stake, I don't see Serena bending over backward to stand up for *you*."

"Just stop this, okay?" Tony's voice had grown hollow from stress, and he collapsed into the chair next to Audrey's before continuing. "Serena is not at fault here, and she doesn't deserve to have our affair made public. Audrey, you know what kind of a black eye that would give her, having her personal life dragged through the courts and local papers. There's no way I'd do that to her, not even to save myself."

Audrey's voice took on a tinny, nearly shy quality as she said, "She put herself in harm's way from day one. You said yourself that she enrolled Dawn at Rowan knowing you worked here. And no one forced her to sleep with you."

Tony leaned forward, taking both of Audrey's hands in his. "That would have never happened if I hadn't had the nerve to move here," he said. "Don't you see? I moved here out of a selfish urge, first and foremost, to try and get Serena back. That was such a limited view. It's not about *getting* her back, it's about respecting her attempts to lead a better life. I can't do much, Audrey, but I can at least do that much for her. And I'll start by keeping her out of this mess."

Gripping his hands more tightly, Audrey inhaled deeply and pulled Tony to his feet. Rising, she leaned forward and kissed him, communicating a mixture of lust, love, and concern with her gentle tongue and full, moist lips. As she pulled out of the kiss, though, her right eye glistened with a single tear. "You still love her," she whispered. "I knew it from the first night you told me about her, but I didn't want to believe it."

Her words felt less like an accusation than an acceptance, but Tony rushed to dampen their meaning. "There's more than one kind of love," he said, lightly stabilizing her chin in one hand. "What I feel for you—"

"Will never compare to what you feel for her," Audrey replied, pulling out of his grasp and staring at him longingly. "If it did, you would have told Larry and Champion the whole story, no hesitations."

"Audrey, I—"

She was already backing out of the room, her back still straight, her proud expression straining to suppress the pain inside. "I love you, Tony Gooden, but I know when to say when. I hope someone can replace Serena for you someday, because it clearly won't be me." He was still grappling for words when she pivoted suddenly and was gone.

Ten minutes after Audrey's exit, once he'd had time to hide in a bathroom stall and expel the warm, shameful tears, Tony stepped back into the lions' den. Taking a seat on Larry's couch, he looked up at his boss and Champion with dry eyes. "Gentlemen," he said stoically, "do what you gotta do."

41

Serena stood face-to-face with her oldest daughter, applying Dawn's makeup with careful expertise. Stepping over to her bathroom sink and grabbing a mascara pencil, she broke the uneasy silence lingering between them. "It's not that I don't trust you, baby," she said, reaching out for her daughter's chin again and steadying it between a thumb and forefinger. "It's just that your father and I both have to understand your side of what happened. Like I've told you, you're not to pay these fool reporters or Rowan lawyers any mind, but if I'm going to speak up on your behalf, I have to be able to explain what Mr. Gooden did to you."

Mother and daughter were as close as lovers preparing to clinch, so much so that Dawn averted her eyes from Serena's patient gaze. "I've told you the whole story like five times, Mom." Struggling against Serena's attempt to hold her chin still, her voice dropped to a near whisper. "What more do you want?"

Serena inhaled deeply, then released the breath as she applied the mascara. For ten days she'd performed this delicate dance. Every other day or so, she approached Dawn in a different way: *What exactly did he do? What did he say, again? Where did he touch you? Why do you think he did this? Why is he saying this is untrue?* With each probing question, each loving hug, she had offered her child an unspoken opportunity. *If you made this up—for any reason, it doesn't matter—just tell me now. We can back off this more easily now than later.*

Though her story of Tony's seduction wavered in its consistency—in the first version he'd wordlessly squeezed both breasts, in the second he'd laid a hand on one after describing exactly what he'd like to do to it—Dawn refused to bite. While insisting that she didn't want to relive it, didn't want Serena constantly hounding her, Dawn insisted that she'd told the gospel truth or at least the spirit of it. And when Serena saw the fragility, defensiveness, and wounded wariness in her baby's eyes, she knew that her preferred reaction—shaking some sense into the girl until an honest account fell from between her lips—would only make matters worse.

She was saving her firepower for Jamie. While she couldn't prove a thing yet, her interrogation of Fritz had rewarded her immediate skeptical reaction to Dawn's accusations. Jamie hadn't been stupid enough to tell his spiritual mentor any details, but Fritz had his suspicions. He'd stumbled upon Jamie and Dawn on three separate occasions in the week before the incident. Each time they'd been holed up somewhere in Fritz's house—once in the bedroom that had become Sydney's temporary home, twice in the half bathroom that adjoined Fritz's cramped kitchen.

"I saw nothing alarming," Fritz had recalled when Serena confronted him at the mosque that day. "You understand? I had no sense there was anything improper going on, just a lot of talking and feverish discussion that they didn't want overheard." When she insisted that this alone was odd—though Jamie loved his stepdaughter, he'd never been big on conversation with her—Fritz had nodded quickly. "Exactly. I felt something odd was going on, but Sister Serena, I did not want to pry. Jamie was doing so well in processing your adultery, and if anything, I felt it showed growth that he was spending time with Dawn at all, given the rift between you two."

The secret conferences were Ugly Revelation Number Two about Jamie in recent weeks, coming right behind Levi's news about the apartment her husband had rented for Angelita and Andrea. Serena had already confronted him about that mess, and Jamie had been surprisingly sanguine about the whole thing, admitting he felt it was best to have his "other" family nearby so he could provide them with consistent emotional support. "You and the girls will always come first," he'd insisted. "Assuming we can get Gooden the hell out of our lives, of course."

The demands of life—work, motherhood, the lawsuit, crying herself to sleep after reading the latest news accounts of Tony's suspension from his job—had left Serena without the energy to take on another battle with Jamie. To the extent she held out any hope of rehabilitating her marriage, she knew that confronting her husband about Dawn's allegations would be a high-wire act. Make the wrong accusation, ask the wrong question, and any remaining trust between them might be erased forever.

These and other ugly realities inhabiting her, Serena bit her lower lip as she turned Dawn toward the bathroom mirror. "There," she said, stepping back and sizing her daughter up. Fully dressed in her red-and-white silk dress and black heels, her face now perfectly made up, Dawn was sure to be one of the most striking girls at Rowan's Black History Month program. "Girl," Serena said, beaming, "I only wish I could have been so fine in my day."

Blushing, Dawn leaned in toward the mirror, admiring her mother's handiwork. "How long did it take you to get this good at makeup, Mom?"

"Oh, just a few years," Serena replied. Taking a deep breath, she finally launched into her long-delayed plan, the one she'd hoped wouldn't be necessary. She informed her nearly sixteen-year-old daughter that she couldn't take driver's education until she turned seventeen.

Forty minutes had passed by the time they pulled into the school's parking lot, and Dawn still hadn't said a word since they'd left the house. Sitting in the passenger seat with arms crossed, she didn't budge as Serena climbed from the car.

Standing in front of her open driver's side door, Serena leaned down and aimed her words at Dawn. "You've been doing really well in school, honey. Let's not mess with that by being late for the concert. The choir's counting on you."

Her arms still crossed, her eyes wet, Dawn glared at her mother, emotions on her sleeve. "How you gonna drop that crap on me right before this program, Mom?"

"Look, my timing may have been off, okay?" Serena's conscience knocked, setting off a momentary twitch in her right temple. "That's no excuse to show out, young lady. Now get out of the car!"

Dawn stormed ahead of Serena through the crowded parking lot, her deep-set frown holding as she nodded stubbornly at passing teachers and friends. Serena stayed close on her daughter's heels until they entered the school auditorium. A few rows from the back, Jamie and Sydney sat with their necks craned toward the main entrance, looks of relief flooding their faces.

Serena paused and stood there, just inside the entranceway, as she watched her daughter's predictable next move. Bustling forward, her gold necklace and diamond earrings flying, Dawn bobbed, weaved, and even elbowed her way to her stepfather's row. Even from where she was, Serena could tell from the tense look on Dawn's face and Jamie's narrowed eyes that it was not a particularly respectful exchange. In seconds Jamie had kissed Sydney's forehead, whispered something into her ear, then scooted out into the aisle and taken Dawn by the elbow. Pausing there, he caught Serena's eye and nodded briefly before turning and dragging Dawn in the opposite direction. By the time Serena reached Sydney's row, Jamie and Dawn had flitted out the exit door near the stage.

She told her baby daughter a quick, necessary lie—"Mommy has to use the bathroom, I'll be right back"—then continued down the aisle, following her husband and daughter's footsteps. Flitting out the exit door, Serena came to a sudden halt the minute she stepped into the hallway. Looking left and then right, she sought any sign of her family.

At the other end of the short hall, she saw a long arm fly into the air, its owner gesturing wildly but struggling to keep his voice down. "Get a hold of yourself, girl!"

Scooting down the hallway, her back to the wall, Serena shut her eyes, absorbing the conversation.

"You owe me, Poppa Jamie! The car you said you'd buy me, that won't do any good if I can't drive it! You gotta talk some sense into her. I'll be damned if I'm gonna wait a year to get my license! It's not enough that she ruined my relationship with Glenn, locking me up like I was some wide-eyed virgin."

Serena could hear the impatient pleas in Jamie's tone. "Dawn, let's talk about this later, okay? Your program starts in a couple minutes—"

"I don't care about that! I mean, I don't mind singing in the choir and stuff, but come on, you know she's tripping about this driver's ed thing. And you owe me!"

"You may have misunderstood her," Jamie said. "I'll handle it, though, okay?"

"You better." Dawn paused as if taking a beat to check their surroundings, then lowered her voice so much that Serena struggled to follow her. "This ain't turning out like you said it would."

Jamie groaned, then said, "I told you, baby, there's nothing to worry about. Right now everyone believes you, not Mr. Gooden. Why do you think the school suspended him without pay? Everyone believes you, Dawn."

"Everyone," Dawn sighed, "except Mom."

Serena fought tears as Jamie responded. "What did she say?"

"Nothing direct, but I'm not stupid," Dawn replied. "She knows something's not right."

Wiping her eyes, Serena took the last few steps down the hallway—some of the longest she'd taken in years—and rounded the corner. Crossing her arms and letting new tears flow, she looked into her husband's wide eyes and said, "Oh, you're so right about that."

"Oh, God. Mom." A hand plastered across her mouth, Dawn froze in place.

Looking between his wife and stepdaughter, Jamie let several beats pass, his hands clenching into fists. "What are you going to do?" he asked, his eyes meeting Serena's accusing stare with the equivalent of a middle finger.

Serena hugged herself, then glanced at the floor. "Dawn, go join the choir members in the band room, now. You do that, maybe I'll forget my idea about postponing your driver's ed."

After glancing quizzically between her parents, Dawn stepped out of her heels, grabbed them up, and took off down the hallway.

Serena looked at her husband, shaking her head. "So, after your spiritual rebirth, after the confessions we made to each other, you used our child to set Tony up?"

Jamie straightened his back, amplifying his height advantage over his wife. "I'm human, Serena, no church or mosque could change that. You may as well know, I'll never have it in me to forgive Gooden. First, he ruined what should have been the happiest day of our lives, crashing the wedding. Then he has the nerve, the *balls*, to bring his ass to Cincinnati and swoop in the minute you're feeling vulnerable?" He swept a hand forward, wiggling it dismissively. "No, there's not a real man alive who could let that go." He curled his upper lip as he asked, "You'd have preferred it if I'd literally killed his ass, huh?"

Though she knew someone could happen upon them any minute, Serena didn't fight the urge to let her head fall into her hands. Cathartic tears washing her palms, her words burst forth in strong shudders. "Oh, Jamie. Oh, Jamie."

He stepped toward Serena, a comforting hand extended, then retreated when his wife backed out of his reach. "This was the only way to get him out of our lives, Dee," he said. "I know it looks bad, but I need you to stand by me on this. At this point, it wouldn't do any good to have Dawn recant. Think how it'll make her look. She might get suspended from Rowan. Expelled, even."

A sense of acceptance welling up within, Serena crossed her arms again and looked at Jamie with drying eyes. "Dawn will be all right, I'll see to that. She's a kid. Principal Jacobs, the school board, even the courts, they'll all understand."

Jamie pressed a palm against the nearby wall, gathering himself as if he'd been knocked off balance. "So Dawn's welfare is all you're worried about," he said, his eyes hardening. "Well, as your husband, don't forget this is about you, too. For me to take the fall for Dawn's accusations, Dee, you'll have to tell everyone *why* I wanted to ruin Gooden. And bear in mind, I'm not just talking about your colleagues and friends. I'm talking about your parents, about Dawn and Sydney." His eyes probed hers. "The last thing you want is for them to relive some of the shit in your past, right? You think you'll help them avoid those same traps, admitting you cheated on me?"

Though Jamie's questions had turned her creeping confidence back into a quivering blob of fear, Serena set her jaw and turned away from her husband. On one level, she felt the same sensation she'd suffered the day she learned about Angelita and Andrea; it was as if she were again watching this action from a remote location, taking in a movie.

This time, though, Serena was determined to write her own script. Forcing herself to take one step after another back toward the auditorium, she raised her voice for Jamie's benefit. "The concert's starting." When he shouted at her, insisting she answer his questions, she shrugged before turning back to face him.

"You really think so little of me," she asked, "that I'd let my need to please my parents, to please my coworkers, scare me into giving you a pass on *this*? A few more days of these accusations, and you'd have had Dawn committing perjury."

Jamie's Adam's apple constricted and he flexed his fingers. "It would have been worth it to get rid of Gooden, Dee." He advanced on Serena, his arms crossed as if to control himself. "Don't throw your good name away for him."

Serena flung herself back around and stepped back toward the auditorium as fast as she could, but not before she caught Jamie's parting shot. "You won't say anything! You enjoy being *Serena*

Kincaid too much." The truth of the accusation slammed into her back, reminding her of the many times she'd tried to stuff her skeletons, both old and new, into any available closet.

You better hope I'm the same woman, Jamie, Serena thought as she moved briskly toward the row where Sydney was seated. Her husband had no clue as to the answer, but then Serena wasn't sure she did, either.

 G lenn and Ben sat side by side atop the desk in Tony's office. With their arms crossed and their legs swinging anxiously with a matching rhythm, their resemblance was even more stark than usual. As he crammed the lid onto the last of the boxes they'd helped him pack, Tony glanced in their direction. "We're ready to hit the road, fellas."

As Ben slid forward, Glenn stayed atop the desk, smacking a fist into his other palm. "This is all my fault, Mr. G."

Throwing an arm over Ben's shoulder as he stepped within reach, Tony forced a smile in Glenn's direction. "Come on now, we've had this talk. This was going to happen eventually, regardless."

Glenn's only movement was the defiant swing in his neck. "I'm not going for that, sir. If I'd just let Dawn down easy—"

Tony checked his watch, sighed. "You know, Glenn, if blaming yourself for my suspension helps you treat women with more respect, then okay, blame away. But I don't blame you." It was the absolute truth; the drama surrounding Dawn's allegations had simply been the wake-up call, the announcement that Tony had built himself a world bursting with conflicts of interest.

As an executive overseeing Rowan he'd 1) worked alongside his girlfriend; 2) interacted regularly with his old flame's daughter;

and 3) slept with his foster sons' principal. Granted, he might have kept these balls in the air a little longer, especially if the academy had stood by him after Dawn's accusations, but Tony knew he had to go. There were plenty of other places he could do good, assuming they didn't mind hiring alleged perverts.

As the twins helped him load the half-dozen boxes onto a small dolly, he tried not to think about the inconvenient realities awaiting him. His pride had forced him to submit his resignation just a week into his suspension, but at the moment he had no clue where his next paycheck would come from. And given the play Dawn's allegations had received in the local press, he knew he'd have a hard time skirting that issue when the twins' social worker came calling next week. He was already calculating ways to convince her that an unemployed pariah could be a worthy foster parent.

The office tower's hallways felt cold and brittle as he rolled the dolly past one silent colleague after another, the twins following behind him with pinched, defensive frowns. He'd already said his good-byes to Larry and Audrey earlier, and everyone else seemed intent on acting as if he were already gone, eager to get past an awkward moment.

Zora was waiting dutifully when they stepped into the cold, the trunk of Tony's Passat popped and ready for his boxes. The twins helped him load everything in, then they slipped into the car as Zora stepped out and joined the twins in the back.

Tony hopped into the driver's seat and looked to his right, where his father sat in the front passenger seat. "Well, the worst part of the day's behind me."

Wayne removed the toothpick he'd been chewing from his mouth before nonchalantly whispering, "Tony Gooden, you've just been punked."

"Pop," Tony replied, sighing, "you are too damn old to even know what that phrase means."

"You'd be surprised how many forty-year-old women still watch a little MTV," Wayne said, leaning back into his seat. "As long as the women I date watch that stuff, I have to stay up on it, son." He glanced over his shoulder, noting that the twins and Zora were immersed in their own conversation, some argument about whether Eminem or Jay-Z was the better rapper. Satisfied that he and his son were as good as alone, Wayne turned back toward Tony. "Now, in case you didn't catch my meaning, I still disagree with this move of yours."

Tony knew his morning meditation had done its job, because he didn't feel the slightest twinge at his father's resurrected argument. "I know, Pop, you think I should stay and fight."

"Absolutely." Wayne nodded toward the backseat. "What kind of example are you setting for them, running from a false accusation?"

Tony shifted out of park and tapped his accelerator. "The message to them is this: I care more about them having a peaceful senior year than I care about my career."

Wayne cleared his throat and grabbed a handkerchief from the pocket of his overcoat. "Poor Audrey was right. You really do love that woman."

"Pop, please," Tony pleaded as he zoomed out of the Whitaker Holdings parking lot, refusing to pause for so much as a look back. "I thought you and Zora came down here to be moral support for me and the twins right now. This isn't helping."

"Fine," Wayne said, flipping his hands into the air. "So, how 'bout them Bengals?"

Tony slapped his father with a weary glance. "Just ask me a genuine question, but leave Serena out of it, please."

Wayne lowered his voice again. "You need a loan, something to tide you over until you find something else?"

"I have some savings," Tony replied after checking the rearview mirror to ensure the twins and Zora were still in their own little world. "Profits left over from the sale of my condo back home. If that runs out, which it will in a couple more months, I can always take out a home equity loan."

Wayne leaned in closer to his son. "To keep them," he said, jamming a finger against his seat, "won't you have to be gainfully employed?"

Coasting to a stop at a red light, Tony shrugged. "I'm gonna beg for mercy like Liza Minelli's husband on a bad night, Pop. Hopefully the social workers will go easy on a brother."

Wayne's brow furrowed as he tried to picture his son receiving such unmerited favor. "But, how much mercy can they have while you're under this cloud of suspicion—"

The insistent buzz of Tony's cell phone interrupted Wayne. Sticking in his earpiece, he glanced at the phone's face and grimaced when he saw the call was from Larry. "Beautiful. Doesn't he realize he can't fire me after I quit?" He glanced at his father as he pressed the accept button. "Hold on a sec."

Larry's tone hummed with nervous energy. "Tony? Is that you?"

"That's the number you dialed, right?"

When Larry made a grumbling noise in response, Tony waited for his former boss to respond in kind, but was disappointed. "I'm sorry, man," Larry finally said. "I'm in a crowded hallway here, can barely catch your voice. Look, I tried to reach you at the office, and they told me you'd just pulled away."

Tony realized the car had grown silent, that the twins and Zora were listening as intently as his father. He felt his teeth grit as he said, "Larry, I told you I was leaving as soon as I got my office packed up. Now how may I help you?"

The loud voices and echoes in Larry's background intensified and he raised his voice. "I need you to come down here."

"Down where? What are you talking about?"

Larry paused, sounding as if he was speaking to someone on his end of the phone. "Would you give me some space, please? I'm on the phone here." His voice grew louder as he said, "Tony? I'm back. Look, I'm down here at the city prosecutor's office. I got summoned an hour ago, didn't have time to call you until just now."

Pulling the Passat into the parking lot of a Dunkin' Donuts, Tony came to an abrupt stop. "So, is there a point to all this or what?"

"The Kincaid girl's not bringing any charges against you," Larry said, the words bursting forth like a springtime shower. Tony could feel the smile on his old boss's face. "She and her mother were waiting here when Audrey and I showed up. They're admitting the accusations were false, the whole nine."

Opening his door with a jolt, Tony spun his feet onto the ground and slapped a hand to his forehead. "Oh, my God," was all that came out before a statement he never thought he'd utter. "I don't know what to say."

"You don't have to say anything right now," Larry replied. "You just need to turn that little Volkswagen of yours around and move your stuff back into the office."

Standing and trading confused glances with his family, all of whom were still huddled in the Passat, Tony searched for words and still came up empty.

Larry had no such struggle. "Let me tell you something," he said. "I know I have to tread lightly, but I am *so* ready to rub Champion's face in this. Matter of fact, tell you what. We're gonna call his ass together, from my office, as soon as you can meet me over there. I told him we should have backed you a hundred percent!"

"I know you did," Tony replied as he paced alongside his car. Having sensed this was a sensitive conversation, his family remained dutifully inside the Passat, minding their respective business. "You stood by me from the minute the accusations hit, Larry, and I love you for it, brother."

Larry gave a hearty laugh. "You ain't got to love me, brother; just get your butt back to the office ASAP, that's all I ask."

Sighing, Tony gathered his will with two quick actions. First, he turned back toward his car and eyed the twins as they sat there watching him. Then, as he pictured Serena's face during their last conversation—likely the last they would ever have—he gave it to Larry straight. "I appreciate your asking, man, but as much as I want to, I'm not coming back."

43

When Dawn emerged from the door leading to her family doctor's suite of offices, Serena snapped to attention. As her daughter crossed the physician's waiting room, Serena detected a new lift to her child's shoulders, a rejuvenated spring in her step. She stood as Dawn arrived at her chair and placed an arm around the girl's neck. "So?"

"Mom," Dawn replied, her voice a touch catty but her smile warm, "can we just go?" Her eyes sent a clear message: *I'll tell you everything in the car.*

Once they were in the parking garage, Dawn slipped her mother a copy of the birth control prescription she'd obtained. Recognizing the brand and feeling comfortable with the doctor's choice, Serena sighed as they arrived at their Volvo. Opening the driver's side door, she looked over the hood at Dawn. "You do realize this is not a license to go buck wild, right?"

Her increasing restraint winning out, Dawn was silent until they had each shut their respective door and were entombed inside the Volvo. "Mom, how many ways do I have to say it? I haven't been with anyone since Glenn. And this was your idea more than mine."

"Only because it beats the alternative if you go and do

something impulsive again," Serena replied. "Which I'm not advocating."

"You act like you haven't heard a word I've said the past few days," Dawn said, huffing. "I said you were basically right."

Serena had heard every word from her daughter's mouth lately; she was just having a hard time believing that Dawn's creeping case of common sense would hold. Two nights after she had exposed Dawn and Jamie's scheme against Tony, Serena had finally forced a bare-knuckle discussion: how could her own child betray her the way she had? Dawn's initial attempts to hang tough crumbled quickly, ending with her bawling and choked pleas for forgiveness.

"It was both of them, Mom," Dawn had insisted, in a reference to Jamie and Glenn. "I was so angry at Glenn for dumping me, I just wanted to 'get' somebody, and Poppa Jamie caught me off guard, said he'd owe me big if I helped him out." After suffering from Jamie's favoritism of Sydney as well as Serena's heavy work schedule in recent years, Dawn was grappling with an equally cruel blow: realizing she'd been used by the stepfather she'd always hoped would view her as his own flesh and blood. The child had nearly been inconsolable, and that very sight left Serena a hot mess as well. By bedtime, they'd gone through a full box of tissues and the tips of their respective noses were red and raw.

Serena had forgiven Dawn's disloyalty with very little effort or thought, but by putting her child on the pill she hoped to at least head off some of the traps that had tripped her up in life. Beyond that, all she could do was impart as much common sense to Dawn as possible, in hopes her daughter would delay her next round of intimacy and insist on being as safe as possible when the time came.

"Sex is emotionally exhausting," Dawn was saying now as they rolled through the parking garage toward the exit. "I mean, I know I'll meet the right guy soon enough, but it doesn't have to be tomorrow."

Thank God. Serena could feel her parents' prayers surrounding her and Dawn even now; as such, she decided to let her child's words hang in the air. An "atta-girl" would only make Dawn realize how uncool her newfound wisdom was.

Serena had just taken her change from the parking attendant when her cell phone buzzed with a call. Pulling into traffic, she attached her headset. "Hello? Oh, hi, Will!" She smiled wide at his words, thanked him profusely for his decision, then hung up after reminding him to complete all the necessary paperwork. Detaching her headset, she glanced toward Dawn. "Want to know who that was?"

When Dawn shrugged genially, Serena said, "That was the gentleman I've just hired to become the assistant treasurer of the school system."

Dawn's eyes narrowed quizzically. "But you're the treasurer."

"And this gentleman, Will Morgan, will be my assistant. There are so many duties I've taken on these past couple of years, honey, and I finally realized my life—our life—would be easier if I got some help with them."

Dawn frowned. "How will he make 'our' life easier?"

"Well, for one I won't be working as much," Serena said. "Instead of working late a lot of evenings, I'll be able to leave at five-thirty or so, because Will can do a lot of the things I stay late to do."

Dawn ticked her head toward her mother's. "You convinced the stingy school board to hire someone new, just for me and Sydney?"

Serena chuckled. "Well, I didn't exactly frame it that way, sweetie, but that was my plan, and it worked." She looked into her daughter's pleasantly surprised gaze. "You can thank me later."

The conversation took a lighter turn as mother and daughter drove to Serena's parents' home. By the time they pulled into Jan and Charles Height's driveway, they were laughing so loud they nearly ran over Jamie, who stood in the center of the blacktop with his hands behind his back. Dressed in a chalky gray pinstriped suit and a white shirt with no bow tie, he stood erect with determined, focused eyes.

As was still the case now, weeks after being caught by Serena, Jamie and Dawn were unable to connect. For his part, he tried by attempting to catch her eye and share a nod, but Dawn wanted no part of it. With her lower lip curled up against her teeth, Dawn honored Serena's earlier suggestion and ignored her stepfather instead of telling him just how betrayed she felt, just how much she wished he would fade into nothing. Her restraint proved Serena right; when Jamie realized his stepchild had passed him wordlessly and wouldn't be turning back, his shoulders slumped like a punctured tire.

Deflated or not, though, Jamie planted his feet anew and met Serena's eyes as she neared. "Hello," he said, dropping his arms and revealing the bouquet of red roses in his right hand.

Serena stood a few steps back from her husband, her hands against the side of her navy blue skirt. "You're here to drop Sydney off?"

"Yes. She's already inside, Dee." His eyes still trained on her, Jamie dropped to his knees and extended the bouquet toward his wife. "Serena, we've come through too much this past year to let things fall apart. I know what I did seems unforgivable, but, please, let's not undo all that we've been working toward."

As much as she wanted to turn him away, as eager as she was to be free of men altogether for the foreseeable future, Serena's will to ignore Jamie was stifled by a sudden cry from her parents' front door. "Granny, look," Sydney exclaimed. "Daddy's proposing to Mommy all over again! I told you they're still in love!"

Caught between Jamie's outstretched offering and her daughter's hopeful yell, Serena was paralyzed by her desire to make her child happy. Quick to capitalize, Jamie turned over his shoulder to wave at Sydney before pivoting back toward his wife. "You know the girls need us," he said, his voice deep and confident, his face spreading into a smile. "Let's do the right thing."

44

D espite an oval pair of ebony-tinted sunglasses, a furry pink hat, and a matching winter coat, Tony recognized Serena as soon as she stepped inside the coffee shop. Seated at a raised corner table, he played it cool, doodling on his BlackBerry until her gaze naturally wandered over to him.

She was silent as she approached and pulled out the chair catty-corner to his, so that they faced each other diagonally. Respecting her need for distance, he kept his eyes on his BlackBerry screen. "Good morning." It was a Sunday, and Serena's kids were at church with her parents while she and Tony were here, at a Panera Bread shop near the University of Dayton's main campus.

Setting her sunglasses down as Tony passed her a coffee mug, Serena asked, "Where do the boys think you are?"

Smiling, he braved a glance in her direction. "Where do the girls think you are?"

Chuckling, they each revealed the alibis they'd built for their respective families. "The girls think I'm at the office catching up on work," Serena said. "That excuse won't work much longer, though, now that I've hired an assistant."

"Oh, the games, the lies," Tony replied, shaking his head playfully. "My job's easier than yours. I just told the boys that I had a 'hot date' with a woman who's in Dayton. Which you are, at the moment."

Serena felt her shoulders hop with amusement. "Whatever, brother."

"Look," Tony said, turning serious once Serena had returned with her mug of decaf. "I really appreciated your call, and your agreement to meet."

Serena leaned forward, her hands clasped to ensure they didn't get intertwined with Tony's. "You deserved an in-person apology, and I need to know if there's anything I can do to heal the damage Jamie and Dawn did to your reputation. Is everything all right with your foster parent status?"

"We're getting by," Tony replied. The withdrawal of Dawn's accusations had backed some of the heat off of him, calmed the social workers a bit, but then there had been the unfortunate issue of his unemployment. The authorities hadn't been terribly impressed with his modest rainy-day funds; as a parental figure, he was expected to generate an ongoing income.

"Kinko's saved me," he told Serena as she shook her head at the thought of him in one of those pale blue uniform shirts. "Never saw myself working in customer service and earning a few steps above minimum wage, but at least no one's walked in and recognized me yet."

"You won't be there long," Serena said, consciously resisting the urge to place a warm hand atop one of his. "You really have to forgive me, Tony. I let you down."

"I don't want to hear it," he replied, waving her off. "You were torn between your love for your daughter and your trust in the man you tried to build a life with. Who was I to compete with that?"

"So," Serena began, her gaze sheepishly aimed into the table's wooden sheen, "do you think you and the twins will stay here in Cincinnati for good? Or, do you even see them staying with you once they turn eighteen?"

"Well," Tony said, "as you've seen firsthand, the boys have some growing up to do, especially Glenn. I think it's smoothest if we stay here until they're through high school. Plus, it gives me time to work with this therapist Zora talked me into seeing."

Serena felt her neck tack to the right, her curiosity welling up. "What are you seeing a therapist for?" She felt like a fool for hoping it had something to do with her.

"I have this problem, you see. They're, uh, known as . . . women?"

"Very funny."

"No, no," Tony said, not wanting to waste time on miscommunication. "All I mean, Serena, is that I've always had difficult relationships with the women in my life, but I didn't want to understand why." He told her of the therapist's approach, how the sister was the first person who had made him confront the entire range of emotions he'd experienced while processing Millie's abandonment through the years. "My old man was my prime influence growing up," he said, "and no self-respecting man of his generation believed in working with shrinks, especially when there was nothing obviously wrong with me."

Serena playfully flicked her tongue between her teeth. "Except for the unhealthy size of your water-head, even if it is due to your God-complex."

"Yeah, well, everyone always saw that as self-confidence. This Dr. Walker has put me in the mirror. I've got a few issues to let go of where my mother is concerned. I know, I know," Tony said. "You always knew that, but now I do, too. You happy for me?"

"Of course." Serena took a deep breath. "I'd like to take the journey with you, Tony."

His chest burning with repressed hope, Tony sat up straighter in his chair but kept his tone detached. "Say what?"

"What if we set a regularly scheduled date, an appointment to meet here one Sunday morning a month? I want to hear how you work through forgiving your mother, see you grow up overnight while you try to raise those two he-men you call boys."

Despite the many ways in which his character had deepened and broadened since the day of Devon and Kym's wedding, something about Serena's platonic request repelled Tony. What were they going to do, just deactivate their sexual chemistry? "Sure, we can do that, Serena. We'll sip tea every month and trade stories like two old girlfriends. I assume I should just leave my family jewels and whatever's attached at the front door?"

Embers glowed to life in Serena's eyes and her back bristled. "You promised me you wouldn't pressure me about Jamie—"

"I haven't asked you one thing about him," Tony replied, his tone cooling again as he gestured calmly. "Serena, I came here with the understanding we'd have one good, clear discussion. I *might* have survived that. Now you're offering me the chance to see you month after month, with no indication of whether that leads anywhere?" He inhaled, pawing toward some sense of peace. "I don't know that I can handle that."

Serena gave in to her simplest urge, one with the fewest repercussions. Placing a hand on top of Tony's, she lowered her voice. "Do you really think it would be healthy for us to jump into something physical, when I've just separated from my husband and when you just split with Audrey?"

Resting his elbows on the table, Tony rested his forehead against a wrist. "Spoken like a woman who's had some therapy of her own."

Serena blinked in surprise. "How else do you think I could have come this far, separating from Jamie for what may be the last time, even though it's breaking Sydney's heart and wagging tongues on my job?"

Tony raised both of Serena's hands to his lips, pecking a kiss onto each. "I respect everything you're saying. I just don't know that I'm man enough to live up to your arrangement." The very idea of seeing this woman time in and time out, never knowing whether she'd ultimately have the will to file divorce papers on Jamie, felt unacceptably risky.

Serena's eyes darted to her watch and she scooted her chair back. "What are you saying?" Her short heels clacking against the wooden floor, she searched Tony's eyes. "If I make this drive again in four weeks, will you be here?"

After shutting his eyes tight for a beat, Tony rose and helped Serena into her coat. "Make the drive," he said, pecking a platonic kiss onto her cheek, the type that kills a man filled with passion. He withheld any promise; Serena would have her answer the next time she walked through these doors.

Epilogue

*E*ighteen months after being trampled to within an inch of his life, Tony finally felt as if he'd fully recovered. The limp, the occasional fear of crowded spaces, the recurring nightmares: all were now relics of his past, fading in the rearview mirror. Now that he had shaved his beard and gone back to wearing a skintight fade, he bore no visible signs of his recent journey.

As his water skis glided over the turquoise surface of the Atlantic, a mile from the sparkling white shores of Grand Bahama Island, Tony realized for the first time that he now took his health for granted. Bending and bowing his body, keeping a tight grip on the cord connecting him to the zooming speedboat, he caught himself and marveled at his abilities. Just six months ago, the lingering pain in his left leg would never have allowed him to keep his balance on these skis, much less move with the agility and strength waterskiing required.

With the boat whisking him along, Tony reveled in the physical challenge and began planning the rest of his weekend adventures. There were so many to choose from—snorkeling, parasailing, windsurfing—and he aimed to partake of as many as he could squeeze in.

When the boat dropped him back at the shore, Trey, Mitchell, and O.J. came running down to the dock. Dressed in the same outfits as Tony—knee-length swim trunks in loud fluorescent colors, white muscle T-shirts, and thick flip-flops—they critiqued his skiing style before turning back toward the shore. With the bright sun painting the clear blue sky and the air full of the ocean's salty flavor, the midwestern quartet floated out to a main road and hailed a cab to Freeport's International Bazaar.

They piled into the cab, still trading wisecracks. "Okay, I'm thousands of miles from home—Daddy needs a drink," O.J. said, winking with pleasure at Tony. Now that he was an assistant minister at his church, the DJ could little afford to hang when he was at home. His friend's joking aside, Tony sensed that in time his boy would be in charge of his own house of worship.

Tony and the fellas had agreed to this weekend getaway three months earlier, around Independence Day. With their mid-thirties bearing down, on top of the responsibilities of wives, children, and work, they felt they'd earned the right to act like college brats for three days somewhere far, far away. For the twenty-six hours since they'd arrived, they'd lived up to that ideal while respecting the commitments waiting at home. Much alcohol had been consumed and many women had been flirted with, but only Trey planned to get biblically familiar with anyone.

It was late afternoon, and a light breeze wafted through the air as the partners in crime bopped through one of the bazaar's many strips of shops, bars, and restaurants. "So what you think?" Trey asked, hands raised victoriously over his head. "Should I call up that sweet little maid from the hotel?" The attractive sister, who looked like Naomi Campbell crossed with J.Lo, had taken a quick liking to the blue-eyed hipster while cleaning their suite.

Pastor O.J. did little to fluff Trey's ego. "Don't get too ahead of yourself with that babe, hoss. She only took after you 'cause she got shut out by the rest of us. I mean, Mitchell and I are married, and ol' Tony here seems to have misplaced his Johnson altogether!"

"Oh, no!" Mitchell clapped a hand onto Tony's shoulder. "You gonna let him hit you like that, Mr. Too Good?"

Keeping his eyes straight ahead but not breaking stride, Tony shrugged. "O.J.'s forgotten a little conversation he and I had a couple months ago. You know, the one where he complained about not getting no booty since he put a ring on LaRae's finger?"

"Hey, Gooden," O.J. said, pointing a finger anxiously and looking as if his mind was replaying every embarrassing fact he'd revealed. "Chill, man. I was just messing with ya."

Tony elbowed Mitchell, leaning in toward his friend's ear. "See how the truth backs a brother off you? Anyway," he said, looking O.J. in the eye as Mitchell and Trey's laughter surrounded them, "I'm still a man, pastor, don't worry. I'm just too busy to get tangled up in mess these days."

He hoped he didn't sound self-righteous, but truth was truth. Even though the twins had now graduated from Rowan Academy and moved back to Chicago with him—where they'd enrolled free of charge at Chicago Technical, courtesy of their "grandfather" Wayne—life in Chicago was just as demanding as it had been in Cincinnati. Tony agreed to let the boys move into a dorm sophomore year, but for this first year of college he'd forced them to stay with him, if only to ensure they were adjusting to life as men.

Once they'd settled on their first selected bar for the afternoon, Tony ordered a round of drinks for the entire table. "This is my contribution," he shouted as he peeled off three traveler's checks and handed them to the waitress. He knew his round of drinks was paltry compared to O.J.'s donation; Mr. Radio Star had paid for the gang's entire condo. "Don't ask me for nothing else."

"It's all good, baby," Trey replied, cracking a grin and rising from his seat. "I got to run and drain the one-eyed snake y'all; be right back."

Tony rolled his eyes. "I don't want to hear you whining if we drink your free beer while you're gone." As his friend stalked off in search of a bathroom, Tony took a second to appreciate his friends. If only Devon—who'd backed out of the trip when his wife, Kym, insisted he attend a family wedding—had come along, all his closest boys would be gathered in this one spot.

He had much to be grateful for, though. For a while there

he'd come close to canceling out Trey's friendship altogether. Two things had pulled them through: the disintegration of Trey's own relationship with Jade, who was ultimately frightened off by his host of kids and baby mamas, and Tony's decision to move back to Chicago with the twins. Given that the tension between them centered around his desire for Serena, Tony's gradual acceptance of life without her had drawn him closer to his old friend.

An hour turned into several as Tony and his boys knocked back liquor, swapped memories, and engaged in the types of jokes they liked to pretend they'd outgrown. Tony was halfway through a plate of loaded nachos, eager to soak up the alcohol flooding his system, when he realized he and Trey were alone at the table. Scanning the bar, Tony nodded toward his friend. "What happened to the fellas?"

"Mitchell wanted to check out that jewelry store next door, think he had his eye on something for Nikki," Trey replied. "O.J. bolted without saying much; I assume something he ate didn't like him, know what I mean?"

"Whatever," Tony said, checking his watch. "Day's getting away from us. We got a few more bars to sample before getting in a nap, right? Gotta be rested before hitting the clubs tonight."

Trey leaned forward, his palms pressed flat against each other. "T, you sound like a brother eager to get into some action tonight. I thought I was the only one on that tip."

Tony slipped his Ray-Ban sunglasses down over his eyes. "I'm not dead, Trey. I didn't want to talk about it in front of those two, but I might just be up for some action tonight."

Trey raised a blond eyebrow. "But T, whenever I try to get you out in the streets with me back home, you always pass."

"I just don't have time," Tony said. "I was never like you, Trey, one who had women naturally flocking to me. I was a calculator—figuring out what it took to get next to whatever women I was interested in. Granted, once I did the work, I could usually get what I wanted, but it still took effort." He considered taking another pull on his latest margarita, then thought better of it. "Between watching over the boys and swatting away the knuckleheads who keep stepping to Zora"—his sister's increasing influence as a women's rights activist had outstripped her status as a novelist, but the brothers just kept coming for her—"I don't have time to go around playing games."

"Hey, I respect that," Trey replied, "but if you're ready to go buck wild now, does this mean you're completely over . . . well, you know."

Tony's jaw twitched and he raised a hand. "Trey, come on, don't do this. You do value our friendship, right?"

Trey stared in Tony's direction, but it was clear he was looking at someone standing behind his friend. An anxious but gleeful smile on his face, he shrugged in Tony's direction. "Never mind, man, never mind. Just be cool."

Tony bolted forward so quickly he knocked over his margarita. Letting the sticky liquid dribble down onto the floor, he fixed Trey with an instructive stare. In the pit of his stomach, he knew Serena would always be a sore subject. Although he had followed through for six months with their periodic get-togethers and had been a complete gentleman each time, he'd put a stop to them when Serena finally filed divorce papers. Serena still hadn't been ready to talk about a future for the two of them; in fact, Tony sensed she needed the luxury of life without a man to please and place extra demands on her. He'd had no choice but to wish her well and pray he could move on with his life.

"I made the right decision," he told Trey, the insistence in his tone sounding unsettling even to his own ears. "I did the right thing, and I'd prefer to never speak about it again. Okay?"

From over his shoulder, a bubbly but strong voice said, "Well, okay."

His head filling with white noise, Tony pivoted in his seat to find Serena standing over him. Dressed in a silk aqua short-sleeved blouse and a matching knee-high wraparound skirt with a pair of leather sandals, she was untouched by the passage of time save for the length of her hair; her waves of nearly straight curls ran to her shoulders, coming to a stop at her breastbone.

Tony was still mute, reared back in his seat, when she spoke again. "I'm as tired of talking about your time in Cincinnati as you are, Tony," she said. "So I promise, take a minute to discuss it with me now, and we'll let it go for good."

Still turned in her direction, Tony glanced toward Trey's seat, hoping for a few seconds to gather his thoughts, only to find that his homeboy had pulled the same disappearing act as Mitchell and O.J. Under his breath: "Well, wasn't that damn sweet of them."

In seconds he grabbed his wallet and followed Serena out into the street, where they melded wordlessly into the surrounding crowd of enterprising natives and aimless tourists. For the first block their silence was all the communication needed, she walking with the confidence of a woman reborn, he stealing wary glances from behind his sunglasses to confirm this was really happening.

Serena kept her eyes straight ahead when she finally cracked the ice. "So, tell me what you know."

He licked his lips, taking a deep inhalation of the conch-fritter grease wafting through the air. "I know that Jamie picked up after you, that he moved in with his son and the kid's mother. I know Dawn is still at Rowan, that she's on track to graduate and wants to attend cosmetology school."

"You heard right," Serena replied. "Her plans aren't exactly what I envisioned for her, but I guess I'm learning it's not always healthy for children to try and live up to what their parents want for them. If she doesn't feel it, she won't succeed at it."

"I think our family therapist mentioned something about that recently," Tony said, shrugging. When Serena did a double take, he didn't fight the smirk that emerged. "Yeah, the shrink did such a job on me, I even let her take a crack at the boys. Glenn especially needed help reevaluating his treatment of young ladies." He looked at Serena directly, slowing his pace. "He's really come a long way. I aim to keep him from ever treating another girl the way he did Dawn."

"Well, it won't be easy," Serena replied, a half smile on her lips. "And you may as well know, all you can do is try and influence him. What he does in the end is up to him."

"I'm learning," Tony said, reaching out and taking her hand as a reflex action. They traded notes about their "low-maintenance" children. Sydney was still upset over her parents' divorce, but counseling had lifted her spirits, her grades were still high, and she had come to understand her parents' love for her hadn't changed. Ben had already starred in one play produced by the university and was hard at work writing his own production, all while maintaining a nearly perfect grade point average.

They passed a deserted but clean alleyway, and Serena pulled Tony toward its nearest corner. "You were frustrated with me the last time I saw you."

His hands wrapped into hers, Tony guided her toward the nearest wall. "Where'd you get that crazy idea?"

"Maybe by the fact you never even called before moving back to Chicago." Six months into Tony's stint as a Kinko's manager, Larry Whitaker had called and convinced him to serve as chief operating officer of the newly approved Chicago Rowan Academy. Picking up where he'd left off, Tony was immersed in the school's construction, the hiring of staff and faculty, and coordinating the public relations campaign so central to the school's launch.

"I couldn't be a phony," Tony replied. "I knew what was best for you, Serena but it didn't feel like what was best for me."

Serena looked up into his eyes, the initial protective wall receding by the second. "I'm glad that you worked out your differences with Mr. Champion and Larry—"

"I never worked a thing out with Champion," Tony said, a touch of defiance in his tone. "When Larry rehired me, it was with the condition I not have to deal with that arrogant fool. I didn't forget how quickly he sold me down the river."

"Well, at least my prediction came true. You weren't at Kinko's long."

After slipping off his sunglasses, Tony ran his hands up and down Serena's shoulders, kneading her flesh like dough. "You were right about more than that. And if I made you feel guilty about looking out for yourself, about taking your time before turning your, Dawn, and Sydney's lives upside down, I was wrong."

She held Tony's gaze, drilling into his soul with the wattage of her stare. "Well, you may have figured out by now that I've gotten what I needed out of being alone."

Tony grinned. "Praise Jesus."

Serena pressed a finger to his lips. "Don't sleep, I am still a bit touched. I'll always have to be handled with care."

"You know that's never scared me off," Tony replied. "I'm far more fragile than you've ever been." He gathered himself, his body tensing with a question. "So I know we're not having a Mars-Venus moment, you are ready for me now, right?"

Serena smiled at the question, then reached up and palmed the back of her future lover's head. "A few more seconds, Mr. Gooden, and you'll have it all figured out."

A sunny sky overhead, the streets around them teeming with sensual stimuli, the young, attractive couple slowly merged, the start of another piece of their journey under way. Stepping forward into the unknown, each was aware of the many uncertainties, the myriad barriers ready to bash their bliss to bits. For Tony and Serena, though, the time for flat-footed calculations of their odds had passed. From here on out, they'd be floating on faith.

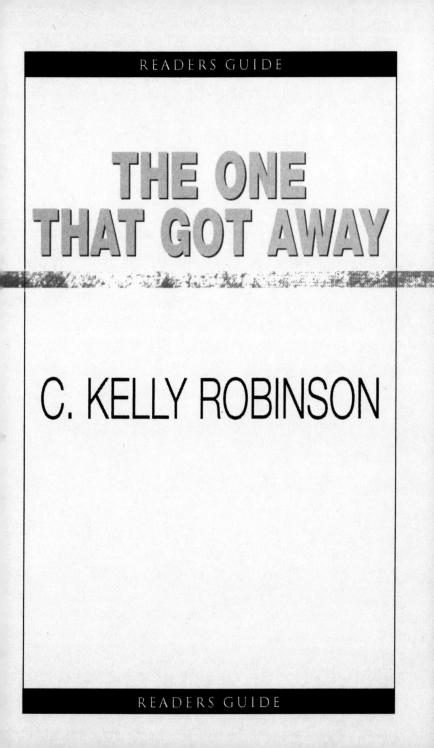

THE ONE THAT GOT AWAY

C. KELLY ROBINSON

A CONVERSATION WITH C. KELLY ROBINSON

Q. What inspired you to write this specific book?

A. Really now, who doesn't have a "one that got away" in his or her past? The idea had percolated in my mind for years, and eventually I was inspired with a full story around it.

Q. How did you come to make Tony, who was a supporting character in your previous novels (No More Mr. Nice Guy *and* The Perfect Blend), *the lead character in* The One That Got Away?

A. If I may so myself, Tony Gooden came screaming onto the literary scene in my second book, *No More Mr. Nice Guy.* He was the guy most female readers loved to hate, serving as Mitchell's instructor in the art of running game on unsuspecting women. In the years since that book came out, I've had friends and readers ask me about Tony's back story; how did he wind up with such a cold, calculating soul when it comes to women? I guess those questions rolled around in the back of my head for a while. Eventually, I envisioned that Tony had suffered the loss of "one that got away" in his past, in a way that had reinforced other trials—not knowing his biological mother, having a distant relationship with his stepmother—that fed his surface-level, play-boy treatment of women. This was a chance to take a flawed but

interesting brother and show him grow a little bit by confronting his past.

*Q. Was Serena inspired by anyone in your own past? Does C. Kelly
Robinson have "one that got away?"*

A. You're talking to a confessed introvert, so dozens of attractive girls "got away" from me in my innocent youth. I've never
harbored any illusions about finding them and winning them
over, but I'm no different from many of my friends who have
exes or old dates they'd just as soon avoid today.

*Q. Do you think most couples whose emotional connection outlives
their initial relationships or romances should eventually wind up together? What should readers take from the way Tony and Serena ended
up?*

A. I know of several friends and other couples who were high
school or college sweethearts, split up, married and had kids
with someone else, only to wind up back together by their thir-
ties or forties. It can happen with folks whose connection is so
special, but it's probably not healthy to plan on it.

Q. Anything else you wish to share with your readers?

A. Just to say thank you again for supporting my work through
these first five books. I won't let up in working to produce stories that entertain and enlighten. And if you have a manuscript
of your own, stay at it one day at a time—it's the only way to
ensure your voice can eventually be heard.

QUESTIONS
FOR DISCUSSION

1. Is there a "one that got away" in your life? Looking at Tony and Serena's interactions at the wedding, did anything remind you of awkward run-ins you've had with ex-boyfriends or girlfriends? Do you have any rules you follow when encountering these situations?

2. Whom did you find more sympathetic between Tony and Serena? Did your view of whether they should end up together change over the course of the story? Why or why not?

3. If life is about choosing between "good brothers" and "dogs" or "players," where did Tony and Jamie each fall along this scale? Who were you rooting for Serena to wind up with?

4. Did learning about the abuse Jamie suffered in his childhood change your opinion of him at all?

5. What's your take on Serena's relationship with Dawn? How would you or have you handled your own teen-age children differently?

6. Did Serena first sleep with Tony because she was 1) vengeful after learning of Jamie's betrayal, 2) still attracted to him sexu-

ally, or 3) unbalanced after skipping her antidepressant medication?

7. What did you think of Serena's decision to take one last shot at making things work with Jamie? Can you relate to her motivations for wanting to stick it out, even though she still had feelings for Tony?

8. When Dawn surfaced at Ben and Glenn's apartment, should he have stayed out of the situation given his volatile relationship with Serena and Jamie? How should he have handled the situation?

9. Should Serena have violated Dawn's confidence by asking her mother to speak to her about abstaining from sex?

10. Was Audrey too aggressive in chasing Tony? Did she overreact to his decision to respect Serena's privacy when he was charged with harassing Dawn?

11. What sort of a future do you predict for Tony and Serena?

12. Were there any supporting characters—e.g. Trey, Jade, the twins, or others—who surprised, enraged, or impressed you? Why?